TAG

SHARI J. RYAN

Annie's Book Stop
anniesplainville.com
508-695-2396 MA 02762

Booktrope Editions
Seattle, WA 2014

COPYRIGHT 2014 SHARI J. RYAN

This work is licensed under a Creative Commons Attribution-Noncommercial-No Derivative Works 3.0 Unported License.

Attribution — You must attribute the work in the manner specified by the author or licensor (but not in any way that suggests that they endorse you or your use of the work).
Noncommercial — You may not use this work for commercial purposes.
No Derivative Works — You may not alter, transform, or build upon this work.

Inquiries about additional permissions should be directed to: info@booktrope.com

Cover Design by Shari J. Ryan

Edited by Katrina Mendolera

This is a work of fiction. Names, characters, places, brands, media, and incidents are either the product of the author's imagination or are used fictitiously. Any resemblance to similarly named places or to persons living or deceased is unintentional.

PRINT ISBN 978-1-62015-533-2

EPUB ISBN 978-1-62015-561-5

Library of Congress Control Number: 2014919080

In dedication to my parents:

Mom and Dad, I would not be who I am today without you. You've given me the tools to thrive and the support to feel successful in my goals.

Mark and Evilee, I'm very lucky to have you in my life. You have gone above and beyond to make me feel cared about and make me a part of your lives, which I couldn't be more grateful for.

Love you all, always.

A Special Thank You

I'd like to thank our service men and women for the sacrifices given to protect and serve our country. For the blood, sweat and tears you shed, you are not thanked enough for what you have volunteered to do.

I am lucky enough to be a part of a military family and to be a part of people's lives who have served this country proudly. It is and always will be an honor for me to know you, and to call you my friends.

Acknowledgments

To my stellar book manager, proofreader and friend, Jennifer Gilbert, thank you for being my first reader and my biggest cheerleader. Your relentless efforts in helping my books succeed have never gone unnoticed. You go above and beyond and always outdo yourself. There aren't enough ways to say thank you in the world to make myself clear on how much I appreciate what you do.

Katrina Mendolera, an incredibly talented editor, my books would be nothing more than words on paper without the constant hard work and passion you bring to my stories. You have been a terrific friend and I can't thank you enough for the amount of work you do to help make my books shine.

Ken Shear and Katherine Sears, over the past year you have made many of my dreams come true and given me the opportunity to achieve more than I ever could have thought possible. Thank you for allowing me to be a part of this remarkable publishing company.

Marni Mann, who I now call my narrative consultant, thank you for your sage advice in crafting this story. Not only have you been a true friend, but you have also been a wonderful mentor.

Randy Gilbert, thank you for offering to be my awesome cover model. We all know a cover sells a book . . . so I'm holding you responsible.

To my beta readers: Kristina, I treasure our friendship and your honesty. Your honesty has helped me to grow this book into a better story, and for that, I couldn't be more thankful. Gerrit and Jess, thank you for taking the time to offer your expertise in helping me smooth out some technical areas of the story. Lisa, as always, thank you for passionate feedback. It gives me the motivation to push myself a little harder. And last but not least, Tanya, I treasure the friendship we've grown to have and I thank you for taking the time to read this book and offer me your feedback.

To my friends and family, I thank you for the constant love and support you have shown me over the past few years. Living out a dream doesn't come without sacrifice and while I may seem as though I've fallen off the face of this earth, please know I love you all.

Lori, thank you for always reading every excerpt, every quote and every new idea I send you, and thank you for giving me the motivation to keep writing. Love you.

Josh—my dearest. You are the sweetest and most understanding husband in the world—I'll get to those dishes in the sink tomorrow. I promise. Love you, always.

Boys—Bryce and Brayden, as you get older, I cherish the moments when you look at my books and call them: mommy's books. My heart warmed when you, Bryce, told me you want to write a book someday. Brayden, even though you don't know what it means to write a book, you look awfully cute walking around the house holding one.

TABLE OF CONTENTS

PROLOGUE 11

CHAPTER ONE 14

CHAPTER TWO 23

CHAPTER THREE 28

CHAPTER FOUR 36

CHAPTER FIVE 41

CHAPTER SIX 48

CHAPTER SEVEN 60

CHAPTER EIGHT 69

CHAPTER NINE 80

CHAPTER TEN 91

CHAPTER ELEVEN 99

CHAPTER TWELVE 102

CHAPTER THIRTEEN 109

CHAPTER FOURTEEN 115

CHAPTER FIFTEEN 127

CHAPTER SIXTEEN 136

CHAPTER SEVENTEEN 145

CHAPTER EIGHTEEN 151

CHAPTER NINETEEN 158

CHAPTER TWENTY 165

CHAPTER TWENTY-ONE 170

CHAPTER TWENTY-TWO 176

CHAPTER TWENTY-THREE 184

CHAPTER TWENTY-FOUR 194

CHAPTER TWENTY-FIVE 205

CHAPTER TWENTY-SIX 211

CHAPTER TWENTY-SEVEN 219

CHAPTER TWENTY-EIGHT 226

CHAPTER TWENTY-NINE 231

CHAPTER THIRTY 236

CHAPTER THIRTY-ONE 241

CHAPTER THIRTY-TWO 243

EPILOGUE 253

PREVIEW OF *RED NIGHTS* 255

PROLOGUE

A SHADOW GROWS on the ground in front of me, and I know only one of us is walking out alive. It *will* be me. The echo of gravel crunching beneath his feet puts all my senses on alert. I hear the hollow short breaths wheezing from his weary lungs. The pursuit is up, and I dig my fingertips into the brick wall behind me, bracing myself to face this asshole once and for all.

The shadow slinks into the light and a knot pinches in my stomach as a translucent red dot wobbles through the space in front of me, which seems to rest directly on my chest. My focus is pulled further into the conjoining street, and I'm able to draw an invisible line between the red glow and the hollow barrel held in his right hand. My throat swells around my tonsils. I *can* do this.

But then there's Krissy.

Blood-stained fingers of his left hand are woven around a knife and splayed across my sister's mouth, the blade pointed straight down into her collarbone. One wrong move and she's done. I never would have thought her luck would be so poor.

The corners of his lips curl upward into a sinful grin, revealing even more blood. He's only holding the knife up to her throat for effect — so he can drag out every second of Krissy's miserable death.

Her dark cobalt eyes are large and appear silver from the reflecting street lights, which illuminates her fear even more. Her chest heaves in and out. In and out, faster and faster, fighting with the last breaths she will take. Time has stopped around us. The world is out-of-focus, and it's just her and me—the little girl kneeling next to me at our dollhouse, the little girl sitting at the other side of our tea party table, the young woman whose shoulder has gathered so many of my fallen tears. The loss of her will make my life meaningless once gone. *I will always protect you,* I want to say. But it's too late.

His hand concealing the pistol lifts again, and the red dot moves up and down from my chest to my neck, swaying with each of his breaths.

"Last chance to tell me where Daddy is," he snarls in a gravelly shout.

If I knew, I would have told him way before things ended up like this. My sister should not have to die in his place, and neither should I. I would happily take that bullet for my sister, except I assume he has more than one bullet.

I slip my hand into the back waistband of my pants and curl my finger around the trigger. I have one chance. Please, God. Save her. My hands spring forward, and I pull the trigger without having time to focus on the target.

The bullet grazes the side of his torso and a simultaneous bite of pain burns through my shoulder. I've been shot, as well. The right side of my body is immediately numb. My knees buckle and my body tumbles to the gravel as if pulled down by a magnetic force.

His grin returns and it glows sinisterly in the dark. He takes one look at my sister and pulls the knife through her throat with one smooth glide. My heart hammers against my ribcage. I can't feel anything, yet I've never felt so much.

Krissy's thick, wavy onyx-colored hair spills over her flushed cheeks as her head crashes to the pavement. Her eyes are still staring at me, but the girl inside will soon be gone.

The asshole looks back at me. I'm next. And that's fine. I don't close my eyes. I will stare death in the face. I am braver than what stands between me and whatever exists on the other side of this life.

Sirens scream in the distance and the glow of lights bounce off the surrounding walls. I had called the cops when I found his note on Krissy's bed, and I told them where they supposedly were. I'm almost caught up to them, and I'll do whatever it takes to save Krissy.

While it only took them several minutes to find us, they were seconds too late. Krissy's neck was already slashed.

As I acknowledge the sirens, the asshole points his blood-covered finger at me, and the corner of his lip pulls up into a sneer as he shoves the knife into a holster on his leg. He darts around the corner, clutching his wounded area with both hands.

TAG 13

I drag myself over to my sister's lifeless body. I sweep the hair off of her pale flesh and place a kiss on her forehead. "I will kill him, Krissy, even if I die trying. And if I don't die, I will live for both of us, and I will retaliate on everyone who has done you wrong. I won't ever trust anyone again. I'm so sorry I let you down."

I lay my head on her chest, listening to the slow beats of her heart. I pray for the next thump until there is only silence within her.

Now I pray for her peace, and I wish death upon her murderer.

CHAPTER ONE

CALI

LOOK AT ME. You know you want to.

I slide my pen in-between my teeth and arch my left brow slightly. Eye contact. *Check.*

I love a good first day of college, even if I should have already graduated a year ago. The scent of floor cleaner, paper, and whiteboard markers waft through the air. Everyone is dressed neatly in back-to-school attire and brand new shoes. These are things students seem excited about; looking the new year head on with a fresh start. I look at it as a ticking time bomb. There's no telling how long I'll be able to stay at this school. Sometimes it's a week; sometimes it's a couple of months—usually not much longer. It's been a couple weeks since I moved here, and I have a feeling I won't be breaking any records in this location.

The classroom is moderately sized, fit to seat thirty students at most. The seats are being filled in slowly, and the professor is playing with a pen at the podium, studying each student who enters the classroom. Most professors decorate their rooms with articles, pictures, and diagrams. Not this guy. The walls are all empty except for the whiteboard behind the podium. But even the whiteboard is blank.

"Welcome to Cognitive Psychology," the professor says. His voice is gruff and intentionally sultry—it sounds forced, like he's reeling in his bait.

I've gotten too good at this no blinking game. It works the fastest; large doll-like eyes are his weakness. Therefore, I earned his attention five minutes ago, and I can see a nervous twitch developing behind his creepy dirt-brown eyes. What an act. A teacher should be used to students staring at him.

I glide the pen slowly out from between my teeth and curl my tongue around it before sliding it out from between my lips.

He clears his throat. *Check.* "I'm going to be handing out the syllabus now. Why don't you all take a few minutes to look it over, and I'll be happy to answer any questions you might have." He lifts the stack of papers from his desk and wets the tip of his thumb with the side of his tongue. I bite down on the bottom corner of my lip in response. I know he can see me.

Lucky for him, I'm sitting in the front row. He stands before me with an unsteady hand and fumbles through the papers before handing one to me. A strand of his perfectly quaffed auburn hair falls over his forehead. Keeping my focus steady, I inventory every freckle on his face, noting the slight cleft in the center of his chin and memorizing the location of the slight bend in the middle of his nose. I can hear the fluctuation of his breaths. They quicken as his hand reaches out to mine.

My fingertips sensually stroke over his tough ivory skin as I tug at the papers. "Thank you, professor." I place the tip of my finger between my teeth. "Did you forget to introduce yourself? Or was I too . . . preoccupied to notice?" I look him up and down, playing into the game I already know he likes to win.

He stumbles backwards until he knocks into the podium. "Class, I apologize. I seemed to have forgotten to introduce myself. My name is Professor Lance," he says breathlessly as he scribbles his name out across the board. His handwriting looks as though it belongs to an eight-year-old boy, which confirms his sloppiness.

"Ah, much better, professor . . . Lance." I speak loud enough so my voice carries over the muffled whispers behind me, forcing him to shift his weight awkwardly from foot to foot. *Check.* I have this game in the bag.

Might be the fastest one yet.

When he passes by me to the next aisle, my hair is tugged and my head is pulled backward. I swivel my body around in my blue plastic seat and offer a guileful grin.

"Cali, seriously?" Lex sighs, giving me an exaggerated eye-roll. "Leave him alone. He looks like a nice person."

"*Those* are the most fun, Lex." I thrust my chest out and release an exaggerated sigh. "You wouldn't believe me unless you tried it." She won't try it. So unknowing. So innocent.

"You need help, lady," she says with a sidelong smile.

I waggle my eyebrows and turn back around. *It isn't me who needs help*, I want to say out loud. Lex thinks this is a game I play, but she doesn't realize I'm only here at this school for one reason. And it's not to pick up random guys like she thinks I like to do. It's all part of the act I've had to make believable. Even to her.

"He's married. And not interested," she whispers in my ear with a hint of hostility. "You know, like that guy from last night? You're becoming a home wrecker." She thinks I took that guy home last night. Another part of the act.

"Is that a challenge?" I whisper back. I love proving her wrong. She has yet to acknowledge my expertise on the male brain. I've only been in this town for a couple weeks, but Lex has followed me around like a lost child ever since we met at the administration office when I came to register for classes shortly after I moved here. She's an intern there, helped me settle in, and then attached herself to me like glue. I guess my life is entertaining for her, or at least the life I've pretended to lead.

I study his every word, his every move and his every blink over the course of the next hour. When the bell in the hallway chimes and the class filters out, excitement rushes through me. But Lex ruins that when she slaps my arm, nudging me out of my study. "Let's go, Cali. Lunch." I can sense she's becoming bored with what she thinks is a game.

"Meet you there in five," I say, pulling my arm out of her reach. She groans, ultimately giving up the fight, then turns and bustles out the door with the rest of the eager lunch-ravenous students.

I drop my notebook into my bag and stand up slowly. Once again, I clinch my lip in-between my teeth. Then I sling my bag over my shoulder. Perfect. Last one to exit the room.

Three. Two. One—

"I'm sorry I didn't hear *your* name?" he calls over.

I shake my head, locking my most innocent looking gaze on his eyes. "Nice to meet you," I say in a hushed voice. "I'm Cali Sullen." A nervous smile tugs at his lips. *Captured.*

It's clear he doesn't recognize me, which is surprising since Krissy and I looked so much alike. There was a three-year difference between us, but she looked a little older, and I look a little younger, making it

TAG 17

easy for us to pass as twins if we wanted to pull it off. I twirl a strand of hair around my finger and widen my eyes. "You didn't ask any of the other students their names. Why me? Do you . . . like what you see? Is that why?" I curl my lips into a slight smirk, knowing I likely twisted his fucked up mind into pretty little knots.

"I. Ah. Ah. Have a nice day, Ms. Sullen."

I fidget with the buttons on my shirt and drop my gaze to the ground. "Um. You too, professor?" I spin on my heels and rush out the classroom. I've added the icing to this cake. I love fucking with men who I *know* are fuckers.

I slump down into the warm leather driver's seat of my car and pull down my mirror to reapply lip-gloss. When I look at my eyes, I feel ashamed. I feel like Mom would be disappointed in me. Then I wonder if she would be proud of me for protecting the innocent. Although, I'm not sure retaliation falls under protection. In any case, I try to avoid my reflection—the uncontrollable bitch who stares back at me. It's hard to remember back to when I wasn't like this—when I wasn't on a constant revenge kick—when Mom and Krissy were still alive. I feel like when that life ended, this new shitty one was its replacement.

The vibration of my phone disrupts my stony glare, and I slap the mirror shut. I answer and press speaker while coiling my other hand around the steering wheel. "Hey."

"Where are you, Carolina?"

"School," I respond matter-of-factly.

"You need to drop out and leave."

I bite my tongue. We're like oil and water, but I try to keep our arguments at a minimum. He's gotten so much worse over the years since Mom died. "Dad, I'm fine where I am."

"The hell you are," his voice lowers into a whisper. "He's inbound to your location."

Shit. I impulsively check the rearview mirror. It's clear. This asshole isn't going to stop until he kills every last person in my family. It's why I call him Reaper. He's been after Dad for years for a reason I don't know, one in which I obviously can't be trusted with knowing. I've begged to know why his location is always confidential, but just the same as the many secrets in my life, it's on a need to know basis. Since Reaper can't find Dad, he's been trying to work his way through Krissy and me. And since I'm the last daughter standing, I will continue to be his target until one of us has the last shot.

"Okay," I reply earnestly. "Four days and out."

"No. I want you out of there now. I want you to head to Boston. Is that clear?"

I press end and drop the phone back into my bag. Dammit. I reopen the mirror and look back at my reflection. The bright blue hues that used to reside within my irises are now dull, making the color appear gray. My eyes are always half-lidded, and my complexion is pale. I'm worn out, and I'm constantly in battle with the mission my attention is focused on. I'm doing this for the right reason. Krissy. The end of her short nineteen years were filled with lies, deceit, pain and suffering. And now I'm going to make sure anyone and everyone who caused her pain will get back what they have given.

I flip the mirror shut and duck back out of my car. I guess I don't need four days. I can do it today. I send Lex a text message telling her something came up, and I have to leave for the day. She responds with a sad face and tells me she'll see me tomorrow. But she probably won't.

I poke my head back into the classroom I left minutes earlier, spotting my target. It's his lucky lunch hour. I enter into the room and close the door quietly behind me, pressing my thumb into the lock button at the same time.

"First name?" I ask in a tempestuous voice.

"Zach." He visibly swallows the rising lump in his throat, and I now realize how much I'm going to love this moment, knowing he has no fucking idea what's about to happen. "Can I do something for you, Ms. Sullen?" I allow my eyes to draw a slow line from his lips down to the bulging seam in his pants.

"Yeah." I let the strap of my bag fall off my shoulder and drop to my feet as I unfasten the top button of my blouse, giving him the *okay* to move in toward me—which he does, timidly. His eyes dart back and forth between my face and the doorknob. "Locked," I whisper.

His hand wraps around my back, and he pulls me into his hardness. "I don't like games, Ms. Sullen."

That's not what I heard.

"That's too bad." I lean forward and skim my teeth against his ear lobe, breathing heavily for extra measure. "Because, I love them."

I utter the words into his ear, and his grip tightens in response. His other hand cups my chin and he pulls my lips into his. He smells like coffee but tastes like mint. He's rough in all the wrong ways, and he's impatient as well as unpleasantly forceful.

His hand slips down the back of my jeans and palms my ass as he lifts me up, forcing my legs to straddle around his thin, bony waist. My shirt is pulled up over my head, and his tongue connects with my skin, tracing a line over my collarbone. His movements are animalistic and untamed, and his slobbering is making this hard to work through.

I lower my lips to his ear. "You want me?" I honestly scare myself with how well I can pull this off.

"You're a bad girl, Ms. Sullen."

You have no fucking idea.

"Have you ever raped anyone in here?" I ask while running my tongue over his earlobe. He hesitates, and I graze my lips down to his jawbone. "I get off on that kind of shit. Did you know that?"

"In that case, yes." Got it. "She asked for it, though."

"Krissy, wasn't that her name?" I nibble on the skin below his ear, letting my teeth linger on his lobe so my words vibrate within him. "So, if I stop you from going any further—" I pant a little, for effect. "Are you going to pretend I'm Krissy?"

"You-you knew her?" he stutters.

"I guess you could say that. But don't let it distract you from this."

He pulls away and looks at me for a brief second, studying the look on my face. I'm a good actress, though. All he sees is a seductive grin and my wanting eyes. "I'm not distracted, and I don't need to pretend," he says, breaking up the moment of silence. "After these little teasing games of yours, you will be mine, one way or another. You can call it rape, but I'll call it retribution for you coming in here like this and looking like that." He looks me up and down shamelessly and bites down on his bottom lip.

I uncoil my body from his as I hop down, pushing him away so I can take a few steps back. In a honeyed voice, I say, "Before you rape me, I need a second." I pull my phone out of my pocket and click upload.

"What the fuck did you do?" he asks. "Get over here you fucking bitch." He grabs my arm and pushes me over to his desk. He pounces on top of me from behind and claws at my bra, so I let out a few cries—

pretend cries. But he doesn't know they aren't real. He flips me around and tries to shove his hand down my pants, which gives me the perfect opportunity to attack. I lift my leg and wrap it around the back of his knee. Then he lifts me up to his chest, and I wrap my arms around his head, putting him in a choke hold.

"It's your move," I let out a small laugh. "But I warn you. You make the wrong one, and I'll kill you."

He releases his hands, so I release mine, but then he shoves me to the ground. I rebound quicker than I fell, though, and while I want nothing more than to attack him again, I'd much rather get the hell out of here. I slide my shirt back on and fix the few stray hairs curled up on the top of my head. Then I pull my lipstick out of my back pocket and glide it slowly over each lip. I've pushed him to the point of no return, which is precisely where I intended for him to go.

"What the fuck is your problem, psycho?" He moves in behind me, and I back kick, shoving the stiletto of my boot right into his perpetrator.

"Fuck you. That's what," I respond, turning around to stare down at his crouched body and flushed face. "Oh, and you don't have to worry about hiding that rape from your wife, the dean, or police anymore." I slide my phone back out of my pocket and play up my smug grin while checking the screen. "YouTube works so freaking fast nowadays. I'm pretty sure this is record timing, actually. Don't you think?" I ask, playfully. I show him the display on my phone screen. "Damn. I'm good. This is totally going viral." I laugh a little more, knowing I'm pushing him far over the edge.

His jaw drops open as he adjusts himself and backs up until his knees buckle at the desk chair. "What the . . . " He stumbles over his words as a white pallor clouds his strawberry licked cheeks. "Why would you . . . ?"

"Krissy Tate? The girl you raped—you know, your straight A student?" Confusion washes over his already flushed face. I've been waiting for this moment for so long. "I lied about that not being a distraction. You see . . ." I lift my hand to check out my nails, dragging this out to build up the suspense. "I'm her sister. Carolina Tate." I shove my hand out to him. "Nice to meet you, asshole."

"Oh shit," he says with a sickening sneer. "You two do look alike."

TAG   21

"You think because you're a psychology professor you can work a girl's mind over?" I quirk my brow. "Did you ever wonder what would happen when one of them worked *your* mind over?"

I straighten my sweater and lift my bag up from the ground, ending this encounter once and for all. "By the way," my voice rises in tone as I turn around and tap my finger into the air for effect, bending my thumb down as if pulling an invisible trigger. "If I were you I'd go ahead and off yourself. I mean . . . your wife is gone." I count the reasons on my fingers. "Your career is gone." I press my fingertip into my chin and grin for the final shot. "Oh, and you're looking at some serious jail time—you know, the place where *you'll* be raped by massive dudes every day? Fun times ahead, I'm sure." As I saunter toward the classroom door, leaving him dumbstruck with his hand cupped around his mouth, I make sure to leave him with a proper message. "Consider this little visit . . . payback for what you did to my sister."

* * *

I pull my Elios pizza out of the microwave and drop myself onto the couch for what's going to be my nightly entertainment. But right as I'm about to shove a greasy slice of pepperoni into my mouth, my phone buzzes on the coffee table. Dammit. I snatch my phone up, staring at the caller ID for a second—a random number, as always. But no one else knows my number except Sasha. So I know it's Dad.

"Hi Dad. Don't worry, I'm leaving soon," I say, sounding as unfazed as I normally do.

"I received some information today, Carolina." *Hello to you too.* He sounds worn and tired, making me wonder where he is now. "Did you approach that professor at Krissy's old university?"

"Depends," I say playfully.

"What did you do?" Dad whispers, as if someone were tracing our call—not that whispering would keep the listener from hearing this.

"Just had a little talk with him." I can't hide the pride in my voice.

"Dammit, Carolina. I was told about the YouTube video. He's dead now, and who knows if that will be traced back to you?" He forces a long heavy sigh into the phone, making his annoyance with me clear.

"Leave. Tonight. You hear? There's a flight heading to Boston at twenty-one-hundred hours. Flight number AA220. Your ticket will be waiting for you. I want a text in two hours confirming you have your ticket." I flick the TV on, hoping one of the local stations is reporting on the death of Professor Lance.

"Okay," I say as the call ends. *Love you too, Dad.* Ass.

I shove the slice of pizza into my mouth and turn up the volume. Sweet. I love when people take my advice.

Breaking News: Dead at thirty-five. Psychology professor and a recently reported rapist, Zach Lance was found in his classroom dead. The cause is unclear at this time, but rumors of a drug overdose appear to be the cause, leading us to believe this is an alleged act of suicide.

Job complete.

I press Sasha's number in my phone, and she answers after one ring. "Cali-girl, did you see?"

"Good riddance, huh?" I say, listening to her breathe a sigh of relief.

"Maybe it all finally caught up to him," she says. "I still can't believe Krissy didn't tell anyone." She was like that—she always kept her head down, but the weak link usually seems to be the target. And she was twice—unfortunately in the wrong places at the wrong times. "Cali, did you have something to do with this?"

"It was suicide. Nothing more," I reassure her. Or at least I try to reassure her. But if anyone in this world knows me and what I'm capable of, it's her. "I gotta run, Sash. Talk to you soon." I hear her kisses being blown into the receiver as I click end.

CHAPTER TWO

CALI

I READJUST the heavily weighted carry-on over my shoulder as I scan my gaze down the departure screen, confirming the flight number Dad gave me. Looks like it's on time—there's a plus.

With sluggish strides, I pick up my ticket then make my way through security, needlessly earning myself numerous once-overs.

"Ma'am could you please remove your sunglasses?" the woman with the wand asks me. I let out an exaggerated sigh and slide them off my nose. The light burns my eyes, and I squint in reaction to the pain. "You do know you are inside, and it's dark out, right?"

I narrow my eyes at her and cock my head to the side. "Have you considered it may not be to hide my eyes from the sun?"

"We'll need you to step aside. You need to be searched."

I do as they ask, spread my legs apart and lift my arms out to the side. "Search away," I say with as much sarcasm as I can squeeze into two words.

I'm patted down by two different TSA agents and asked to walk through the full body X-ray booth. "Nothing," the second woman shouts over to the first woman who has returned to the metal detector.

Who would have thought? This isn't my first rodeo, peeps. "Duh," I blurt out. I snatch my bags and shoes off of the belt and brush by the guards. "Hope you enjoyed copping a feel," I say, blowing them each a seductive kiss.

I shove my feet into my boots and continue walking while checking my ticket again to see what gate I'm supposed to go to.

As I arrive at Gate 88, I scan the small area, noting it's going to be a very full flight filled with people who all look as if they're going to a funeral. What is it with Bostonians and wearing all black in the winter?

At least I'll fit in there.

I plop down in a corner seat in the waiting area as I feel my phone vibrating in my pocket. I pull it out and respond to the question mark I've been waiting for from Dad. I respond with:

I have my ticket. Leaving soon.

-Cali

Or so I thought.

I've been seated among the dozens of other passengers for the past two hours, watching the gate times change a number of times before I see the plane actually arrive. Just as I'm powering my phone down, preparing to board, an awful stench burns my nose from a few inches away. A middle-aged man with greasy black hair and a thick lip-covering mustache who smells exactly like the inside of a port-a-potty has found a reason to sit directly beside me in a row of empty seats. When my eyes unfortunately meet his, he takes the opportunity to speak to me. "Heading to Boston?" he asks. I raise my eyebrows and force a tightlipped smile. I simply follow that with a nod and give him a *no shit* look. "I heard winter's coming early this year," he continues.

"Cool," I mumble with a sigh. I pull a magazine out of my bag and open it in front of my face, hoping to block my vision of the man's blackened-stained grin. But it's only seconds before I'm taken back when his finger sweeps down the bare skin of my collarbone.

"What does that mean?" he asks, pointing to my tattoo.

With a smooth motion, I lay my magazine down onto my lap and place my hand over his, giving him the false notion that I'm a gentle person. I take the opportunity to offer him a slight smile before I twist his forefinger backwards as far as it will go before the expectant snap. "I'm sorry," I say sweetly. "Did I tell you it was okay to touch me?" I pull down a little harder, and he smiles in response to the pain. But as I hold my hand there, I see the smile begin to fade.

"It's a free country, chicky," he sputters as his tongue knocks around between his bare gums.

"Why would you think it's okay to touch me?" I ask again, keeping my voice calm, yet stern. He licks his lips and looks me up and down, responding with only a look. "Do you go around touching girls half your age because you feel it's okay?"

He clears his throat and looks around to see who's watching or listening, but I don't move my eyes from his. "Why not?" he says, shrugging his bony shoulders. "Besides, you're *definitely* asking for it."

He thinks I'm asking for it? I'm wearing a fucking scoop neck, black long sleeve shirt, jeans, and combat boots. "The only reason it's okay, is because no one has ever probably told you no. But it occurs to me that after I snap your finger off your hand, you won't be able to touch people inappropriately anymore, will you?"

He hoots with laughter, dragging in attention he probably shouldn't want. "You think you could break *my* finger, little chicklette?"

I pull his finger a little further, and his smile grows. "Ow, stop. You're hurting me," he puckers his lips and winks at me.

"Oh, look, it's your right hand. You a righty?" I turn his hand over and see deep callouses bubbling on his palm. "Yes, you are. So, if I rip this thing off, you wouldn't miss it, right?" I turn his hand back over and glare into his beady eyes. He's questioning my words. He's unsure of my capabilities. And that's fine. "Sound okay to you? Or are you going to leave and stop touching people?" His smile fades and his eyes widen. I release his hand and offer him a smart-ass smile. "Oh, and the tattoo means death. It's a Maori Warrior symbol. They used to eat their enemies once they slaughtered them. Cool, huh?"

I see his Adam's apple struggle to move. He lifts his bag from the ground and nearly trips over his own feet, darting away.

I reopen my magazine to the page I was reading and refocus my attention on an article as I hear a soft chuckle coming from the other side of me. I turn to see who was enjoying the free entertainment and I'm faced with a man who looks to be either a wrestler or in the military—black shaven hair, stiff jaw and bulging muscles on every inch of his arms. His eyes are currently focused on a book, and I suppose he could have been laughing at that, rather than me. But as I question it, his large shamrock green eyes lift and look right at me. A slight grin tugs on the corner of his lips, and he winks so quickly I'm questioning whether it was me who might have blinked. Before I can react, he stands up and walks away.

I swallow hard and refocus my attention on the magazine once more. Stupid attractive man causing a moment of feebleness. I didn't react, though. He winked at me. I think. And I didn't make a snide comment or scowl. Weakness.

I let out a few short breaths, regaining my composure. He's gone. It's fine.

The boarding zones are being called, and I check my ticket again. Zone two.

After twenty minutes of watching the first class and business class passengers try to cut each other in line in order to race onto the sardine can faster, zone two is called out over the loud speaker.

I place my sunglasses back over my eyes and lift my bags over my shoulder. I hand the flight attendant my ticket and she looks at me for a moment before taking the crinkled piece of paper from my pinched fingers. "Ma'am, please remove your sunglasses." What is with the prejudice against sunglasses? I pull them up over my head and shove my hand out further, waiting for her to hand my ticket back. "Thank you for your cooperation, ma'am. Have a safe flight." She hands me my ticket and I pull my sunglasses back over my eyes. I hear the flight attendant huff with annoyance as I enter the jetway. Last time I checked, there weren't TSA rules about wearing sunglasses in an airport.

I walk down the thin aisle in the middle of the plane, all the way to the back row where the scent of urine and shit wafts through the air from the bathrooms. Whatever. I'll breathe through my mouth for the next several hours.

The plane fills in slowly, but when I hear the doors close, I realize the two seats beside me are still empty. Could I be so lucky to have this row all to myself? Sweet.

I sink into the window seat, pull my headphones out of my bag, and plug them into the armrest. This could almost pass as comfortable. I reach back into my bag and pull out a pill bottle, pop the cap off and tap the container into my palm until two capsules roll out, then I toss them into the back of my throat and swallow hard, praying they take effect before takeoff.

My knees bob up and down as I try to relax the rest of my body, but as always, this isn't working. If only I could knock myself out and wake up in Boston, this would be so much easier. My hands are trembling under my clamped grip over the armrests, and I clench my eyes shut. *If I can't see it, it isn't happening.* I repeat my mantra a dozen more times before the engines ignite, but it doesn't work. I suck in spurts of air to make sure I don't pass out from forgetting to breathe, but the air feels so thick in my lungs, it's hard to breathe. I forcefully blow it out and try to suck it back in harder. I should never get on another plane again.

My seat sinks slightly, and I know someone's next to me now. Great. "Hey," a muffled voice blends in with the loud music booming in my ears. I ignore it, though. I'm not here to make friends. "Hey. Can you hear me?" The voice sounds again. I shake my head, giving this person the message that I'm not responding. Just as I'm satisfied with thinking they figured it out, something drops into my lap, compelling me to open my eyes. It's a nip of alcohol. What the hell? I look beside me, making instant eye contact with the striking shamrock-green eyes that were looking at me in the airport. I pull the buds out of my ears and quietly mumble, "Thank you."

His top lip curls into a small grin and he leans his head closer to me. "I didn't want to tap you or anything. Don't wanna lose a limb tonight." His grin grows, unfurling a perfect smile. "That'll help you make it through the flight." He points to the nip. "I'm Tango. Yell if you need anything." He presses his palms onto the armrests, preparing to stand up, but then shoots me another look. "Although, I suspect you won't know you're even on this plane in a few minutes." His smile returns and part of me wants to grab his arm and ask him to stay.

"Thank you," I say again.

"No worries." And with that, he quickly returns to his seat.

Wait. Come back, a normal person would say.

But I'm not normal.

I open the nip and take a whiff, making sure it smells like vodka. It does. And with my confirmation, I down it with one swig. It only takes a couple of minutes before my eyes close and my mind shuts off.

CHAPTER THREE

TANGO

MOVING ON to bigger things. I have to keep repeating this to myself and maybe then I'll believe it. Walking away from the people I love, knowing I'm not coming back is pretty fucking hard to wrap my head around. I mean, I know this could have been the case at any point over the past six years, but now things are pretty much set in stone—pun intended. My family thinks I'm dead. It's what they were told. And when someone in authority tells you a loved one died, it's sort of believable. I sat in the black sedan that pulled up to my parents' house a few weeks ago. The black tinted windows concealed the truth: me, still being alive, so it was okay if I tagged along. I didn't have to be there when it happened, but I felt like I deserved to witness the pain they were being put through because of me.

I'll never forget the one and only time I was one of the marines giving the news. Since that day, a black sedan has always represented death to me. Regardless of the straight face we were trained to maintain when giving that type of news, my heart shredded into a million pieces and I didn't even know the parents, only their son who I'd fought beside. I offered to be the one to give them the news. It was the least I could do for him.

It was different watching two marines in dress blues step out of the car and approach the front door of my childhood home. A white glove pressed on the doorbell, the chime that would set off a world of pain in the two people I love the most in this world.

My mother pulled the curtain away from the window to see who was outside. The curtain dropped from her hand quickly, but the door opened slowly. I heard her yelling for my father.

The two of them stood side by side, clutching their hands over their hearts as the men in blue bowed their heads out of respect. Fuck. It took so much out of me not to jump out of the car and throw my arms around both of them. But it was either then or very soon. And if I pushed it off, they would have suffered more.

My mother fell into my father, shrieking and screaming. I could hear it through the closed window. "God no. Give me my baby back." Her anger quickly turned to the Marines. I couldn't hear specifically what she was saying, but I'm assuming it was something along the lines of, "This is your fault. How could you? Don't ever come back to my door again." It's what my buddy's mother said to me when I gave her the news. I can't say I blame her.

After minutes of condolences and getting punched in the chest by my five-foot-tall mother, the men returned to the car, slipping inside flawlessly without ever changing their expression. But I knew what they were feeling inside.

"Sorry man," one of them said. Sorry doesn't even begin to do this situation justice.

Two days after my funeral I joined a mercenary service in hopes of keeping my remaining time occupied in some way. I didn't want to sit around, waiting to expire—it would have been too depressing. Anyway, within a day of enrollment, Eli Tate contacted me, requesting my service. I accepted on the spot. This gig is high paying and I can send the money to my sister anonymously. It could pay for her college tuition. He told me I would start in two weeks. I'd fly out from Los Angeles on her flight and start the job in Boston when we landed. Since my truck had to be driven across the country anyway, I took a week and a half and flew around the states, scratching things off my bucket list. Nashville, New Orleans, Vegas, and I had to see the Statue of Liberty in New York at least once during my life. It's probably good my list was short, though, because I had to cut my two weeks to twelve days due to some YouTube incident she caused.

In any case, I keep telling myself that with each ending comes a new beginning, good or bad. But I can't forget that with each beginning comes another end as well.

At least she's a sight for sore eyes. I imagined someone more rough around the edges, unruly hair, no makeup, baggy clothes—an overall unkempt look—a stereotype I guess I subscribe to regarding these types of self-proclaimed bad-girls. However, she couldn't be further from this generalization, which immediately tells me she isn't a self-proclaimed anything. She's likely a straight up badass with a bad attitude. Although, I can't blame her after what I read in her file.

I probably shouldn't be watching her sleep. I shouldn't be wondering what music is playing through her headphones, and I probably shouldn't have given her that alcohol. By the size of her little frame, it doesn't seem as though she'd be able to handle what I'm assuming is Valium and then the shot of vodka I gave her.

Well, at least if this job doesn't end well, looking at her will make everything I'll have to give up worth it. God, listen to me. I've been in that desert for too fucking long. I'm horny and I need to focus on the issue at hand. Although, she is the issue at hand, so technically it's okay to focus on her.

I pull out my phone and review the files once more. I wonder if she even knows what type of danger has been following her around for the past three years. She doesn't seem like the clueless type, but someone in her situation wouldn't necessarily carry the confidence she seems to be portraying. This type of shit can make a person crazy. And for some reason, this makes me already like her. Because, what I've seen should be making me crazy, but I haven't let my mind take the best of me yet. At no point in the past six years have I given myself a minute to reevaluate the reasons I think I'm going straight to hell.

I can tell myself over and over that everything I did was for my country. I can even believe it. But at the end of the day, watching too many pairs of eyes freeze over as their souls are sucked from their bodies never became easier. I'm not a murderer, but that's how every person in Iraq and Afghanistan sees me. Yet, in the U.S., I'm a war hero. This is such a screwed up world we live in, and people don't understand how badly each of us Marines wants nothing more than world peace. *To Serve and Protect*—the protecting part comes easy to us, but it's the *serve* part that comes with loaded expectations.

CALI

The thump of the runway below the wheels startles me awake. My eyes shoot open and I see a blur of pavement racing outside the window. My heart slows and I have the urge to kiss the ground below me. Maybe I should try to stay here in Boston for more than a few months this time since I. Hate. Flying.

After the fasten seatbelt light goes out, I unclasp my seatbelt and step into the aisle. I open the overhead compartment and reach in for my bag. Things shifted during the flight and my bag has tumbled to the back corner of the bin. Of course. I climb up on the seat while slinging my smaller bag over my shoulder and then pull the other bag out of the overhead compartment, letting it fall over my opposite shoulder while hopping back down.

"That's one way of doing it," a now familiar voice says from a row ahead of me.

I shrug my shoulders and shove my headphones into the side pocket of my bag. "Thanks again for—"

"Don't mention it," he interrupts me as he pulls his bag out from the overhead compartment and turns toward the exit.

I walk through the jetway and find myself in an empty airport. My eyes drop down to my leather-braided watch and I twist the hour hand forward three hours. 5:00 a.m.

I pull my fleece out of one of my bags and drop my stuff onto one of the many empty seats before curling up in one of them. I slide my sunglasses off and pull my phone out of my pocket. After I power it back up, I see I don't have any messages yet, which means I have nowhere to go. Dad always sets up a safe location for me to stay. But nothing yet. I look around again. Nothing is even open. I lean my head back and close my eyes, still feeling slightly numb from the Valium and vodka cocktail I ingested six hours ago. I'll just sleep until my phone buzzes.

"I don't think there are any connecting flights down here?" I open my eyes and I see Tango exiting the restroom.

"I'm not connecting. Just waiting," I say flatly.

"Me too," he says.

Who would he be waiting for outside of a closed terminal? Although I guess he's probably wondering the same thing about me.

"Mind if I wait over here?" he asks, pointing to the chair across from me.

"It's a free country," I smirk.

"Is it now?" He reaches down into his bag and pulls out his phone. He types something, looks at the screen, and fumbles with his watch to change the time. He drops his phone back into his bag, crosses his arms behind his neck and stretches his legs out in front of him. His eyes close, allowing me to take a better look at this very chiseled, very beautiful specimen of a man.

Is this guy trying to play me? I lift my bags and pull them up to my lap. I stand up, looking around for a place to go, and my eyes settle on the light flickering on inside of the Dunkin Donuts. *Beautiful.* Coffee.

As I non-verbally confess my love for coffee with a simple look, I amble toward the little shop, hearing, "Large iced with cream and sugar," from the distance. I turn around, bewildered by his nerve. His eyes are still closed, but a smile is dancing across his five o'clock shadow. I roll my eyes at him. But he doesn't see.

I move up to the counter at Dunkin Donuts and place my bags down to pull my wallet out.

"What'll it be?" the cashier asks. Her eyelids are hardly open and the black circles under her lashes tell a story of a night that must have ended only hours ago. Her hair is piled up into a messy bun on top of her head and her shirt is wrinkled and buttoned in the wrong button holes. My response takes longer than she appreciates, and she rests her elbows on the counter as her chin falls into her hands. Her eyes open a little more as she looks up at me, waiting for my decision.

"A medium hot coffee with cream, no sugar."

"Will that be all?" she drones.

I glance back over my shoulder. His eyes are still closed, but I swear I still see a smirk tugging at his lips.

"I'll also have a small hot coffee, black."

She hands me both of my coffees and my change. "Hope your day runs on Dunkin," she recites, ending with a yawn.

I walk back over to the seat I was sitting in and find his seat empty. *Ass.* Now I have two fucking coffees. I should have known better. I sit back down and reach my hand with the small coffee over to the trash bin beside me.

TAG   33

"Whoa," he gasps, walking up from behind me.

"What, are you playing hide and seek?" I mutter under my breath.

"No. Peek-a-boo." He pulls a bag out from behind his back. "Cinnabon?"

"Those things are evil. The calories in those will eat you alive."

"Eh, it could be worse," he winks.

"Coffee?" I hand him the small hot coffee rather than the large iced coffee he asked for.

"This isn't what I wanted."

"Oh. It isn't?" I arch my eyebrows to play confused. "Oops. Sorry, complete stranger who asked another complete stranger for a coffee."

"I'm not a stranger. I already bought you a drink."

"A nip hardly resembles a drink."

"Well. Then, we're still strangers." He hides the Cinnabon bag behind his back, making me secretly drool over the delicious scent of those sinful things.

"Oh well!" I hand him his coffee. "I better start moving." I check my watch again. Where is Dad with my damn housing information? This guy is clearly getting a little too comfortable in my presence. And I can't have that.

"I thought you were waiting for someone?" he asks, sounding as if he doesn't care. But if he didn't care, why would he ask?

I did say that. "I was wrong."

"No. That's what some call lying."

"What do you care?" I snap back. I wrap both hands around my cup and take a sip of the steaming deliciousness.

"I'm kidding. Relax." Is he laughing at my hostility? *Asshole.* "You always so hard-edged?"

"Do you always act like you know people after talking to them for five minutes?" I retort.

His eyes widen and his brows rise, giving me a look as if *I'm* a lunatic—which I am, so I'll give him that. He drops back down into the seat across from where I'm sitting. "If you want to be technical, I talked to you seven hours ago on the plane." He takes a sip of his coffee, his hand almost completely concealing the cup. Actually, he kind of looks like a grown man taking part in a tea party. I guess I could have at least gotten him a medium. "So, no. I don't always act like I know people after five minutes. It's usually ten or twenty." And we have a stand-up comedian here.

It's getting harder to seem unfazed by him, probably because he fazes me. Nevertheless, we both know in about ten minutes we'll never see each other again. Well, at least *I* know this.

"Well, it was kind of nice of meeting you, Tango," I say, getting ready to make my official exit from this uncanny encounter.

"What about that text message you've been waiting for?" he asks.

Oh, for God's sake. Dad fucking sent him.

"Daddy send you?"

"Quick one, aren't ya?" He furrows his brow with a look of degradation. "He was worried about your recent—" he fake coughs. "You know . . . you convinced your sister's rapist to commit suicide?" He shoves his hand into his coat pocket and pulls in another sip of his coffee, causing an awkward silence. "Impressive if I do say so myself. But drawing that much attention to a girl as pretty as you, won't do well for keeping you safe."

"Look, Tango, if that's even your real name, which I doubt, I'm sure you're a nice security guard and all, but I don't need one."

"Cool. I understand. We're still going to be roomies and besties," he says in a ridiculously girlish voice.

"What if I don't want to live with you?" An amazingly sexy man, who will see me in my freaking pajamas with no make-up, all while shoving pizza into my mouth at eleven o'clock every night.

"I guess you can stay locked in your room all day, then." He shoots me a cunning grin.

Fuck. Why me?

"Let's go, my dark princess," he teases in a breathy voice.

"Freeze, Iron Man." I place my hand out to stop him. "I have a rule about name calling."

"Well then, Miss Carolina, shall we?" He juts his elbow out for me to loop my arm through. This guy is a real piece of work. I can't imagine where Dad found this one. Although I can't ignore the temptation that's dangling in front of my face—this is the first bodyguard who looks like he was born in the same decade as me, and he's apparently a charmer. But he's still a bodyguard. Rules are rules, even if I made them myself.

I shove his arm away and lift my bags over my shoulders. "I'm not going with you. How do I even know my dad really sent you?"

"That's fine. You're welcome to sit here for . . . ah . . . forever and wait for a text message you won't receive. Or, you can come with me. I'll pretend to leave the option up to you. How about that?" He smirks, or winks, or maybe both. Whatever he did makes my stomach twist into an apprehensive knot.

I really thought we were done with the bodyguards. I figured he would have learned after the last one. But as usual, Dad wants to keep me in a bubble.

"What's your story, Tango?" I ask before I slip inside of the revolving door, pausing the conversation briefly before the frigid Boston air slaps me in the face. When he steps out, I continue. "So? Wrestler, ex-cop, ex-con? Those are my dad's favorites."

"None of the above."

I stop and look at him. "Then, what are you?"

"Your friend. That's it."

"You aren't my friend. I don't do friendships with bodyguards." I turn back around and drop my bags to the ground so I can wrap my arms around myself. My clothing is suitable for California, not Boston. Another brilliant move today. Yesterday. Whatever day it is.

CHAPTER FOUR

CALI

A WHISTLE BLOWS from behind me and a glistening silver sedan screeches to a halt in front of us. Tango jumps in front of me and opens the door. "Ladies first," he gestures for me to slide in.

I grab my bags and sweep past him, knocking into him on purpose as I drop my things into the opened trunk. I'm so irritated right now. I can take care of myself. I'm twenty-two and I don't need a babysitter. He can call it whatever he wants, but that's all this is—babysitting.

I slide into the car and stop at the first seat, forcing Tango to go around the other side. If this is the way it's going to be, I'm not going to make it easy. I'll drive him away. I'll make him go running for the hills, wishing he didn't accept this offer. My previous attraction to him is gone or hiding from the guard who has taken his place.

I fold my arms over my chest and pull my sunglasses back over my eyes. I don't have to hide here, but I don't want to face reality either.

Tango drops his bags into the trunk and slips in through the opposite side, settling into the leather seat. He gives me a once over and smirks. I'm glad he finds my presence so amusing.

"Aren't you going to tell me to put my seatbelt on now?" I say in a childish voice. That's what all of the past bodyguards have done—treated me like I was five.

"I don't give a shit if you put your seatbelt on. You're the one who will go through the windshield if we're hit. Your problem, not mine."

I throw my head back and close my eyes. The driver closes the trunk and hops into the driver's seat, sealing this deal. The car guns away from the curb and takes each turn at least twenty-five miles per hour.

We've been driving for more than fifteen minutes, which is quickly putting a kink in my quick escape plan. Normally, I don't like to be this far away from the airport. And it looks like we're heading to suburbia, which is even worse. A twenty-five-minute ride drops us into a newer development filled with apartments. Hopefully, I'll be living in one, and he'll be living in another. But I know well enough that that wouldn't be the case.

We step out of the sedan and I wait for the trunk to pop open so I can pull out my own bags. I don't need someone carrying my shit for me too. I hear the pop, and I wrestle with the trunk to force it open at a quicker speed. I yank my bags out and throw them over my shoulder.

"Where to, Jeeves?"

Tango effortlessly pulls his bags out of the trunk and holds them both out in front of him, accentuating his largely defined triceps. He nods to the driver and heads toward the closest building.

With much reluctance, I trail behind. We drop our bags in the center of the capacious living room, and I glance around, familiarizing myself with my new living quarters. The smell of fresh paint mixed with a vacuum soap smell drifts through the air. The floors are covered in a light-colored carpet, which offsets the similar but darker shade of paint on the walls. Basic furniture lines the perimeter of the room and a small oak coffee table sits perfectly in between the round of furniture.

I look into the two bedrooms and drop my coat on the bed in the larger bedroom. The room is staged with the essentials: bed, closet, and desk. Looks like a dorm room.

I pull out my phone and send a message to the last random number Dad sent me: *Thanks a lot, Dad.*

I throw my phone down on the stripped bed and return to the living room for my bags. I find Tango in the corner of the room popping some pills into his mouth. *Hmm.* I groan silently to myself while wondering why his striking presence is becoming more infuriating by the minute. I thought I just told myself I was over the good looks. He's a guard, not a model. I don't like guards.

I snatch up my bags quietly, careful to avoid any further conversation for the moment. I need some time to digest all of this.

I close the door behind me and look around to acquaint myself with each boring empty corner of my new bedroom. I hate moving. I drop my bags onto my bed, observing the slight resistance within the springs.

Now this looks comfy.

Whatever. I'm sure I won't be here long.

TANGO

I sent my confirmation to the number I was given by Eli: *She's in my possession. All clear.*

Damn. She's a firecracker. I haven't ever turned down a challenge, but taking on an assignment with a hot chick who has a bad attitude is a new one for me. It's definitely different than any of my previous missions—mostly since I never had to work with a female. Plus, knowing my hormones and how they react, I'm not sure I'm capable of completing any job with a chick hanging over my shoulder.

Thankfully, there was no place for flirting or relationships in the Marines, so it was rare when it happened. Definitely didn't happen with me. Plus, I haven't really had time to focus on women outside of the Marines since I was deployed more than I was home. Well, unless I was at the club.

The club. God, it's been so long since I've been to one. Thinking back to it now, it probably wasn't the best place to focus on women. They looked at me the same way they looked at every other dude who walked into that place. Money. Money. Money. But for some reason I was able to convince myself to forget this whenever I was in there.

Being around Cali now, she is the purpose for me being here, and she is the focus. I feel like I've been told to stare at a briefcase full of money and not touch it. Not imagine what it would be like to experience having that type of money. Not to spend it and do both good and bad things with it. Although with her hiding in her room and avoiding me—for all intents and purposes, the briefcase will remain closed, keeping me from staring at the goods—which will probably make this a lot easier.

Fuck. I need to get laid and probably not by the task at hand. I should find a club around here. I wonder how hard it would be to convince her to join me. I can't exactly leave her, so I'd have to bring her.

On second thought, imagining this scene isn't hot. I could see Cali knocking out a stripper or two for the simple reason that they might look at her the wrong way. Scratch that thought. Back to this situation sucking ass.

CALI

My phone lights up with a return message saying, *Invalid Number.* Of course.

I unpack the few things I have and organize them in the closet. I remove my laptop from my other bag and place it on the small metal writing desk.

I settle into the firm wooden chair in front of my laptop, waiting for it to power up. While waiting, I glance out the window at the mess of trees butted up against each other. It's the only positive feature about this place so far. I can't help but to feel jealous of those trees. It's almost as if they're teasing me with their freedom. They're allowed to dance in the wind and enjoy the security of being near other trees who live exactly the same way. It's a simple enjoyment I'm not allowed to experience. Although, the last few weeks were the longest I've been without a bodyguard. And it was wonderful, exuberating really. I made an asshole kill himself. I can't think of anything better than that.

The ping of my inbox pulls my attention back to the screen. I don't keep my email account on my phone like most people, mostly since Dad has always given me hundreds of reasons why it's a bad idea. Not that I like to listen to him, but I can see some legitimacy to some of his reasons. My laptop is pretty secure and it's a little harder to lose than my phone. I click on the e-mail icon and twenty unread messages show up in a bold stream. Most of them are from Lex. I think it's safe to assume she's wondering where I've gone. She'll forget about me in a week. They all do. I open the e-mail from Sasha. She knows not to ask me where I am or who I'm with, but she still sends me an email every day telling me about her life in a corporate office, and the hot men cloaked in expensive clothes, who all appear to be oozing with money. She's the center of attention in her office, being the only female in her department. She's stunning, which I'm sure is blatant to all of her male co-workers. She also works part time at a small restaurant in the center of town every night. She doesn't like to be bored, so she spends every free minute she has working.

Our moms were best friends when they were our age. Sasha and I were born only a few months apart, making us as close as sisters, which is why she knows enough to know not to ask anything. She's connected to me, which is why I can't be around her. Reaper knows her. And he'd do anything to find me. After Krissy's funeral, I made Sasha move out of her apartment and change her number.

She seems happy in her new town now and finally admitted to having her eye on someone at the restaurant she works at. I guess he's the chef or something. From the way she was talking, I had a feeling someone had to have been attracting her attention for the past few weeks. She was careful to tiptoe around the subject, though, probably knowing how miserable I am right now. Probably knowing how little I care about who's dating who . . . even if it is her. She's aware of the 'no boyfriend' rule I've declared for myself. I don't want to be the cause of another innocent person's death. Therefore, I will remain single, alone, and dejected for the time being, but that doesn't mean she can't live a normal life. She doesn't realize it makes me happy to know she's making friends and meeting guys. I want her life to be normal. She wasn't born into this mess and shouldn't have to live like she was.

I send her a quick note telling her how happy I am for her. I want her to live the life I hope to live some day. I want her to marry and have a family—to leave the thought of my horrible past in the past.

I click send, which brings me back to the rest of the unread emails. Most are spam. I delete all of them except the last one—the one that has gone unread for the past year. Krissy's last email to me. I can't read it. I don't know if I can handle what she didn't know was going to be her last words to me. Even thinking about clicking *read* forces a burn behind my eyes. I have spent the last year crying whenever no one was looking. Every time I feel like my tears are drying up, something else pops up that reminds me of her. I still can't read this. I don't know if I'll ever be able to.

CHAPTER FIVE

TANGO

I'M SURE we won't be here long, so I'm not going to think twice about the fact that this room is meant for a miniature person. The ceiling is angled, and I can't even stand up straight in most corners of the room. I haven't seen the other bedroom, but I'm assuming it's twice the size with a full height ceiling.

Unfamiliar with this area, I pull my phone back out and open a map. I'm sure she's starving and when a woman is hungry, things only go south from there. And this chick would probably prove that theory correctly in the worst way possible. My truck won't be dropped off until later, so I need to find shit in walking distance. Although, I'm guessing she wants to stay locked in her room, and if that's the case, I'll grab a pizza and leave it at her door. On second thought, knowing my luck . . . she probably doesn't eat pizza. I'm sure it has too many calories. Ugh. What have I gotten myself into?

I pull open my bag and straighten the neatly folded pile of clothes, knowing they'll be staying like this until I need them. I guess I could have told her not to bother thoroughly unpacking. Although she's been on the run long enough, so she probably lives like I do. And if she does, I'm sure she knows living out of bags doesn't get old. It's actually comforting—knowing I can pick up and leave at a moment's notice.

I take off my shirt and toss it onto the bed as I reach into my bag for a clean one. My hand sweeps against the small picture frame I've kept in here since I left for the Marines, and it makes my heart ache. Last time I looked at this I was in Afghanistan. The picture reminded me of what I was fighting for—my motivation to make it home. But now it's the reminder that I still have one person who knows I'm alive and loves me—my motivation to keep pushing forward, even knowing

I can't see her again. It's moments like these when I stop and realize what has happened over the past few months. How did I end up here? I had such a promising career. I was a lifer in the Marines. I wasn't great in school, but I excelled with everything I touched in the military. It felt like my destiny, which made combat easier to accept. I was doing what I was placed on this earth to do. But now that I've been discharged, I have no direction. I have no real plan. I'm just crossing the days off as they go by. It's easy to be strong when resilient people surround you. Having no support, though, it's weakening.

CALI

My stomach snarls with hunger, reminding me I still haven't eaten anything since the slice of microwaved pizza I scarfed down last night. Maybe I can sneak out without the hulk noticing.

I pause when I pass by his room. He's hunched over his bag folding clothes. A man folding his clothes? That's different. All I know is he's preoccupied.

I continue down the hall, concentrating on not making a scuffing noise with my feet. He probably has bionic ears too, though. All of my previous bodyguards seemed to.

I twist the knob on the front door and pull, but the door doesn't give. My focus is drawn in a line upward from the doorknob, noting three deadbolts. One even has a keyhole on the inside.

Motherfucker. He actually locked me in. He's the worst one yet.

Not a bodyguard, my ass.

"You need something?"

I whirl around, faced with a white t-shirt tightened over a well-defined chest. I close my eyes to block out the sight. "No."

"Cool." He turns around and heads back toward his bedroom.

"I'm fucking starving," I yell after him. My voice carries louder than I intended, but I'm so irritated right now that my self-control is being pushed to the brink.

"Why didn't you say so? I was about to order a pizza." He walks back into his room and immediately returns, pulling a cream-colored Henley over his head. "But if you're that hungry, I'll assume you don't want to wait for delivery."

"I don't remember asking you to join me for lunch." I cross my arms over my chest and fall back against the door. "I don't need a babysitter, Tango."

He pulls his coat off of the sofa and throws it over his shoulder. "Well, I'm hungry too. And since I'm supposed to . . . ahh . . . keep you company, we'll call it, I can either go with you or we can wait an hour for delivery." He shoves his hand into his front pocket and pulls out a key. The key that will release me from this new bubble I seem to be confined to. "Oh, and even if I wasn't supposed to . . . ahh . . . keep you company, it's a free country, right? And there's only one food joint within walking distance."

"What if I place a restraining order against you?" Like that would even work.

He throws his head back and lets out a brash husky laugh. "Good luck with that one, Carolina."

I growl with annoyance. "It's Cali."

"I'm sorry, but I think the name Carolina is beautiful. It's fitting. You shouldn't be so annoyed to hear it." He looks at me without shame, which tells me the compliment was sincere. I never really saw anything beautiful about myself. And I have a bad attitude to boot. So I'm not exactly sure what he meant by it. But it was sweet, I suppose.

He slides behind me and unlocks the front door. "Well if it helps, you can call me whatever you want, princess."

I bite my cheek, refraining from another comeback. He wants me to keep fighting. It's obvious he's enjoying it.

I don't flinch, I don't react, and I don't respond. I take the lead and head out the main entrance, realizing we likely have no transportation here since we were dropped off.

"Look. You're in danger—we both know this. We're okay here for the time being, but I don't want to go too far. There's a sandwich shop around the corner. Will that work for you?" he asks.

I follow behind him, pondering the likelihood of being able to run. My focus darts around to familiarize myself with these new surroundings. It's pretty barren, full of trees and no shops in sight. "I need to find a pharmacy after we eat." If I don't refill my prescription, I'm going to implode from pain.

"There's actually one around the corner," he says.

"You from here, or something?" I ask.

He pulls out his phone and stops walking. Whatever he's reading seems unimportant since his face doesn't twitch. His eyes hardly scan the words. His chest doesn't constrict any faster, and the visible pulse on his neck holds at a steady rhythm. He drops his phone back into his pocket and continues walking. I cannot read this guy.

We step into the sandwich shop and the bell sounds on the glass door, announcing our arrival. The scattered customers all stop mid-bite and turn their attention to us. The examination is brief and they all turn back around to continue on with their eating.

TAG   45

I approach the counter and wait for the woman to greet me. "What can I grab for ya, hon?"

"Small roast beef with everything on it and a water." I reach my hand into my front pocket to pull out my card, but Tango reaches his hand out in front of me with his card. Dad has been good at depositing money into my account since I can't exactly settle down and do something normal, like find a job. I suppose it's his attempt at repentance for making me suffer alone. Maybe he thinks it makes me look at him as less of an asshole for the life he's given our family. I can't be bought, though. "I can pay for my own food," I grumble in Tango's direction.

"Daddy's orders, princess." He hands the woman the card and says, "Add a large pastrami with cheese and sauerkraut. Oh, and a large soda."

She takes the card from his hand as her eyes linger on his face. Her puffy cheeks turn a rosy red and the lines around her lips tighten while she fights the urge to smile at the Incredible Hulk.

"Small roast beef with the works, large pastrami with cheese and sauerkraut, with a watta and soda," she yells into the kitchen with a thick Boston accent. It makes me want to laugh, but I realize that wouldn't go over well in a crowded shop full of other Bostonians. "You two aren't from around hea, are ya?"

"California," I say.

"Missouri," he says.

So, he won't give me any answers, but a lady at the sandwich shop asks him something and he answers right away. He's definitely being an ass to me.

She turns around, pulls the two plates off the counter, and hands them to my boyfriend-looking bodyguard. I snag my plate from his hand and drop down into the nearest seat. He slides in across from me, and his knees knock into mine under the table. He doesn't apologize or excuse himself. He just smiles and laughs softly—it weakens me a bit. But then my mouth takes over with its automatic reaction.

"Excuse you?" I snap.

"I didn't do anything?" he retorts, completely unaffected by my attitude.

"You just knocked your legs into my knees."

"It wasn't an accident. Why would I say sorry?" he laughs. "You should really calm that temper of yours."

"And you should learn some manners," I respond.

I knock my knees back into his and momentarily have the desire to keep them there, not minding the warm feeling it causes in my belly. But instead, I slide out of the booth. I carry my plate over to the counter and plop down on a stool. "You can watch me from over there, I'm sure." I might be laying it on too thick, but I don't know how else to lay it on. "Excuse me," I say to one of the waitresses behind the counter. "May I have a knife to cut my sandwich, please?"

"Of course," the waitress responds as she places it down beside my plate.

I place my elbow down on the bar and rest my head in my hand. Some days, I wish Dad would disappear and leave me with a life of my own, rather than in the coattails of this fucking career he chose for himself. I didn't choose this shit. No one ever asked me if I wanted to be followed around my entire life. Dad was the cause of Krissy's death, and he's out there carrying on with what he does best. Well, now it's only me. My life will always be under some kind of microscope because of him. But Tango, he's pretty much the fucking icing on top. To send me an amazingly hot man to ogle, only to be informed that he's my new babysitter, is pretty screwed up. It's like Dad wants me to be miserable.

Tango doesn't take a hint. He sits on the stool beside me and twists the chair so his knees are only an inch from my right thigh. His proximity is making me uncomfortable, but not in the worst way. Then again, yes, it is the worst way. He's making me uncomfortable. People aren't allowed to have that affect on me. "Look, maybe we aren't getting off to a great start," he says, shoving a fry into his mouth. "I'm doing my job. We both know that. But people still make friends at work. You know?" He sounds serious, which makes me realize he has no idea how unlikely a friendship would be with me.

I tip my water bottle into my mouth and take a long swig, looking into his eyes, trying to read him. I pull the bottle from my lips, making a slight popping sound, and look back at my plate of food. "Why do you want to be my friend, Tango?" I ask in all seriousness.

Out of the corner of my eye, I watch as he shoves another fistful of fries into his mouth and chews for a minute before responding. He clutches his hand around his napkin and looks at me. I turn to look at him, waiting for his answer, and watch as his dimples deepen a touch. "Because I think you're a pretty cool chick."

His words force warmth to spread through my cheeks and everything inside of me wants to say something nice in return, but that would be going against everything I think I should be doing—keeping him at arms length. "You might not think that if you really knew me." And the heat is gone. I have to keep reminding myself that a friendship is impossible with him. The words Mom burned into my head constantly replay whenever I even think of befriending someone new.

She would place her hand on my cheek, look me in the eyes, and say: *know everyone . . . trust no one.* I promised not to forget those words. It was the last thing she said to me.

CHAPTER SIX

TANGO

THIS GIRL IS seriously in pain. I've seen pain. I've seen a mind destruct. My mind has had its moment too, but this girl has lost everything without ever having a say or a choice in the matter. I know she's snarky for a reason, but it's her way of remaining strong. And I admire that. Every second I spend with her, I understand her a little more. I understand her more than she realizes. She's so wrapped up with feeling alone in this world she likely hasn't considered the possibility that there are other people living with similar feelings, even if the situations are different.

She doesn't trust me, and I can't blame her. I can see the struggle in her eyes to even accept me as an acquaintance. And again, I can't blame her.

CALI

He's pretending to act occupied as I pick up my prescription for Vicodin, which I appreciate. I've been taking painkillers for a year, and the scar is only half of the reason. The other half is emotional pain. I've been pacing the aisle for twenty minutes as they verify my information and transfer my prescription from California. I'm sure he knows the list of meds I'm on, and I'm sure it will give him a good inside track as to how fucked up I am.

I lean over the counter to see if they're any closer, but I don't see anyone at all. I push back off the counter and walk down one of the nearby aisles, searching for painkillers and sleep stuff.

"You in pain?" Tango asks, turning the corner from another aisle.

"Always." I mean that in so many different ways.

"Do you have an injury?"

Here we go. First step to friendship is admitting weaknesses about yourself. "Yes." That was easier than I thought.

"Hmm. That wasn't in your record."

I twist my head toward him and stare him down until he looks back at me. My teeth grind against each other until my gums hurt. "What else have you *read* about me?"

"Your birthday is August 2nd, which makes you a Leo—the ferocious lion of zodiacs," he snorts. "Big surprise there." He pulls a box of pain relievers down from the shelf and examines the back as if he's never seen them before. "I know you've been through hell." He places the box back on the shelf and picks up another one. "I know that you want a friend, but you're scared of having one. I know you're in physical and mental pain. But it's not because I read it in your file, I know because it's written all over your face, and it's tattooed on your collarbone." He tugs on my sleeve, and I consider not pulling away, but the look in his eyes makes me feel something and it's not something I should be feeling. I jerk my hand away from him as if it were an uncontrolled reflex.

"I was shot in the shoulder. They couldn't extract the bullet because it's too close to an artery." I squeeze a box of painkillers tightly within my grip and graze him as I walk back to the pharmacy counter.

He rushes to my side. "Who was supposed to be with you when that happened? Is that what this is all about? Someone let you down?"

I clap my hand over the bell to grab a pharmacist's attention quicker. "Excuse me?" I shout into the back room.

"We'll be with you shortly, hon," one of the pharmacists replies from behind the wall I can't see around.

"Tell me, Carolina." He pulls on my arm again, and I don't pull away this time. I look up into his eyes and I swear I see what compassion is supposed to look like.

"Yeah. The last guy didn't exactly do his job. Let's just say, I don't trust anyone—I can't trust anyone, for a reason." My words cause a jitter within his eyes—a look as if he's trying to understand.

He nods his head as if he does understand. "Sorry to hear that," he says simply. Sorry is as much compassion as I pull out of these bodyguards. It's why I don't typically talk about myself. Why bother? They don't *really* care. With the exception of maybe one or two, most of the previous bodyguards usually remained quiet, like a soldier on guard. I didn't speak to them, and they didn't speak to me. It was manageable. But Tango is slowly pulling me into his web, and I don't know if this web is already a tangled mess or a beautiful dew droplet covered mesh of security.

"Tate?" My name is called from behind the pharmacy counter. "ID, please." I hand the gum snapping, pharmacy assistant my ID. She studies it for a second and looks back up at me. Then back at my ID. "New tattoo?"

"No, it's not. Is my prescription ready?" She looks at me and tilts her head to the side as if I said something to offend her. She extends her arm out and hands me the bag.

I turn around to leave and I hear the girl mutter, "Have fun snorting that."

I pull in a deep breath of air through my lungs until I feel the skin stretching over my chest. "Excuse me?" I turn around to face her. Anger is bubbling through me and I'm not sure if I'll be able to suppress it. I'm good at going from zero to one hundred when it comes to seeing red.

Her lips pucker and she shrugs her shoulders. "I call it as I see it." She crosses her arms over her chest and straightens her neck, trying to front some kind of confidence after she broke pharmaceutical conduct, I'm sure.

"It is incredibly rude to make assumptions like that." I understand I look damaged, and these comments seem to be finding me more often than not lately, but I need to gain some solid ground again. I'm losing myself in this chase I've devoted my every waking moment to.

I feel Tango's arm sweep against mine as he places his hand down on the counter next to me. "Is there a problem with your prescription?" he half asks me, half asks the pharmacy assistant.

I stare at her for a moment longer, waiting for an apology maybe. I don't see one coming, however. "I'm entitled to my opinions," she sneers.

"You're entitled to act as a professional, not an antagonist. Say what you want to me, I don't care. However, for everyone else's sake, your supposed future profession will take you further if you learn to keep your misconceptions of others to yourself."

Another employee must have heard the confrontation, because I see a large burly man with ashen hair and a matching thick beard turn the corner, walking toward me slowly with a slight limp. He places his hands down on the counter and breathes heavily, trying to catch his breath from his twenty-foot walk. "I'm the manager, is there a problem here?"

"No, but thank you for asking." He studies me for a moment. And I'm starting to gather who might be responsible for creating the open hostility around this place. It's evident that a nose piercing and a couple visible tattoos warrant a drug addict label.

"Could I see your prescription for a moment?" No one looked at me this way in California. People had tattoos on their faces there and piercings in unpredictable places. No one gave them a second look. But here in this sheltered suburb of Massachusetts, I've been given twenty once-overs since I arrived six hours ago.

I hand him my bag and focus my eyes on his nametag. "Davis? Is that your name?" I ask.

He nods his head with confirmation as he turns the bag over to see what prescription I had filled.

"Do you trust your employees?" I ask.

He doesn't blink before answering, "Of course I do."

"I'm sorry to hear that," I retort quickly. His eyes twitch and he looks from side to side at the idiot girl who was helping me and the other college student filling the drug containers.

"Excuse me?" he says with a slight crackle in his voice. A slight sheen of sweat glows over his forehead, and I can sense a growing discomfort within him.

"This one over here," I point to the girl, "she was pocketing pills before I approached the counter. She also told me that you let her take whatever she wants." It's not really true, but it's what she deserves. His eyes dart over to her. Her cheeks redden as she shakes her head back and forth, disagreeing with my accusations.

He hands my prescription back to me. "Thank you. Have a nice day." He's definitely trying to shut me up. Other customers are now standing behind me, looking over my shoulder trying to catch a better view of what's going on.

"That one over there," I point to the guy filling the pill bottles. "I bet you the quantity in this bottle doesn't match what the prescription calls for." I know this is a risky assumption, but if they want to judge me by my looks, I'm going to do the same back to them. Neither of them look like they should be behind a pharmacy counter. He takes the bag back from my hands, rips it open, and retrieves the bottle. The pills ping one by one on to the metal pill counter. The number appears in red digits, displaying: 35. "My prescription called for forty-five pills. Right?" I'm silently cheering myself on for winning this one. Karma. Definitely karma at its finest.

He recounts my pills and pours them into the container. "I apologize on behalf of my staff."

Tango's fingers press into my arm as he pulls me to face him. "Let's go."

* * *

I close the door of my bedroom and fall into the unforgivingly hard chair in front of my laptop. I unlock the latch and lift the screen. I find a picture of Reaper on my hard drive and drop it into the Internet search engine. I love that we can search with images now, since it helps me keep track of where this asshole is. A list of similar images pops up on the screen. The most recent one shows footage of him in a bank in Maryland. The image is dated as of three days ago.

Rage boils through me each day that I know he's running around loose, chasing me and chasing Dad. I know I could have ratted him out to the cops and helped them locate him, but everything within me needs to feel the retaliation myself. I know he'll eventually be put away or killed, and since it's me he's after, the chances are partially in my favor for causing the latter part.

My eyes lock on the image stretched across my screen. I click my mouse on the zoom button, bringing myself closer to my sister's murderer—*the only man I've ever loved*. I shouldn't have trusted those smoldering translucent blue eyes, shadowed by his dark straight brows. His perfectly tousled toffee-colored hair, and the flawless full lips made for touching were all it took to make me fall for him. Looks are so damn deceiving.

I shake my head at the smirk playing across his lips. He doesn't even know he's being photographed, yet it's as if he's always playing nice for the hidden camera. It's all a game to him. I close the page and open up a new one. I search for the closest shooting range. It's been a week since I've been, and this pent up anger isn't going anywhere. I need to unleash. It's sad to remember the day a paintbrush was good enough to relieve stress. Now, I'd probably snap one in half with my first stroke.

I reach into my bag and pull out a Sharpie and scribble the address of the nearest range on my hand.

I walk into the main living area, noticing Tango sitting at the breakfast bar with his phone. "Do you shoot?" I ask.

His forehead wrinkles with a downcast expression, questioning me. "Shots?"

"Yes."

"What kind of shots?" he asks. I'm sure he thinks I'm talking about alcohol.

"9mm Rounds."

He sucks in a mouthful of air and holds it, processing what I've said. "Well then." A satisfied smile inches across the bottom of his cheeks.

"Can you shoot? Or are you going to sit in the observation room?" I question. I'm sure he knows how to shoot. He wouldn't be a guard without that training.

"I've shot a couple of times. I'll give it a try." He stands up from the barstool and pulls his coat off the bar.

"A bodyguard who can't shoot?" I know that's a crock of shit.

"I'm not a bodyguard," he corrects me.

*   *   *

He made us wait a couple of hours for a reason I was unsure of, but when we walked outside, he lead us through the parking lot and up to the front of a newer black pick-up truck. "Whose truck is this?" I ask, hesitating before following his lead and walking around to the passenger side. I figured we'd be taking a cab to the range.

"Mine." I hear the pop of the locks unhinging from inside and we both climb in and settle into the nylon bucket seats. "I had it driven here, but it was running a bit late. It's why we needed to wait out the last couple of hours," he grins.

It smells like a combination of a pine air-freshener mixed with cologne. I've smelled worse in a man's vehicle. Actually, it's kind of nice. I sink into the seat and drop my purse to the floor. I'm usually stiff as a board when I get into someone else's car. The inability to trust always seeps in, and it causes me to feel claustrophobic, but for some reason, I don't feel like that at all in his truck.

He twists the radio knob and surfs the channels until he finds a country station. "Keep the windows closed," he says, stifling a snicker. "I'll be laughed out of this state if anyone hears this music."

"I grew up in Texas, so this kind of sounds like home," I say, offering up more information than usual.

He looks at me through the corner of his eye and clears his throat. "Yeah. I know."

"I sort of wish you didn't know *everything* about me." I keep my focus on the blurred lines on the highway, suddenly feeling very exposed.

"I don't know *everything* about you."

"Seems like it," I say gently, trying to keep my hostility at bay.

"How about I tell you what I know? Anything I don't mention is something I honestly don't know about you."

"Sure." I actually really want to know. Although, what I *do* know is this is where I find out if he really thinks I'm a *cool chick*, as he said, because he does know everything about me. Or, I find out he only thinks I'm a *cool chick* because he doesn't know anything more than what is on the surface.

"Your name is Carolina Anne Tate. You're five-foot-three, one-hundred-ten pounds, you have three freckles on your nose, shoulder-blade-length black wavy hair, one tattoo on your right arm, two on your left arm, and the most gorgeous blue eyes I've ever seen." His words pull me to look at him. But he's concentrating on the road and won't look back at me. He seems unaffected by his own words, as if it were a robotic description. Though, I doubt he describes all of his client's eyes as beautiful.

After keeping my eyes locked on the carved edge of his jawline for more than a few seconds, I gather he isn't planning to look back at me, and I turn my attention back out my window.

"Hmm," I sigh. "Is that all?" Please tell me that's all.

"Your mother died of breast cancer when you were nineteen. Your sister died a couple years later. And you haven't seen your father in three years."

My sister died? That's not exactly how I'd put it. "Is that all?"

I feel the brakes compress as we near a stoplight. He turns his head and his eyes center on mine. "Yes." He didn't blink, twitch, or stall. He's being truthful. If there's anything I've been raised to do well, it's to read someone's facial expressions. He's a challenge, but I have to think his lack of nerves is a telltale sign of truth.

"What did you do before my dad hired you?" I ask while I have his eyes still locked on mine. Dad always said, eyes are the best lie detector on the human body, and he still hasn't blinked.

As I assumed he would, he twists his head forward and almost simultaneously, the light turns green. He turns the music up and pulls his sunglasses down from his head, placing them over his tell-all eyes. I can't obtain a fucking thing from him. Maybe he trusts almost as little as I do, which probably won't make this working relationship any easier.

We pull into a dirt lot, and the silence between us enhances the crunching of the gravel below his tires. The pines overshadowing the building tell me this place is for locals—this place wouldn't be found unless someone was looking for it.

Without any exchange of words, we enter into the shooting range. I place my hand down on the front desk and pull my license out with my other hand. My eyes scan the back wall, admiring all of the weapons. My focus stops on my favorite: "the 40 Cal Smith & Wesson, please."

The man studies me before complying. His dark eyes, chiseled jaw, and starched flattened shirt and pants tells me he's either seen his day in the military or in some kind of law enforcement position. He's looking at me as if he wants to get inside my head, like any other law enforcer I've ever met. He clears his throat and sucks his breath in, puffing his chest out before leaning over the counter onto his elbows. My lip unintentionally curls at the close proximity he's claimed toward me. "Seems like an awfully specific request from a girl like you."

"And what kind of girl am I exactly?" I chuckle once and stand up straight, crossing my arms over my chest.

He pushes off the counter and turns to the back wall and retrieves the weapon. With his fingers bent around the neck of the pistol, he places it down on the counter. "Keep the handgun in front of you at all times. Don't point it at yourself or anyone else. If we see you doing this, you will be removed at once. Please confirm that you agree to this policy."

"I agree." I reach for the pistol as he releases his grip.

"I'll have the same," Tango says. Maybe he really doesn't know much about shooting. If he did, I'm sure he'd ask for something larger or more powerful—typical guy move.

The man asks for his ID, but he doesn't study his face or try to read his thoughts. He mindlessly pulls the pistol out from behind the counter and places it down gently. He doesn't recite the policy or ask him to agree.

Whatever. *Let it go,* I have to tell myself.

"I'm Chuck. If either of you have any questions or need anything, give me a shout." He leads us to two side-by-side alleys and hands us each a pair of safety glasses and ear protection. "Have fun."

I waste no time lifting the pistol, squinting my right eye closed, aiming, and releasing. With each shot, my body relaxes a little bit more. Once I've gone through my first round of shots, I remove my glasses and reload. I notice Tango hasn't shot one round. He's watching me intently, studying me.

"Something wrong?" I ask.

"That was pretty crazy." His focus moves from mine over to the target. Fifteen rounds put down range and hitting center mass of the target. "You practice a lot?"

"Yes." I insert a fresh magazine and rack a round into the chamber. I've practiced weekly since Krissy was murdered. I won't ever miss

TAG

another shot. If I didn't miss that one shot, Krissy might still be alive. Anyone can tell me her death wasn't my fault, but I will forever blame myself for not saving her. "You planning to shoot?"

He turns to face the target. He closes his left eye, opens it, and closes his right eye. He holds the pistol out in front of him and shoots aimlessly. The bullet grazes the outside of the target, and he grunts with annoyance.

He shoots off another three the same way, and I'm honestly shocked he doesn't know how to shoot. My shock is turning into curiosity, though. Things aren't adding up.

He suppresses a laugh and throws his head back. "This is so fucking embarrassing." His cheeks are visibly red and you can't fake that.

I can't believe I'm doing this. "Here, I'll show you." I clear my pistol before placing it down next to me, being careful to follow protocol so Chuck doesn't find a reason to throw me out. This is going to look ridiculous. I'm at least eight inches shorter than he is, trying to wrap my arms around his to show him how to aim. I point to the top of the pistol. "See this u-shape?" I point out the sites.

"Yeah."

"Look through it." I wrap my fingers around both of his biceps, which feel like stone beneath my touch. "Extend this arm out," I say, pressing down on his right arm. "Now bend your left elbow slightly, while cupping the bottom of your right hand." I shove my knee in between his legs. "Leave some space here for balance." I'm more or less hugging him right now, and it feels . . . nice. Maybe even more than nice. I force myself to refocus my attention, and I take a step back. "Now take a breath, release, and when you feel yourself relax and all of the air is out of your lungs, slowly and steadily squeeze the trigger." I place my hands over his chest, sending a thrill of nerves to coarse through my body at the slight touch of his hardened muscles.

The round shoots straight through the neck of the target. "Not bad for a beginner," I say. Is that a smirk tugging on my permanent scowl? It can't be. What is he doing to me? What. Is. He. Doing. To. Me?

He shoots a few more rounds. Most of them are scattered around the outside of the target, and a few make it in to the inside range. Nevertheless, all of them are better shots than the first ones he let off.

After an hour of releasing all of the steam my body has pent up for the past two weeks, we turn in our pistols.

"Nice shot, honey," the attendant behind the counter says. Now he's giving me compliments?

"I know," I respond, before walking out the door.

For leaving the shooting range only sixty seconds ago, my brain is already bubbling. Thoughts prickle my mind and I feel out of control. I feel like my mind has taken over and I'm not responsible for what I'm about to do. Since I don't have the ability to trust people, I sense eyes and ears in every hovering shadow, and my gut tells me Tango's lying—likely lying about more than just not being able to shoot a weapon. I shove my hand into Tango's chest and push him against the wall of the building. Caught off guard, he complies with my force. "Whoa!" He puts his arms up by his head. "Chill. Will ya?"

"Look me in the eyes and tell me you don't know how to shoot. Tell me that was all an act."

"Why does it matter if I can shoot or not?" His expression is firm. The skin around his cheeks doesn't tighten, and he doesn't lower his hands. But he's not afraid of me. On the contrary, he keeps giving in to me. I want to know why.

I pull out the knife I swiped from the sandwich shop earlier, knowing it would bring me some kind of comfort. I've kept it in the sleeve of my fleece. I couldn't travel with any weapons, and it was the first thing I saw that could be used if needed. I raise it up to his neck. "Tell me who you used to work for?"

His arm swings down and his hand clamps around my wrist, twisting it and pressing it against my back. I attempt to swing with my other hand, but that one gets slapped against my other wrist. With one hand, he encapsulates both of mine, holding them against me in a way that prevents me from moving. With no effort, his now free hand reaches around me and pulls the knife from my hand. He pushes me forward until we reach his truck, still keeping my hands locked behind me. He opens the door and lifts me up with his arm while easily shoving me inside.

He closes the door and locks it, crating me in from the outside world again. My eyes scan the door for the lock button, but I don't see one. Fire is blazing through my nerves, and my rage is overpowering what control I have left.

He opens his door so calm and casual and slides in while gently closing his door. "What the fuck was that, Carolina?" His fingers wrap

TAG 59

around the steering wheel, and the whites of his knuckles glow through his reddened skin. "A knife? Seriously?"

"You're a liar. Just like the rest of them." The words flow freely. I went too far. I realize this, but my anger is not something to play with. If he actually read my file, he'd know that. He'd know how screwed up I am. He'd know not to fuck with me. Yet, he did.

We pull into our parking lot and I flip the door handle three times before I turn and give him a blazing look. "Let me out of this fucking tin can," I growl. He reaches over me and flips the lock I apparently didn't see under the door handle. The locks pop up; I open the door and then kick it fully open. I jump out and storm toward the entrance of the apartment. I'm somewhat surprised he let me go so easily, but I take the opportunity and run. Because that's what I need to do right now.

I'm done.

I'm so fucking done.

CHAPTER SEVEN

TANGO

NOT SURE I EXPECTED a knife—a serrated bread knife of all things, to be pulled on me today, but I've encountered worse. She must have snatched it from the sandwich shop. I'm gathering she's a bit more troubled than I was originally led to believe. Maybe I didn't need to go through the trouble of making her think I haven't shot a pistol, but the man in me needed to feel her touch. And I did. Her hands are small, soft and don't match her personality. She smells like a flowery shampoo, and all I wanted to do was lose my face in her silky waves. I shouldn't be feeling like this. This is my life and work, both meaning the same thing. I know better than this. But my problem is and always has been that I look for trouble, and I always love it—the feeling trouble gives me. And goddamn, this girl is nothing but trouble.

She's embarrassed; I can see that. I feel like I know her type. She's lost within her own mind and doesn't know what's good for her. And I'm guessing that's because nothing has been good for her or good to her in the past. Something's gotta give, or this is going to turn bad real quick. I'm guessing if I'm not the *thing* that gives, the *bad* is going to be on my shoulders.

She's moving quickly ahead of me, trying to create the distance she apparently needs from me. It doesn't take much to trigger her, clearly.

CALI

I bust through the front door and then my bedroom door. I'm out of breath after running through the parking lot and up the stairs. I had to wait for Tango to unlock the door since I'm essentially his prisoner now. Although, I didn't have to wait long since he was on my heels the entire time, making me feel like a child. Now I'm gathering my things and shoving them into my bags. I sling my bags over my shoulders and head for the front door, ready to fight if needed. Ready to fire him if needed.

As expected, I'm stopped at the front door where he stands—large, in my way, and taking up the entire doorway. "I can't let you leave," he says simply.

"Get out of my way before I call my dad." My jaw is tense and my pulse is palpitating in my ears. He needs to move. I need to escape. I need to be free.

"Carolina, you can't call your dad." He drops his arms from the threshold of the door, giving me the illusion he might let me by. "He won't pick up his phone." He moves forward, but I don't step back. I won't be intimidated by him. "When is the last time he picked up your call?"

Not once. In three years. We text when he sends me a working phone number. Sometimes he calls to check in, but not since he set me up with this WWE-looking bodyguard.

I disregard his question.

"Let me by." I step forward, leaving less than a foot between us. Most people would laugh if they saw me trying to intimidate this very tall and built man, compared to my five-foot-three self, but I know how to incapacitate him with one move.

But he doesn't move. His head remains straight, but his eyes lower to my face. "You need to stay with me for your own safety," he says, staring into my eyes intently.

"I don't need to do shit," I argue. I drop my bags and take the remaining step before popping my leg out and curling it behind his knee. I simultaneously twist my hand around the collar of his shirt and jerk him forward. His legs give out, and he falls to his knees. He lets out a loud cough, a painful sounding one. And for a second I think I actually hurt him. Remorse sets in quickly, since I didn't expect to actually do any damage. "Feel better?" he asks, looking up at me. He coughs again and nearly folds in half from the deep fight within his lungs. He clears his throat and looks up me. "If you were smart—" He clears his throat again. "You would have moved me from my position if you really wanted to get by me. But now, I'm still here, only lower to the ground, and I doubt you can jump over my head."

Bastard. He's right. I'm losing my mind. I can't even think of a response.

"Carolina, please stop." He pulls in a deep struggling breath before looking up at me again. "Your dad is not in the CIA anymore. He stole something when he was on a mission in China three years ago. He's been on the run ever since then. There are a number of people who are after him, and you for that matter," he adds, as if scripted.

My heart stops beating, and my mind starts racing. *Know everyone . . . trust no one.* Even Dad.

"How do I know you aren't lying?" I sound powerless. I sound as if I've lost control.

I *have* lost control.

He stands up and steps away from the door, leaving it free and clear. But I don't leave. "Carolina, come here away from the door. We don't need anyone hearing this shit." He waves me into the kitchen, and my body obeys before my mind does.

I drop down into a bar stool and let my head fall onto my folded arms. "Where is he?" I mumble into my sleeve.

"You don't know, do you?" his voice grows behind me as he moves in closer.

I snap my head up and twist my body around on the stool to face him. "No, Tango. My mother is dead, my sister was fucking murdered, and I thought my dad was in the CIA. They've all left me in a world where everyone wants to screw me over or kill me." I feel hot tears piercing the back of my eyes. I will not cry. I'm done crying. I shouldn't have any tears left. I pull in short spurts of shallow breaths until I regain my composure.

He slouches down in front of my stool. "Hey," he says, looking up at me. "You were put in this situation. It isn't your fault. But you do need to be protected. If you don't want it to be me, I can call someone

TAG

63

else. Just say the word, and I'll be gone. I don't want to make this harder on you." He places his hand on my knee for comfort. Not hostility. Like a friend would do. I like his touch. It's warm. It's a feeling I haven't felt since Reaper touched me. "Honest."

I swallow my pride, and it goes down like a rusty nail. I don't want to deal with a new guard. I don't want to be watched. But if I don't have a choice, I . . .

I promised myself I wouldn't let this happen again. I promised the lifeless body of my little sister this wouldn't happen again.

My breaths increase even more. I might hyperventilate, so I suck in all of the air I can and hold it, hoping it will calm me down or cause me to pass out. Tango's fingers slip through my fingers, and he pulls me off the stool and down to my knees. "Come here," he says in a heavy voice. His arms wrap around my body, squeezing me tightly against him. "Friends. Okay?" He releases me and pushes me backward a bit so he can situate his face in front of mine. Being this close to him — it does something to me. It gives me comfort. I don't even remember the feeling. "I will keep you safe from everyone, including yourself." He takes my wrist and turns it over, scanning the area where a two-inch scar shows. Maybe he knew from my file, or maybe he noticed it over the past few days. It's unmistakably a scar marking an attempted end. If he did read that in my file, it's obviously something he didn't feel like repeating to me when I asked him to tell me what he knew.

"I like this tattoo," he says, placing his finger over the ink and the scar, both intended to be one mark. Except, all he probably notices is the lapse in judgment—where my pulse stopped beating the day I lost my sister: my best friend. The day I wanted to die with her.

His fingers remain on my wrist, and the warmth of his touch makes me weak. I'm forcing myself not to twitch, not to let him know he's gotten in my head.

"Where is my dad?" I ask, pulling myself away from him and up to my feet.

"Right now, he's in Mexico. He's hiding."

I have become my father's bait. That is why I am being chased. This must be why Krissy was killed?

"What crime did he commit?" I ask, knowing he probably won't tell me.

"I'm not supposed to tell you," he says with what I now can confirm is compassion in his eyes.

I nod my head, trying to understand. But I don't. I can't. This is my life, and I'm in the dark.

Am I supposed to sit here and believe a complete stranger? Maybe he's the one lying. Maybe he's trying to reach my dad through me. Maybe I completely fucked up again by letting him in this close.

"How am I supposed to know I can trust you?" I ask, backing up until I hit the windowsill. "I mean, you come up to me in the airport and tell me my dad hired you. Now you're telling me my dad is a criminal and wanted. Who is he wanted by?"

"From the little amount of information he told me, some people from China are after him. The group he was with at the time have been after him for the last three years."

"For what?" I repeat.

"Please, Carolina. Let me do my job correctly."

"Well, I'm pretty sure you've already lied to me once. And I'm sure I don't need to inform you of the saying, *once a liar, always a liar*. Right?"

"Fair enough," he says, pulling a worn brown leather wallet out of his back pocket. I'm not sure what I'm expecting to see. I'm not sure I know what bodyguards carry for IDs. Maybe I should after all this time. But I don't. He opens his wallet and pulls out his license. "This is the best I can do."

Tango Flynn from Springfield, Missouri. "Great, so you weren't lying about your name or what state you were from." I hand his license back to him. "This doesn't clarify more than your name."

"Look. I can't leave your side. No matter how difficult you make this. I've agreed to this job, and it has to be this way." He slides his wallet back into his pocket and crosses his arms over his chest. "If you want me to pretend I'm not here, I will. If you want company, I'm here. Deal?"

I nod my head in agreement. "We're making a deal, agreeing on me being your captive?"

"I don't know what else to tell you," he shrugs. "Want me to find a replacement?"

"No, I don't," I say without thinking.

* * *

TAG   65

The never-ending day is finally coming to an end. He asked if I wanted him to grab me dinner from down the street, but I'm not hungry. Right now, I want to pretend like he's not here. My stomach couldn't possibly compete with my mind, which is spinning in circles, trying to comprehend truths that have been hidden from me for so fucking long.

I sit down at the edge of my bed and loosen the laces on my boots. I slip each one off and place them next to the bed. As I scoot backward, my head finds the naked pillow, and it reminds me of how unsettled I am here. The last thing I want to do right now is wrestle with sheets, but who knows who or what has occupied this bed before me. I slide off the bed and open my one lonely bag that I hadn't finished emptying. I wrap my hand around perfectly folded sheets and a blanket and place them over the mattress.

With slow, sluggish movements, I move around the bed, struggling to fit each corner over the rounded edges. I smooth the fleece blanket over the top and make it perfect like Mom used to do. These sheets and blanket are my home. The smell, the softness and the warmth—they remind me so much of her.

I took them from Mom's bed after she was transferred into hospice. It took everything I had to wash them, to purposely remove her scent. But if I try hard enough, I can still smell her—the scent of vanilla and roses—the scent of a beautifully amazing mother. Each night when I bury my head into my pillow, I can feel her presence. I know this life I'm living isn't what she wanted for me, and if she ever knew how angry and miserable of a person I have become, it would make her sick.

I sneak out of my room, hoping to avoid any more encounters for the night and lock myself in the bathroom to wash the day off my face. I take my pills in the same order I take them every night and then look at my reflection. How can I be left in a world where I can't trust anyone? Can I even trust *my* decisions? Was she thinking straight when she kept reminding me how trust doesn't exist anywhere?

I brush my teeth then zipper all of my belongings back up into my cosmetic bag. And with one last look at myself, I hit the light switch and cover myself with darkness. I take a deep breath and step into the hall where I hear Tango coughing again. He sounds like he's in pain, so I reluctantly take a couple of steps toward his bedroom. *Does he need help?* When I peek my head around his door, I see him pulling puffs of air from an inhaler. Maybe he's asthmatic? Although it seems unlikely that Dad would send me a guard who wasn't the picture of perfect health. I suppose he might not have known, though.

I knock lightly against his door. "Are you okay," I ask tenderly.

I've caught him off guard, and he throws his inhaler into his bag. "Yeah, yeah. Of course. Allergies," he laughs.

"You must have pretty bad allergies," I say. I take another step in toward him, squinting at what's on his face. It isn't until I take a couple more steps when I realize he has a blood streak stretching from the corner of his mouth all the way to his ear. "You're . . . ah . . . bleeding."

He takes the back of his sleeve and wipes his face, seeming embarrassed. "Chronic cough. I've had it since I was a kid. Nothing to worry about." He keeps wiping at his face, but it's already dry.

"Hold on." I leave his room and go back into the bathroom where I grab a tissue and lightly soak it under the faucet. I return to his room and sit down next to him on his bed. "Here." I press the tissue against his cheek and blot it around the blood-covered area. I use my free hand to hold his chin still in order to be a little more forceful with the stubborn dried blood. "Sorry, it dried," I say. He watches me intently as I help him. The tough guy façade has softened, and his lips are parted, appearing surprised at my kindness, I'm assuming. I feel bad for him. That's all this is. At least, that's what I'll tell myself. Except, touching his face is making my stomach spin and my heart swell. Feeling his rough stubble scratch against my palm is a surprising turn-on, which tells me I have to let go. I have to walk away before something happens that we'd both regret.

His cheeks flush and he seems uncomfortable, so I take the hint and leave without another word.

Once back in my room, I lie down in my freshly made bed, allowing my mind to race, but mostly I'm contemplating the difference between truth and trust. As usual, my thoughts don't make it far before the awaited numbness from the Valium covers me like a warm blanket.

Visions of Mom's auburn hair blowing in the beach wind soothe my loneliness. This world may have taken away everything I love, but nothing can take away my memories.

Mom always took simple enjoyment out of small things. Driving to the beach in Corpus Christi every weekend was all it took to keep her happy. Krissy and I didn't complain. It was peaceful. It was a break from the disruptive clatter in our house of Dad slamming phones, speaking in different languages, and waking everyone up in the middle of the night because he had to leave on another mission.

He was usually missing from the good parts of our life. We tried to carry on without him, and it was normal to us, but I don't think it was normal to Mom.

They met in high school before his career. She told me millions of times how he used to look at her, how she was his world. But after college, and some *governmental internships* as she called them, he joined the CIA. His world dissolved. The CIA was his world, his family, and his life. I know he loved all of us, but he showed it in an abnormal way; a way civilians are unfamiliar with.

I feel my muscles release and my lungs loosen. *I miss you, Mom and Krissy.*

* * *

It's been three days of awkwardness between Tango and me, but I've kept myself busy with my head buried in my laptop, stalking Reaper for the most part. We've ordered pizza the last three nights and have eaten in our own bedrooms, by ourselves. He took me back to the shooting range yesterday and sat and watched as I shot. Maybe he didn't want to embarrass himself again. Well, that is if he was actually telling me the truth about his lack of shooting skills. I'm starting to think it might be easier to stop acting like such a cold bitch, but that means I'd have to be nice to him . . . and that might make things awkward again. I'm stuck here with him for who knows how long, so I kind of need to figure out how to survive this somehow.

I tuck my ego into my back pocket and walk into the living room where his eyes are locked on his phone. This was a bad idea. I can still walk back to my room. But it only takes a few seconds for him to realize I'm standing here staring at him like an idiot.

"What's up, Carolina?"

I shove my hands into my pockets and roll back on my heels. "Sooo." *Never mind. Don't do it, Cali. You're crossing the line.* If I could punch my sub-conscious right now, I would, but it's clear my mouth has a mind of its own tonight. "Want to have dinner with a friend?"

That sounded as ridiculous as it felt. He's laughing, probably at my feeble attempt to break the uncomfortable silence between us.

"Is this like a truce?" he asks.

"Whatever," I respond in a Cali-like-manner, being careful not to give him the wrong impression. "I need to get out of this apartment tonight."

CHAPTER EIGHT

TANGO

MAYBE SHE'S COMING AROUND. Maybe she's going to make this a little easier on me. I hope so, because I've had too much time to think over the past few days, and things are starting to catch up to me. Memories, realizations—the fact that I'm not a Marine anymore. The fact that I'm only a nobody.

Maybe the burn in my lungs has gotten worse because I'm sitting still. It's like it caught up to me because I let it. The doctor warned me it would happen, but I tried to put it in the back of my head, knowing I'd deal with it when the time came.

I'm scared. And if I ever said that out loud to any of my Marine brothers, they'd whack me upside the head. But in truth, I feel like a child left in the middle of nowhere without any knowledge on how to find his way home. The world seems like such a big place when you have no one and nowhere to turn. It almost feels like the world is caving in, warning me it's done with me, and it's time to go.

But I don't want to go.

I'm not done with this world.

CALI

"Whiskey sour," I shout to the bartender. I lower myself onto the sticky wooden barstool and steal a napkin from the bar tray full of sliced fruits and olives. I spit my gum out and crumple up the napkin in my hand.

"I'll just have the whisky," Tango calls out.

"IDs?" the bartender asks.

I slide my hand into my back pocket and retrieve my license—or the license I've claimed to be my own. He studies the picture on the card and looks back at me. "You color your hair?"

"Yes," I respond, fisting the already crumpled napkin into a tight wad. I had my hair dyed blond when I had this ID made, but that was when I was fun, bubbly and outgoing. It was four years ago before my life started going down the shitter. I wouldn't make a good blond these days.

"Nice." He hands the card back to me and studies me for a moment. "Do you go by Sam, or Samantha?"

"Samantha."

"Well then, Samantha. One whiskey sour coming right up."

Tango looks over at me and cocks his head to the side. "A fake? You're twenty-two." I know how old I am, and I know I don't want anyone to know who the hell I am.

I shrug. "So, what's the problem?"

He shakes his head and laughs softly. "Whatever floats your boat."

The twenty-something-year-old bartender hustles around behind the bar, combining the ingredients to make my drink. The people sitting around us are shouting orders at him, but it appears he's working the bar himself. The crowd seems to be swarming in like a school of fish, which means our space is becoming more confined, and our stools are slowly merging together. I glance down at my watch and realize it's five-thirty. Work just let out, and everyone's stopping in to forget about their long day.

I ordered a plate of nachos and declared it to be my dinner, and Tango ordered a plate of buffalo wings and declared it his. Now here we are both sitting in silence, eating and drinking as if we're complete strangers, which as of a week ago, we were.

TAG

We're both on drink number four, and I'm hoping he starts talking as I've learned alcohol driven interrogation typically works the best. I tap my fingers curtly on the bar top, and my chin drops into the palm of my resting arm. I'm officially bored and getting buzzed, which is not a good combo.

"Am I boring you, Samantha?" Tango teases, nudging his shoulder into mine.

"Not at all," I raise an eyebrow with a hint of mischievousness. Time to drag in the bait.

I wave my finger in the air, calling the bartender's attention. "Two shots of Absolute," I say emphatically.

"You're freaking nuts, girl." Tango's words are beginning to slur. But I think mine are too.

The bartender places the two shot glasses down in front of us and stops to wait for the show. I curl my fingers around the cool glass and throw the clear liquid into the back of my throat. The burn warms my insides and tickles my nose. The rush is instantaneous as the feeling of bubbles float up into my head. This is the moment I love—the moment my pain briefly disappears. The moment happiness comes naturally.

Tango shoots the shot into the back of his throat. His expression doesn't change, and the burn doesn't seem to affect him. Of course. He slams the glass down on the table and grunts, "Good shit."

Maybe now he'll start talking.

His eyes look glossy, and I'm thinking the alcohol is starting to do its job. He sits quietly for a few minutes, staring straight through the bottle of Jack perched on the back bar in front of him. I wonder what's on his mind, and I wonder how many fucking shots it's going to take to make him tell me what is on his mind.

TANGO

"What can I do to cheer you up, Carolina?" I ask her, noticing a slight slur in my words. I've made a mental note that the whiskey burn numbs the other burn in my lungs.

"Cheer me up?" she retorts. I can't tell if it's anger or hurt behind her sparkling blue eyes. She lifts her drink and puckers her lips gently around the straw, holding it there briefly before pulling it back out. "I honestly don't know if anything can cheer me up." I'm pretty sure her words just damaged me. No one deserves the shit she's gone through, although I supposed I could say the same thing about myself.

The bartender places the two glasses of water I ordered down in front of us and lets his eyes linger over Carolina for one second too long. I'm pretty sure he just fell in love with her. It's easy to do. I slap my credit card down on the counter, pulling his attention away from her. "We're good, man." I raise my eyebrow slightly, giving the guy the hint to keep on moving and to shift his focus to something else besides her. Although I guess, I shouldn't really be doing that. She isn't mine, and she probably never will be. But fuck, I think I might do anything to experience her—any part of her. I have the urge to touch her lips, to taste her tongue, and to breathe her breath.

I don't know, what am I even thinking right now?

I'm so desperate to reel in any type of reaction from her that I'd probably settle on making her smile. Maybe that would cure me.

CALI

We paid the bill an hour ago, but we've been sitting here making small talk about nothing more than the weather. He seems disturbed or upset, and I can't quite put my finger on it. I settle my arms over the bar and lean forward to stretch my back. I'm ready to get going, but I don't want to rush him since I know he's trying to sober up before we get back in the truck. "You know," he says out of nowhere. "What you've been put through is nothing but crap. You deserve to live a normal life." He shifts his weight and stands up from his stool, slipping his arms into his jacket and readjusting it over his shoulders.

Suddenly, I'm not ready to go. He seems to have gotten so much information out of me, and I've gotten nothing from him. "Before we go, tell me something about your past." I realize my hand is curled around his arm, but I let go as soon as my brain catches up to the present. "You know everything about me, and I'm being followed around by a complete stranger. If you already know how miserable I am, don't go making things worse for me. At least let me know you." My words sound pleading, and they didn't come out how I intended. I shouldn't have had this much to drink. I just screwed myself.

He sits back down on his stool and brings his feet up to the metal post below the bar. He clasps his hands together and taps his right thumb over the top of his left hand. With concentration, he looks me right in the eyes. It's as if whatever information is floating around in his head is painful enough that it might be easier to keep it to himself. "I was a Marine for five-and-a-half years. I was in Iraq for two years and Afghanistan for two years. I ah . . . I was discharged and came home to Eli's job offer." He slaps his hand down over the bar and looks over at me with half-lidded eyes. "And now here I am with you." He stands back up and zips his jacket. "Ready?"

While in the process of trying to find the words to respond with, my phone vibrates, and I'm thankful for the distraction. I slip my phone out of my pocket and the caller ID displays a text from a number I don't recognize, which happens often since Dad is always changing his number.

What's your location?

-Dad

Before I can respond, Tango snatches the phone out of my hand and flips his phone out of his pocket. Within seconds, he's typing something on his phone. "I need to track the nearest satellites." I'm trying to figure out what he's doing or what he means, but I quickly understand when he continues talking. "I have to write this down. I have his GPS coordinates."

"What are you talking about? What do you need GPS coordinates for?" I know I sound frantic. What if he is only after Dad like all of these other nuts? I have no proof other than a fucking license telling me this guy's name is Tango.

"Carolina, that's not your dad." His words make me feel like I got sucker punched. "Do you think your dad would be sending you a message with a traceable phone number? Because this number is definitely traceable."

"You're a liar and an asshole," I shout. "You've been fucking using me just like everyone else. You think if you're in my head, you could get through me to my dad? You think that's what you can do?" The tears have to stop. I feel them stabbing the back of my eyes, so I take the glass in front of me and throw it across the bar, watching it shatter against a pillar ten feet in front of me. Everyone around me stops what they're doing and looks over. A couple men stand up in front of their dates or girlfriends in a protective manner, probably thinking I'm about to go all sorts of crazy. Which, I might. He's been trying to find Dad. That's all this has been about. He lied.

Tango's hand clamps tightly around my arm, and he pulls me out of my seat. I'm fighting him with all of my drunken strength, but it's useless against his overwhelming power. Before I know it, I'm outside and pinned up against the wall. His hands are pressing firmly on my shoulders and his head is arched down so his eyes are inches from mine. "If you're going to kill me. Just do it fast. Just do it now," I say, trying my hardest to hold back the incoming sobs.

"Listen to me." He loosens his grasp. "You need to get a grip. I swear to you that was not your dad. Your dad doesn't have a phone

TAG

75

right now. If he does, it's not traceable. I know where he is, or his whereabouts, at least. He has no way to contact you. I know you don't trust me, nor do you want to try. But I kind of need you to, for your own safety." He removes his hands from me but doesn't shift his position. "Hate me, slap the shit out of me—I don't care. But I am going to keep you safe. And it's not because I work for your dad. It's because I don't want an innocent woman who's already seen as much shit as you've had to, see any fucking more." I thrust my fists into his solid shoulders and shove him out of the way. "Where are you going?" he shouts after me.

When I reach this point, there is only one way out. I turn my head in each direction, looking for my vice until I hear cars racing by. I pick up my pace before he can stop me. I need the adrenaline to lower the rage. I *need* it. I step out into the busy intersection and watch as a car comes speeding toward me. I'm wearing black and it's night. They won't see me until it's too late. I suck in my breath and wait to feel the wind on my face. Sometimes I take a second to consider my options. Should I just end it, or should I wait? I clench my eyes as the wind grows. The horn screams as an arm is wrapped around my stomach and I'm thrown into the sidewalk.

Tango is hovering over me, his veins pulsating over his forehead and anger darkening his eyes. "I've had it with you tonight." He lifts me up without allowing me time to catch my breath, to suck in the adrenaline or to smile from the rush. He throws me over his shoulder and darts back across the street. I kick my legs and punch his back, but he's unaffected as usual. He is the force I can't reckon with and it's pissing me off.

I'm sick of being treated like an object—like a secured jewel. I want to be free. I should flee this goddamn country and go join Dad, wherever he is. It would be so much easier.

After being manhandled and forced back into the apartment, I'm left huddled in the corner of my bedroom like a deflated balloon. I pull my knees up to my chest and bury my face into my arms. I wasn't going to let the car hit me. I like the rush. It makes me forget. It reminds me *I'm* in control of whether or not I live or die.

I hear the front door open and close so I pull myself up and off the ground and stumble out of my room and toward the front door. I press my ear against the wood and hear the ruffling of his feet against the stiff Berber carpeting in the hall, so I rush back to lock myself in my bedroom. I'm not hiding from him. I'm distancing myself.

A heavy fist pounds against my bedroom door. "Carolina!" he says. I don't respond. I don't move from my desk chair, looking out into the dark trees that are now judging me, rather than dancing. "Carolina!" His voice grows a little louder this time, and it's followed by another knock. "Look. We have to go. *Now*." The words normally cause me to spring into action when I hear them from Dad. It means there's a threat somewhere. However, I'm not sure I want to take orders from Tango—not without trusting his true intentions. And God knows, that won't happen. Trust, the word is a joke. "Fine. I'm calling for a replacement. I'm not here to babysit, like I told you."

Fuck. I don't want him to go. I don't want a replacement. Who knows who I'd end up with this time. I'm so alone right now. "Cali, let me in." His voice turns a little kinder, which pulls me toward the door.

I pull my door open slowly, and I'm sure he probably sees the redness in my eyes. "You called me, Cali," I croak out.

"Carolina is a mouthful," he chuckles. "We really have to go. We have to lead him off track."

Him.

Him, who?

Stomach acid builds up and a wave of nausea washes over me. "Who is he?" I run my fingers through my hair, fisting a section into a knot. "Please, tell me, Tango."

"This guy named Rea—"

"Never mind." *Don't say his name. I can't hear it again.* "I'm not running," I say under my breath. "I—"

"You know him?" he asks, dumbfounded.

"Yes," I answer simply, knowing what truth lies behind the word.

"Cali, this asshole has been the number one guy after your dad. Did you know he was your dad's fucking assistant when he was in China? He knows what your dad did and what he has." My stomach drops and I feel like oxygen has been sucked out of my lungs. Dad didn't actually know Reaper and I were dating. This all makes sense now. Dad was gone long before I met him. I was Reaper's bait right from the start. This makes me want to kill him even more now. "Seriously, Cali. You aren't thinking straight. You've had too much to drink. We have to go."

He's wrong. I am thinking—more clearly than I ever have. For the past year, Reaper thought he was the one chasing me. He thinks he's the reason I keep running. The truth is, I'm just waiting for the right time and the right angle. I'm waiting for my opportunity. I know what I have to do . . . and I don't care what happens after I do it.

"I want him dead," I say softly. Tango leans his head against the door and releases a long sigh. "He killed my sister."

"I understand." He closes in on the couple feet of space between us and places his hand over the bare skin of my shoulder. "I'm not saying you aren't capable of killing him. I believe you are, but in the slight chance he outsmarts you, he'll kill you too." He squeezes my good shoulder gently and looks me in the eyes. "Are you sure he was the one who killed her? He isn't the only one after your dad, you know?"

I meet his gaze and wait for the pain to pour out of my soul before I start talking. "I watched him slice my sister's throat with a knife." I watched her blood trickle out until her body was empty. I watched her eyes beg for help while I sat there crying over her. I watched her chest move for the last time. I felt as the warmth in her skin turned to ice. "He was also my boyfriend. I loved him. I trusted him. And I shouldn't have. Look where it landed me—my sister. I need to have this opportunity, Tango."

"You were with him?" He looks sickened by his own question. "You've known he was the murderer all this time?" He straightens his posture and takes a step away from me. "You were a witness?" His voice continues to rise in volume, angry with me for a situation that didn't even involve him. He sucks in a deep breath and tries to calm down. "Why didn't you turn him in when it happened?"

"They still wouldn't have found him." I look at him with intensity. "And like I said, I want to be the one who kills him."

"Okay. Well, then—thank you for your honesty. Now can we leave here, please?" He thinks I'm joking. Or he thinks I'm not thinking this through. Maybe he doesn't realize this is the only thing I'm always thinking about. I want to see the look on Reaper's face when I put a knife through *his* throat. I want to hear him say sorry for murdering my sister. For making her suffer. For making her pay a consequence for Dad's actions. And for lying to me, using me and making me fall in love with him just so he could find Dad.

"No, Tango. I want to stay here and let him think he can find me. Let him think I had a moment of weakness and stopped tracking him. Let him think he can kill me."

Sympathy grows within Tango's eyes. At least that's what I think the look is. Maybe he's thinking I'm nuts. And now comes the part where he disagrees with me, tells me I'm insane, and forcefully pulls me out of the apartment. He reaches down for my hand and pulls me toward him. His arms loop around my back and he pulls me in against him, holding me. With my head up against his chest, I can hear a struggle in his lungs—a whine with every breath he takes. It's a strange noise, but the feeling of warmth sways my attention to the feeling of security within his arms. It shoots a long forgotten feeling into my gut, and I have the urge to look up at him, but I can't.

"We'll stay," he says gently.

"Really?" Is he going to sit here and watch me kill this guy? Because, those are my intentions. I think I was clear about that.

"If I had a chance to retaliate against someone who killed one of my brothers, I would. And no one could stop me." His eyes change—they soften. "Do what you have to do for her. I'll back you up."

I feel wild inside, powered up and ready to attack. I've been waiting for this.

"I have something for you. Wait here." He stands up and jets out of the room. He returns with a bag I haven't seen him with, which I'm now seeing contains two 45 mm handguns. He shoves one of them into his holster and looks back up at me. He reaches for my hand and pulls me toward him. "Turn around." I do as he says without question. Is this trust? He's holding a pistol and told me to turn around. I'm breaking Mom's rule. "Another reason I had my truck delivered to us. Couldn't sneak these babies through TSA."

He loops his finger through my back belt loop and I feel a tug. His knuckles sweep against my bare skin and I feel an electric zap charge through my body. My breath hitches and my eyes close in response to his warmth. My need for him is growing by the minute, but he's here to protect me. Nothing more. I swallow my unsure feelings as he spins me back around to secure a small holster around my waist. Once secure, he slips the pistol in and stretches my shirt down over the holster. "This is only for self-defense," he says, lowering his eyes to my gaze. "That's my only rule, Cali. You wait for it to be self-defense. Rules of engagement. I'm sure you're familiar."

"I thought you couldn't shoot?" I quip.

He smirks a bit as he pulls a folded piece of paper from his back pocket and tosses it to me. I hold it up to my desk light. It's his target from the shooting range. The holes put together make up the outline of a smiley face. I should be pissed that he played me like a fool, and I had a moment where I believed he couldn't shoot, but this is pretty good. I can't contain the smile that's overpoweringly creeping across my lips.

"Well I'll be damned. Is that a smile, Miss Carolina?"

I bite my cheek in an attempt to stop. "You lied," I say playfully.

"And you have a breathtaking smile." His lip stretches up, hinting at a smile of his own. "So, I guess we're even."

His eyes are studying mine and the moment is making my stomach twist into knots again. I'm not sure he realizes he's staring. Or maybe he does as he flinches a bit and clears his throat. "Well. Good night. I've thoroughly secured the apartment. We're safe." He turns and walks out of my room, closing the door behind him.

I'm left here confused and wondering what just happened in the past three minutes. I want to slap my own face. I shouldn't have to keep reminding myself about Reaper and how much I trusted him, as well. He looked at me the exact same way.

CHAPTER NINE

TANGO

I'VE FELT PAIN. I know the intensity of it and the way it controls your mind and body. But watching Cali in this much pain is almost too much to bear. Everything with her needs to be slow and thought out. I can't let her stick around and kill this guy. She'll go to jail. She isn't thinking clearly. But if I try to drag her out right now, she won't comply, and I don't blame her. I know what it feels like to want revenge. The feeling is almost consuming. I can see how she would think she has nothing to lose by killing him. Everything has already been taken from her. But she has the chance to start her life over, and I don't want her to lose that. It's my job to protect her. And waiting here for her sister's murderer to show up, isn't very logical, but I do have faith that even as a form of self-defense, we can take him down before he has the chance to try anything stupid.

I swear I saw some softness in her icy blue eyes earlier. The look made my heart ache. And my heart doesn't ache. Not for anyone. I've been trained to protect the innocent, and that's what I'm doing. I haven't gotten this wrapped up in a mission before, and I've never been affected this much. Usually, I complete the job and move onto the next, but I have a feeling it won't be that easy this time, especially since this is my last job.

I know what I read about her, but there is so much more to know. I know better than anyone, you don't judge a person by what's in their file. If that were the case, I'd be considered nothing more than a murderer of the innocent. Explosives will give you that sort of reputation.

I sit down on my bed and pull each boot off, placing them down side by side next to my bed. I fall backwards onto my pillow and fold my arms across my chest and close my eyes.

As the wheeze in my lungs acts as a white noise, the apprehension begins. It's too empty . . .

TAG

* * *

The streets should be bustling, people moving around, children yelling as their parents rummage through the street market. I've been in too many of these situations, immediately realizing that this isn't going to end well. Looking behind me for my guys, I quickly realize they're gone. Fuck! I flip my right hand over, twisting my rifle to the side to remove the magazine. No rounds. I reach down to my vest. No mags, just empty pouches. I reach to my thigh. No sidearm.

Wonderful.

My nerves tell me what's next as I duck into a doorway just as the pops begin and the rubble starts flying. Fear sets in now as I start thinking of how to survive with no ammo, an unknown number of people firing small arms at me and no team for support. Nothing in here to improvise with except a small table and chair. There's a window on the opposite wall, which I quickly but cautiously run to, trying to see what's on the other side of the building. No one. They must all be in the street. Do I wait until they breach the doorway and try to intercept the front man for his weapon? Capture is not an option; I need to take as many as I can down with me as I go. Death somehow seems justifiable as long as those assholes come with me.

This is it.

As I hear their voices grow louder, my hands tense, ready to grab the rifle barrel when it peeks through the door. If I can get the weapon out of his grip, I can drive it backwards, hopefully crushing enough of his facial bones to render him useless.

My breathing is heavy but slow. I see sharper and hear clearer than normal.

Silence.

The door implodes and I miss his weapon. Within a second, my left hand instinctively grabs the lower portion of his jaw and my fingers clench through his tongue. I grip his jaw like a handle to hold tightly as I disable him.

As I swing my right palm down onto his ear, I hear the hollowed crack below my hand.

* * *

I wake up, half screaming, half shaking, soaked in sweat. Catching my breath, staring at the ceiling above my face, I think of how I've come to hate my dreams, my experiences, and my mind in general.

CALI

The brightness of the sun spills into my room, so I pull the pillow over my head. I need coffee and we don't have any. My phone vibrates on my nightstand as if it were an alarm clock. Every day this damn thing wakes me up with Google alerts for sightings on Reaper. I suppose I was already somewhat awake today, though. I slap my hand over the phone and drag it off the stand until it falls onto the bed. I peek my head out from below the pillow and wait for my eyes to adjust as I pick up the phone and bring it into focus.

It's not a Google alert. A text message from a blocked number displays across my screen.

> *Cali, I'm in Boston. Meet me at 112 Beech Street @ 1:00 p.m.*
>
> *I want to see you.*
>
> *Love, Dad.*

I shake my head, baffled by this message. Dad always calls me Carolina, and he doesn't use twelve-hour time. This is definitely not Dad.

My feet drop off the bed and slide into each boot. I lace them up and pull a new shirt out of my bag. I pull it over my head and open the door. Tango is leaning on the wall opposite of my door, one foot on the wall, and one hand holding out a coffee.

"For me?" I ask, my voice croaking.

"I locked you in and ran down the street. And you were none the wiser." He presses his tongue out between his lips, but doesn't smile. He's cute. *Ugh. Take it back, Cali.* I take the hot cup and toss my phone at his now empty hand. "What's this?" He drops his foot from the wall and handles the phone with both hands.

I take a sip of the coffee and close my eyes, momentarily enjoying the beautiful toasty warmth running down the back of my throat. "Thank you, for this." I lift the cup and tap the air.

"Carolina, what is this?" Oh, we're back to formal names. Nicknames must belong under a drunk category. "This isn't your dad. I tried to tell you last night."

TAG
83

I shake my head and pull my phone from his hand. "My dad calls me Carolina. And the last time he used twelve-hour time was when I was probably twelve. So, yeah. You were right."

"I have an idea," he says, heading toward his bedroom.

"What?" I chase him down the hall. "What are we doing?" I'm hoping we're going to this location. We're going to hunt Reaper down and I'm going to fucking shoot him point blank.

"Go grab your stuff just in case . . ."

He doesn't have to finish his sentence. I get it. I run back to my bedroom and place my coffee cup down on the dresser before changing into clean clothes. I open my bags and scoop up the few hanging shirts I threw into the closet and dump them in my bag. Then I rip the sheets off the bed, roll them into a pile and shove them inside too. Lastly, I unplug my laptop and smother it between the compacted sheets. Zipped and ready to go. I throw my bags over my shoulder and snatch my coffee back from the dresser.

"Ready," I sing in an anxious voice as I walk toward the front door where he's waiting.

He whips the door open and sticks his head out, looking in each direction before moving forward. "Stay behind me, just in case."

Unfamiliar with this area, I don't try to follow the signs on the roads. The only thing my mind is set on is figuring out what we're going to do when we arrive at this location in Boston. We turn onto another highway, and I happen to notice one of the signs we're passing by. It says: *Cape Cod, 20 miles.* I've heard of *the Cape.* It's at the tip of Massachusetts, definitely not near Boston.

"Where the hell are we going?" I ask.

"Away."

"Okay. That's it. I want some additional proof that you're really a bodyguard. I have no idea who the hell you really are, or what your intentions are. I don't trust you, and I don't trust a word you say. You could be kidnapping me for all I know." I kick my feet up on the dashboard and lower my seat back. I pull my glasses over my eyes and fold my arms. There has to be something I can do to change his mind. Maybe if I forfeit my body to him, he'll actually start answering my questions. Sex is usually a good answer to problems and it wouldn't be the worst last resort.

"I can say, I'm sorry. But I doubt it'll matter to you."

"No, it won't matter. You won't even answer simple questions."

"Fine. I'll answer a simple question. Go ahead, ask," he says with a snippy attitude.

"Do you have a family?" Out of every question I could have asked, this one popped out of my mouth first. I feel like slapping myself for not thinking this through a little more.

"I had two parents and a sister, yes." His hands tighten around the steering wheel and his jaw grinds subtly back and forth. Then again, maybe we're getting somewhere. I'm starting to see a slight possibility that he isn't as different from me as I thought.

"Did they all die?" I can't imagine anyone's luck being so poor that they could lose their entire family on three different occasions. It must have been some kind of accident.

He pulls in a sharp breath and chews on the inside of his cheek. "Can we just not go there? I answered your one simple question. Please."

I nod, wanting to say I understand. But now I just want to hear what happened and to tell him he's not alone. Although, he knows he's not alone. He knows I've been through the same type of pain. And I know what it's like to shut down and keep to myself. For that, I can respect his feelings.

"I think I've made my intentions of keeping you safe, clear. You could be kidnapped by worse, you know?" he says.

I pull my glasses down onto the bridge of my nose and twist my head to look at his smiling profile. I smile in return, again.

"Hey now, two smiles. What did I do to become so damn lucky?" He turns on the radio and starts tapping his hands on the steering wheel to the beat of the country music. "I'm going to make you trust me. And believe me." His words come out with a bit of vigor, making him sound a little more conceited than I had originally thought him to be.

"And keep me alive?" I drawl. "How lucky am I, cowboy?" I playfully fan myself with my hand.

"I like this side of you, Carolina."

I see a hint of pink appear on his cheeks, so I lean my face in toward his. "Are you—" I laugh. "Are you blushing?"

He releases an exaggerated sigh. "No, I must have a fever."

I roll my eyes and fall back against the seat. I push my glasses back up to my eyes and inhale a long and full breath. Breathing does come easier when I'm around him.

TANGO

I should be looking at the road. *Look at the damn road.* I have no plan. I have no direction. All I know is, I haven't been to Cape Cod, and that's where we're heading. I have to keep her away from Boston. I have to let this shit play out. I don't trust her not to run off, and I guess I don't trust myself enough to contain her.

She looks so innocent and so pleasant when she's asleep, but when she's awake, she's a ball of fire. Although, I do think the meanness has to be a mask, or just a case of self-defense. Whatever the reason is, I like what I see under the mask.

I glance over at her again now, because I can, because she doesn't know I'm looking at her. I kind of like the way a burgundy hue teases a few strands of her midnight black hair in the sun, and the ends curl slightly over the top of her breasts, almost like they were placed perfectly on both sides. But it wasn't done purposely; she's just perfect like that. Her skin is so fair and so complimentary to every color she encompasses. And her lips. Those fucking lips are partly open, just enough to accentuate the plumpness of her top lip. She really is sexy— sexier than I had realized. But she is my assignment and I need to keep reminding myself of this. Still, it's been four long years since a woman has touched me, and I'm desperately craving that soft, delicate embrace. It would fill a much needed desire. And not just from anyone. I'm starting to think that someone has to be her.

The warning bumps on the shoulder of the road have pulled my eyes back to the highway. Must keep my eyes focused on the road, not her. I have to keep my focus, period.

CALI

I must have dozed off for a bit, the bumps on the road have woken me up and I glance out the window. We're driving over rocks toward a beach. "Why are we at a beach? This probably isn't a great hiding spot."

"We aren't hiding. We're staying away from Boston. While you were getting your bags, I called one of the other mercenaries from the company I work with. I have a feeling Reaper isn't alone. There could be a group of them. And there are only two of us. Let my guys go check it out and tell us who's there before we react."

"I thought you were a bodyguard, not a mercenary?"

"Your dad hired me from the company I work for. The company subs out mercenaries. Your dad read my file, liked my history, and thought I could keep you safe. End of story."

"Hmm. And what exactly is your plan to keep me safe, Tango? Are you just going to be my travel companion as I continue running away from the man I want to kill?" I think I have a right to at least know that.

He opens his door and jumps out of the truck. He stretches each arm out behind his neck and bends over to stretch his hamstrings, giving me the perfect view of his amazingly firm ass. *Ugh.* He reaches back into the truck behind the driver's seat and pulls out two extra large sweatshirts, both covered with the Marine emblem. He slips one on and leaves the hood over his head. I open my door and hop down to where he's standing and holding out the other sweatshirt for me. It doesn't take long to figure out why he's handing it to me—it's about twenty degrees colder here. I take my jacket off and slip the sweatshirt over my head before putting my jacket back on. Crap, it's freaking cold.

He still hasn't answered my question, and now I'm following him like a lost dog, waiting for a response. He climbs up a couple of rocks overlooking the ocean, sits on the tip of one and pulls his knees into his chest. He taps the rock beside him and waves me over. "Come sit."

I climb up the rocks to where he's sitting and drop down into the flattened area beside him. "Ready to answer me now? Or are we waiting for the sun to set?" Annoyance definitely saturates my words clearly enough for him to take a hint.

"Yeah, we could do that." He lets his head fall back into the glow of the sun. His features become more dominant—the light colored freckles on his cheeks and the scar above his right eyebrow. "I'm struggling with the plan I was given orders for," he says, straightening his neck as he peers out into the water. "Your dad wants me to keep you safe. You want to kill the man who is after you. And on top of that . . . this job—" He points back and forth between the two of us. "Will probably expire in a month. So, it's a lot to consider."

"What do you mean? Are you planning to quit?" I ask, somewhat baffled and a little upset that this arrangement is temporary.

"I'm not planning to quit, no," he says, refusing to break his cold hard stare out into the water.

"Then what?" I twist my body to face him; feeling emotionally charged from his half spoken statements.

After a few seconds, he looks over at me but doesn't respond. His hands curl around the back of his neck, squeezing and causing his skin to discolor. I hear him swallow and I watch his lips part. I can see the debate in his eyes, fighting over the words he must want to say. "I'm probably not going to make it another month." He bites down on his cheek and his eyes lose their focus.

"I don't—I don't understand what you're saying or what you mean." This pit in my stomach is telling me whatever he is trying to say, isn't good.

"I have lung cancer. I was diagnosed about four weeks ago. It's too late to do anything about it. The doctors gave me no hope—just a countdown. They said I had two to three months left, but probably more likely around two." His words leave him breathless, and me as well.

I've been a complete bitch, asshole, cunt, and a shithead to this poor man who's going to die in probably less than a month. But beyond that, I feel a different kind of pain—a swelling type of ache in my heart. I've warmed up to him. I've started to like him, even enjoy having him around. I've had thoughts of actually being with him, which is dumb anyway. He's my bodyguard. But he's my friend now too. And even if he doesn't see it that way, I do care about him. But he's dying. Someone else I care about will be taken away from me. Is that what this is? Another fucking sick joke from above?

"I should have guessed something was wrong by the way you've been coughing and wheezing," is all I can come up with to say.

"Look. I wasn't going to say anything. The doctor said it will be painful, but I'll be able to continue living until my lungs stop working. Right now, it's bearable, but when it gets to be too much, I'll stop working and find you a replacement. A good one. Or I can save you the trouble, and find you a replacement now so I don't have to put you through the aggravation?"

The words coming from his mouth hurt me. I purposely don't get close to people for a reason and it's to protect my bitterly trashed heart. I know whatever time we spend together from here on out will likely result in a stronger friendship, maybe more. But I can't let that happen. I'll be the one who has to live on after. I'll be the one left with memories branded into my mind and heart. But, on the other hand, what type of person would I be if I told him to leave now, to go die by himself? He has no family, and he hasn't mentioned any friends. Now I'm thinking of Krissy and Mom, if they were in his shoes, and if they had no one when they were dying. I wouldn't wish that on them, or anyone. "I already told you. I don't want a replacement," I say quietly.

"I know. Want to know the irony?" How is there irony in this situation?

I shrug.

"The thing your dad has could save my ass. And that's as much as I can tell you."

"Wait, what?" I shout. "What does he have, Tango? A treatment for cancer? Is that what he has?" He doesn't respond. But he doesn't need to. I can see the look on his face—it's a combination of hope and dread. I'm assuming the hope part is that there's something out there that could save him. The dread most likely being that he wouldn't agree to track Dad down. "How do you know that's what he has?"

He looks at me with a sidelong glare and I can see contemplation form like storms in his eyes. "I refused to take the job unless I knew what I was fighting for. This job had a high alert, meaning, the likelihood of survival is low. My survival rate is low anyway, so I figured it's the perfect job. I kind of just lucked out, being stuck with you." His lip twitches a bit as a wry smile plays across his cheeks. "I'm guessing your dad hasn't had an easy time finding guards for you," he snickers. "Without sounding too cocky, my history dictates that I'd be a pretty badass guard, and regardless of what you might think, he does want to keep you safe. He told me what he had in his possession, so I'd take the job. But I'm smart enough to know, he'll have me killed if anyone ever found out. However, I trust you wouldn't rat me out."

Without thinking, I blurt out something I'll likely regret—or maybe not. "I'll help you find him."

"No. Absolutely not. I can't have you do that. And we still have to deal with Reaper."

"Fuck Reaper. I'll deal with him later. I want to help you." I do. I don't want to watch another innocent person die. I can't.

"Cali, we could be killed just trying to find him. And what if I die in the process? Where does that leave you? Unprotected and in the middle of nowhere."

"Where is he, Tango? Tell me."

"A few hours south of the Texas border. When he hired me, he gave me emergency coordinates for his location. They aren't exact, but they're within a two mile radius of where he is. It isn't going to be easy to find him."

"We're going. My dad is paying you to take care of me, right?"

"Yes, but that doesn't involve bringing you to his location."

"I don't care. We're going . . . and if you don't take me to Mexico, I'm going into Boston and I'll hunt Reaper down until I'm face to face with him. I will put myself in as much danger as possible here if you don't take me to find my dad."

"Cali."

"Choice is yours. Live or die." I wonder how many buttons of his I'll have to push before he gives in. I know this is dangerous and stupid, but a good deed wouldn't be the worst thing for my current track record.

He looks torn as he subtly nods his head with agreement. "You play dirty. And that's not fair." He squints his eyes with a mischievous glint and playfully pinches my side. The sensation causes me to yelp and burst with laughter, which makes me ask myself what this man is doing to me.

"I think we both know life isn't exactly fair," I say.

I see the stormy clouds return to his eyes, as well as contemplation. "You do know Reaper will tail us and follow us. Right?"

"And that will make it easier for me to kill him," I smile. I'm obviously making this sound easier than it is, but this is the way it has to be. I'm sure of it.

"Why are you doing this for me?" he asks.

I look at his pain stricken expression and I take his hand from his lap, allowing myself to feel the warmth flowing through him and now through me. His hand is large and rough, but still gentle and comforting. It causes my heart to pound and my breath to hitch in my throat, holding me back from saying what I want to say. I wait for the rush to pass and squeeze his hand to release some of my own nerves. He's staring at me, waiting to hear or know why I took his hand, because right now it looks like a sign of emotion, and that's not something I'm ready to divulge. The thought brings my words to the tip of my tongue. "Don't let this seep into your head or anything, but—" I stall just so I can hold his hand a little bit longer. "I think you're a pretty cool guy, Tango," I wink. "Plus, I don't really think you deserve to die . . . especially after the shit I've given you this week. The guilt. It's setting in."

He slips his hand out of my mine and my heart rate slows a bit from the external release. But then he slides his arm around my back and pulls me in against his shoulder, forcing another rush of sensations to overwhelm me. "You don't know how much this means to me. This will be the most selfish thing I've ever done." He presses his lips onto the top of my head. "Thank you." And I'm stunned, speechless and breathless. Did his lips just touch the top of my head? How did we even end up at this moment? I've been horrible to him. How could he even want to put his arm around me, never mind his lips on me? I don't understand.

CHAPTER TEN

TANGO

THE TRUTH IS OUT, and it feels good. She's the first person outside of the Marines who knows. I'm told to keep my mouth shut. I'm trained not to weaken and say something I shouldn't. But at this point, I don't give a shit anymore.

I have been alone with all of this. The doctor's appointments, the diagnosis, the news and my discharge—it was fucking horrible. Training to be the strongest person I can only took me so far as I was mentally breaking down inside.

The damn cough was relentless when I was in Afghanistan. At first, I thought it may have been an allergy, but my staff sergeant and the corpsman thought otherwise. Doc, the corpsman, said it sounded serious, maybe pneumonia. So they sent me to Germany.

Germany was like a little vacation until the doctor walked into the exam room. He put the stethoscope up to my back and listened for a couple of minutes. His face kept shifting and twisting— he looked puzzled. He sent me for a set of x-rays, and I assumed it was to confirm pneumonia, but when he met me back in the exam room, I learned pneumonia would have been the best-case scenario.

"Son, do you see this?" He held up my x-ray against the light.

At first I wasn't sure what he was looking at, but then my eyes focused on a large foggy spot in the middle of my lungs. "That?" I pointed to the puffy cloud that most likely shouldn't be there.

"We're going to run some more tests on you, but this here," he pointed to the cloud, "This is cancer. It's hard to tell without doing some more tests, but it looks like it may have been there for a while, which I find strange since your pre-deployment medical tests didn't indicate a problem." He places the x-ray down and leans on the edge of his desk. "I suppose there is the chance that this cancer started a few months ago and advanced faster than normal, but it's hard to say for sure."

The word cancer ironically made me start coughing. I coughed until I ran out of breath, until blood misted out of my mouth for the first time—right onto the doctor's white lab coat. It was as if my body was trying to spell out the diagnosis for me, making it very clear that whatever this doctor was saying, was true.

I had days more of tests, and an MRI before I spoke with that doctor again. I already knew there was no good news, so it was easier to sit in the waiting room, waiting for him to arrive. He came out to get me and simply waved me over. He closed the door quietly behind us and walked around to the back of his desk where he sat and faced me. He looked at the papers in his hands for a moment, probably trying to stall the inevitable. He finally placed the papers down and looked up at me while removing his glasses—another sympathetic move, I thought.

"Son, I'm not sure there's any easy way to say this, so I'm just going to say it how it is. You have an advanced stage lung cancer, and I'm afraid it's too late to try any interventions. At best, I can assume you will have two to three months to live. The cancer is moving so rapidly that you will probably feel like you have a nasty chest cold until the day it gets bad. But the day it turns bad, will probably be an inkling of—"

"The end. Death knocking on my door?"

He nods his head, confirming my incisive assumption.

Being rude was not my intention, but with the bad news I already had, he had placed a death sentence on top of it. My heart felt like it had stopped beating. I wasn't panicked into coughing that time. I just felt nothing, almost like I was already dead. I stood up from my chair and saluted the doctor. "Thank you, Doc." And I turned around and left.

I asked to use the phone at the front desk and I contacted my staff sergeant. He told me an officer would be waiting for me on base in North Carolina to discuss our 'plan.' The plan being to discharge me and send me on my merry way toward a hole in the ground.

Two days later, I arrived on base. No welcoming committees. No family. No cheering. Nothing. I entered into my unit headquarters building. An officer I had once worked with approached me. It seemed he knew why I was there and not in Afghanistan. He placed his hand on my shoulder, and then I knew for sure he knew why I was in front of him. He pulled a folder off of a nearby desk and ushered me down a hall. "Let's start the discharge process," is the last thing I really listened to. Everything else was robotic and said thousands of times before, I'm sure.

At the end of the meeting, I was asked if there was anything they could do to make this time easier on me. That's when I asked them to tell my parents I had died in the field. Mom and Dad didn't need to watch me suffer for the next two months. They didn't need to feel hope when they knew I had come back from war alive, only to find out I would be dead within weeks. Maybe part of me wanted to be remembered as a hero, rather than a sick man. It was selfish and I regret it now. But it was a decision I can't take back.

CALI

We stocked up at a Wal-Mart—bought some things to help us survive a long-ass road trip and hit the road. We drove through lunch and were both famished around three in the afternoon, which is when we pulled off the highway into a diner smack dab in the middle of absolutely nowhere.

Burned grease and French fries aromatize the joint—some of it smells pretty good, but some of the smells are making me wonder how many times they've reused the frying oil.

Tango and I sit beside each other at the booth, both of us with our chins propped up by a hand. Exhaustion is setting in, probably more for him than me.

The waitress approaches us with two menus and places them down in front of us.

Her black hair is up in a knot at the base of her neck, and a hairnet stretches over the mess, constricting all but a few sprigs of frizzy strands are poking out above her ears. Her lips are a fluorescent pink and her eyelids have been painted with a shimmery teal shadow, complimenting her Alice-in-Wonderland-like uniform. I can imagine why smiling might be more work than serving people here.

"Do ya want to order drinks first?"

"I'll have a coke," I say.

"Mountain Dew, please," Tango says after me.

Her gaze floats between my face and Tango's and I swear I see a smile tug at the corners of her lips. "Ya two are cute," she says. "I'll be right back with ya drinks."

My eyes are pinned on the popcorn ceiling, avoiding Tango's likely-to-be cocky smirk. "We are kinda cute," he says with a subtle wink, the same kind of wink he gave me in the airport.

"Well, I am, at least." I wrap my hair behind my ears and try my hardest to maintain a straight face.

"You didn't respond with anything snide to her. I'm proud of you." He picks up his menu from the table and opens it. "Want to share a menu?" he teases, nudging his shoulder into mine.

"No touching on this road trip. That's a rule I just made." After covering miles of pavement, I've had time to think about this, and I've had to make the decision that I can't fall for him any more than I already have. There's no telling whether or not we'll find Dad, which means he could easily be dead in a matter of weeks. I refuse to put my heart through any more. I can be his friend, though. Just his friend.

He hits me with the menu. "You held my hand at the beach this morning, remember?" he laughs, but a tinge of disappointment washes over his face. "Now you're making that rule?"

I point my finger at him and wink, feeling guilty for possibly giving him the wrong impression. "You're a quick learner, aren't you?"

"Actually, I never can seem to take a hint." His knee sweeps against the outside of my leg and I automatically twitch and shift away from him. "Oh gosh, I'm sorry. My legs are so damn long." He's going to make this so impossible.

I twist my legs over to the other side of my stool. "There. That better?" I ask, glancing at him out of the corner of my eye. His mouth twists to the side, seemingly trying to suppress a smile.

The waitress returns with our drinks, places them down and pulls out her little pink sparkly coiled-notepad. "What can I grab for ya folks today?"

"I'll have the cheeseburger with everything on it," I say, closing my menu and placing it back down on the counter.

"And what will you be having, sir?" the waitress asks. A broad smile stretches across her lips, showcasing smudged pink lipstick on her top four front teeth.

"I'll have the double bacon cheeseburger with no lettuce," Tango says while closing his menu.

The waitress finishes scribbling down our order and then shoves the pencil behind her ear while dropping the notepad into her apron. "Those will be right up."

"Pardon me for asking, but how long have you two been together?" the waitress asks.

"It will be six months this Saturday," Tango says without missing a beat. His lips contort into a silly grin as he leans into me. Then his arm wraps around my neck and he pulls me against the side of his body.

And I melt.

He smells like soap mixed with musky cologne. It forces my body to relax within his hold. I have the urge to lie my head down on his shoulder and breathe him in even more. My body doesn't relax. Not for anything . . . or anyone. The feeling is foreign to me.

This feeling is amazing.

The waitress has walked away and Tango still has his arm around me. "What are you doing?" I ask.

"Having some fun," he responds. He removes his arm from around me and straightens his posture.

"How are you this upbeat when you know you're dying in a matter of weeks?" Kind of blunt, but I have to know.

"Why be miserable? It's not going to change anything. I'd rather seize my days and enjoy what's left of my life."

I can't help but think it takes a certain type of person to view life that way. I could probably learn a thing or two. If someone gave me a death sentence, I don't think I'd be able to continue on. I think I'd lie down and wait for whatever was going to happen. I'd be asking, why me? I'd wonder what I'd done so wrong to deserve an eviction notice from my body. I wouldn't be able to smile, or have fun, or eat like I was starving. I can't even comprehend how he has a smile on his face right now. "That's good that you can do that," I say.

"You can too. You're not dying, but you don't have to focus on everything negative. It can ruin your life, and you just never know when that last day might be." He looks down at the napkin he's fumbling with and then back up at me. "Maybe I shouldn't be saying this, but your sister wouldn't want you to be living like this. Don't you think she'd want you to be happy?"

Why should I be happy when the man I was in love with slashed her throat? "I don't deserve to be happy when she can't be happy." He doesn't seem to have a response. It is logical. It's not like I'm forcing myself to be miserable every day. I just can't find much that makes me happy.

The waitress brings out the tray with our burgers and places them down in front of us.

"My name is Peggy. If ya need anything, just holla," she says as she pulls a wad of napkins out of her apron. "Here ya go."

We've been eating in silence, and I'm devouring this burger, which seems to have caught Tango's attention.

"You always eat like a pig?" he asks. His question almost causes me to choke on my last bite. I narrow my eyes at him; unable to speak with the large mouthful I'm trying to push down my throat. "Seriously,

I've never seen a girl eat like you before. It's nice." I still can't respond, realizing I did take way too large of a bite. "I kind of thought you were one of those calorie counting chicks when I held that Cinnabon bag up in front of your face at the airport."

I finally swallow my food and wash it down with a sip of water. "First, I can't believe you just called me a pig."

"I didn't call you a pig. I said you were eating like one. And I think it's a good trait. Not a bad one."

"Second, I love food. I was blessed with a speedy metabolism, and I don't want to let it go to waste. And third, you were pissing me off in the airport that day. I wanted nothing more than to eat that damn Cinnabon, but you were just a random guy following me around at the time." I smirk. "As a matter of fact, Tango, since you're counting your days, and eating makes me happy, I say we eat like pigs all the way to Mexico."

"I think I love you," he laughs.

TANGO

What am I doing? I think I'm losing control. I don't lose control. I have to fight this urge. I can't put her through any more shit.

I sink back into my seat, mentally preparing myself for this lengthy ride we have to survive together all while keeping our hands to ourselves.

"So just to summarize the rules for our trip," I say to her. "No touching, and eat as much fattening and greasy food as possible."

"Exactly," she says with a tight-lipped grin.

"Well, okay. I'll try," I say. I think both of those rules might kill me, though.

She gives me this look that tells me she knows every thought going through my head, which means she knows I think she's so fucking hot and I'm doing everything I can to keep my hands off of her. What a stupid rule.

CHAPTER ELEVEN

CALI

"WHAT PART OF Mexico are we fleeing to?" I ask. "Cancun, I assume?"

"We aren't going for spring break, Cali. Your dad's coordinates point to the Copper Canyons. Although, I'm assuming he's not just sitting out in the open." He looks over his shoulder at the left lane, glides over, and ups the speed even more. "How long has it been since you slept under the stars?"

The outdoors and I have never quite agreed on much. The one time I slept outside was at my friend's house in her backyard when I was twelve. She pitched a tent and we ate junk food all night and gossiped about all the cute boys at school. A million mosquitos stung us and then her older brother came out and scared the crap out of us with fake growling noises in the middle of the night. That was the end of that. We spent the rest of the night on her bedroom floor. "I can survive."

"We'll drive into the canyons as far as we can go, and we'll have to hike from there. It could mean a couple of nights in a tent, though." Camping. Tents. Bugs. Ugh. "Oh," I say. He places his hand on my thigh, a gesture that calms my nerves and kind of turns me on. "I'll protect you from the bears. Okay?" I look down at my leg, at his hand, and I clear my throat, looking back up at him with an arched brow. He grins in return and his hand slides up an inch higher, but I slap his arm.

He pulls his hand away. "I'm sorry. Sorry. I told you, I'm very forgetful."

"Oh right. I'll just have to keep reminding you." I roll my eyes, trying to force away the smile inching across my cheeks.

He pulls off an exit into a gas station and throws the truck into park at the first pump. "Want a snack for the road?"

"Only if it's a thousand calories or more. If not, I'm all set."

His dimples deepen on his cheeks and he nods his head at my request. As he's stepping out of the truck, he reaches into his back pocket and retrieves a blue book. He tosses it onto my lap. "You'll need this." I open it up and find my picture and information printed on a shiny new passport. I shouldn't be surprised.

"Hey," I catch him before he runs inside. "Why don't we just fly there?" Regardless of how much I hate flying, it seems silly to drive across the country.

"Besides that you hate flying," he says with seriousness. "Reaper is too close to knowing our location and the best way to lose him is to drive. We'd be too easy to track if we flew. He has connections deeper than you could imagine." Oh, I can imagine.

He closes his door and jogs into the gas station. I pull out my phone and look at the blank screen. No texts and no calls today. I'm not sure that's the worst thing, though. I send Sasha a message, telling her I miss her. I look forward to the day when it's safe for me to be around her again. She responds back quickly, telling me she misses me too. She knows I only text her when I have a feeling of looming danger. Then again, I wake up each day, wondering how I'm still alive.

Tango's door reopens and he drops in a box of Krispy Kreme doughnuts and a couple of sodas. "Now this is what I call dinner," I say. "Oh, do you want money for gas?" Not like I have much. Dad hasn't deposited any money into my account in three weeks, which I now understand since he's camping out in the canyons in Mexico.

"Oh, you mean, you actually have money?" he asks, playfully, throwing in a wink for an extra measure of smugness. Every time this man winks, smiles or blinks, my insides become mush.

"Some." My voice rises into a whine.

"I have this, but thank you for offering." He closes the door again, and I feel the truck jerk to the side as he shoves the hose into the gas tank. I hear him coughing from outside the truck, reminding me of the true situation. He's not doing this for fun. He's doing this for a last chance at life.

When he gets back into the truck, I watch him wiping his mouth off with his sleeve. "You okay?" I ask.

His hand moves down to his chest and he presses it with the heel of his palm. His skin is flush, but his cheeks are rosy. "Can I say something to you that I haven't been given the opportunity to tell anyone?" For a minute, I worry about what's going to come out of his mouth, but he doesn't wait for me to respond. "I'm scared." And his two words knock my heart into my stomach. "I don't want to die, Cali." If I were standing, I'd fall to my knees, feeling as though I've had the wind knocked out of me. Mom never told me she was scared of dying. She always told me it was God's plan for her, and she was okay with becoming an angel for Krissy and me. Although, now I question the existence of angels, seeing as Krissy certainly didn't have one the day she was summoned to death. I guess Mom didn't really become an angel. Krissy didn't have a chance to tell me she was scared, but it's all I could see on her face when the knife was pressed against her throat. Tango's the first one to admit this type of fear to me, and regardless of his positive attitude that he seems able to maintain, it shows me the weakness within him. His feelings are the truth; it's easy to see that.

It takes everything I have not to weaken and act sad for him. I have to be strong for him, because if the tables were turned, I know that's what he would do for me, or anyone in his situation. "You're not going to die," I say, unsure whether I should be making such a statement. "This is exactly why we're going to Mexico."

He reaches over to me, looking like he's about to take my hand. And I'd let him if that's what he needs right now.

He does take my hand.

Then drops my hand onto the seat next to my leg, giving him free rein to steal the box of doughnuts off of my lap. I laugh silently and look out the window into the darkness, which reflects his face looking at the back of my head. He's smiling and must not realize I can see him.

CHAPTER TWELVE

CALI

I MUST HAVE passed out somewhere between the Connecticut border and wherever the hell we are now. It's almost two in the morning, and I'm somewhat delirious. I straighten my posture and glance out into the dark sky brightened by the thousands of city lights. I pull down my mirror and use the subtle glow to check my after-sleep appearance. Yikes. I smudge my smeared eye makeup off from below each eye and wipe the remnants on my jeans. Lovely. Maybe I was drooling too.

"Sleep well?" He looks over at me for a second.

"Yeah, where are we?" My voice comes out hoarse and sluggish. I'm totally exhausted.

"Just entered Philly."

"Really? That's it?" That sounded more like a whine, but I'm already starting to feel cramped.

"Lot of traffic going through New York and Connecticut. Things will speed up over the next few hours, though."

"Are we driving through the night?" I couldn't do that. I'd be that asshole who falls asleep at the wheel and drives off a bridge.

"No way. I've had my days pulling all-nighters. We're only driving for another hour or so. We'll have to find a place to crash."

The highway is dark and absent of the lights that shone over us just a few miles back. The tall pine trees are as black as the road, and raindrops cover the windshield, each one coming down faster than the one before, warning us of an approaching downpour. The droplets soon turn to a funnel of water cascading around the truck.

Seemingly alone on this wide-open highway so late at night, the rain is mesmerizing—soothing, actually. The radio had been turned off and the noise of clapping thunder and the splashing puddles being shot

TAG

103

up into the undercarriage surround us. Visibility grows fainter and a sign indicating a nearby motel invites us off the exit. The road is flooded and water is seeping over the island, separating the two lanes.

We pull into the motel parking lot with a blinking vacancy sign, and I see him looking over at me. "Sorry about this—it looks pretty run down, but visibility is rough and it's making me more tired."

"Don't be sorry. It's fine, Tango, really. I've stayed in worse." I'm not sure I've ever stayed in anything more than a two star hotel, actually.

"You're a lot sweeter when it rains, huh?"

"I like the rain."

"Well then, I hope it never stops raining," he says softly.

I feel a rush of warmth wash over me and I'm questioning how long I can maintain this wall I've built up in front of me. He always says the right thing.

We both step out of the truck, and I somewhat expect him to run through the rain to the check-in office. But he doesn't. He waits for me as if the rain isn't coming down like the water from a showerhead on the highest massage setting. He's unaffected. And soaking wet in only a t-shirt. I reach back into the cab, pull my bag out, and sling it over my shoulder. When I hop out, he pulls his sweatshirt out from behind his back and holds it over my head. "Ready?" I want to stop and comprehend the adorable gesture, but we both pick up the pace and jog toward the front entrance.

"Thanks," I say as we approach the front door. He doesn't respond, just places his hand on the small of my back as I walk through the front door. It feels like we're together and it comes off as a natural gesture, but we're not together. Maybe that's just who he is, a gentleman. I'm not sure I've ever come in contact with that type of man, and I'm not sure I'd want anything different now. I decide not to remind him of the 'no touching' rule this time.

Tango moves ahead of me and greets the old man hovering over the counter. He looks as if he might be asleep. He looks like he's beyond the age of retirement. The wrinkles on his face have their own wrinkles, and his jaw juts out, hanging slightly open. He should be at home in a warm bed, not staffing a front desk of a motel. I feel horrible, and I want to help him to a chair and drape a blanket over him. He doesn't flinch when Tango approaches the desk or when he clears his throat.

Instead, a loud snore erupts from his nose and he shifts around a bit. At least we know he's not dead. "Excuse me," Tango says loudly. He still doesn't budge.

Tango places his hand down on the bell and it rings loudly, startling the man as his eyes snap open wide. "Oh uh. Oh, sorry. Uh. I must have—you guys aren't with the cops or nothing, are ya?"

"Hey, man, we mean no trouble. Just need a couple of rooms," Tango says. I think I had this guy pinned wrong, and now I'm wondering why he'd be fearful of us being cops.

"I have one room left." He laughs once with only his breath. "It's your lucky day."

Lucky would have been having two rooms.

"I'd pay with cash. This place is kind of sketchy," I whisper in Tango's ear. He nods with agreement and hands the man sixty bucks. In return, the man hands Tango a gold key hanging from a green rubber keychain with the number 104 in gold print. As we're walking away, the man flops back down over the counter, and his snoring commences almost immediately. Guess we brought quite the excitement.

We follow the hallway through a set of glass doors, and the smoky corridor opens up into a long passageway covered in worn red carpeting, white tiled walls and drop ceilings.

We approach room 104 and Tango slides the key into the lock. The door doesn't open smoothly, so he nudges it with his shoulder. The red carpet ends abruptly at our door and turns into a contrasting forest green shag rug that lines our motel room. There's one full-size bed, one kitchen chair and a pedestal to use as a table, I'm guessing.

The bathroom is so small; a normal-size human would have to stand over the toilet in order to close the bathroom door from the inside. It's almost hard to believe the health inspectors have overlooked it. Although, as I know well, everyone knows someone. Sometimes it's for the better and sometimes, not so much.

"I'm so sorry, Carolina. This place is vile." He pulls the thick white synthetic curtain away from the window, creating a sticky tearing noise. "Just a dumpster with some rats looking around," he laughs.

"Nice. Just like the Ritz, I'm sure."

"Haven't been?" He looks back at me curiously.

"I haven't been to a Hilton, never mind a Ritz," I snicker. Not everyone gets to enjoy the highlife. "My dad sent us money, but it was hardly enough with my mom being a full-time mom and dad for us. She didn't have time to work because of various school schedules. She did the best she could, though." I'm saying way more than I've ever felt comfortable telling anyone. I need to shut up.

"Sounds like you had a pretty good mom, huh?"

"Yeah, she made my first nineteen years pretty good." I nod my head, trying to remember each detail of her face, the certain smile she had just for me. We were her life. She didn't need more than us. We were enough. And she was enough for us.

"So you and Krissy were alone for the two years after your mom died. Then Krissy was murdered?" he asks, looking unsure about each word he says, almost as if he thinks he should tip-toe around the subject. Krissy and I were so lucky to have each other after she died. Dad was around for maybe one day, and then we were on our own. She was eighteen and I was nineteen, so we technically didn't need anyone to take care of us. We slept in our parents' bed for six months after she died. We stayed up late most nights, reminiscing, telling jokes, and feeling like mom was sitting next to us on the bed. The three of us were so close that Mom felt more like a third sister. There wasn't an untold secret between us three. We were all best friends, as close as family could be. And the thought of how much I miss both of them right now kills me, and I feel my eyes fill up with tears just at the mention of their names.

I suck in a deep breath. "Sorry, what were you saying?"

He looks saddened by what I've said or didn't say, or maybe by the look on my face. I drifted off in my own memories for a minute and I've left him standing here staring at me, waiting for a response. "I can see you're tired. I'll sleep on the chair. You can have the bed."

His statement snaps me out of my despair. "You can sleep in the bed too." I lift one of my bags from the floor and place it down on the bed, preparing to search for my toothbrush, while also trying not to draw attention to any meaning behind what I'm saying. We're just two adults and neither of us would be able to sleep in that chair. "You already know the touching rule, so we'll be okay," I say, forcing a smile through the awkwardness I'm creating.

"No, really. It's okay. I've slept in the sands of the Middle East for months at a time." He looks down at the wooden chair and wiggles it around, checking its sturdiness. It's not sturdy.

"Actually sand sounds a lot more comfortable than that chair," I say with a raised brow.

He laughs at my remark and must realize it's true. "You do have a point. Well, if you're sure you don't mind?"

"It's fine. I trus—" Whoaaa. *What the fuck was I just about to say? I don't trust anyone. No one. Trust no one, Cali. No one.*

My cut off word is a clear indicator of having second thoughts about what I just suggested. And by the disheartened look on his face, I'm pretty sure I've made him just as uncomfortable as I am. "I'll be right out." He squeezes by me with his bag, struggling to close himself into the bathroom.

I can be an adult. It's just a bed, plus we were sitting closer in his truck. I pull off my sweatshirt and long sleeve shirt, leaving on just a black racer-back tank top. I guess this is as comfortable as I'll be getting tonight. I climb into the far right side of the bed and pull the covers up to my neck and turn onto my side, facing the door. The bed feels like a slab of concrete and the pillow feels like nothing more than a sheet. Oh well.

I hear the bathroom light switch off and Tango's bare feet pad against the shaggy carpet. I was about to yell at him for walking across the floor with bare feet, but when the moonlight shines over him, I see he's wearing socks. I can also see he's shirtless and wearing jogging pants that hang low around his waist, accentuating the lean muscles that curve and twist in just the right places around his hips. Even with hardly any light, I can now see he has twice as many tattoos as I do. There's one reason he was unaffected by them. Normally, I'd be intrigued to know what each one stands for, but if I continue staring at every one of his bulging muscles, I might do regretful things. I roll onto my back and fold the pillow beneath my head for added support.

"Sleep well, Cali," he says.

"You too," I mumble. The bed shifts heavily from his weight, and I think we're both quick to realize the bed is not big enough for both of us to fit on it comfortably. He shifts to his side and curls his pillow up in-between the bend of his arm. I turn over onto my side to give him some

TAG 107

space. Now we're butt to butt and probably both staring at the wall with the same question running through our heads: *how did we end up at this point in just a week?* I don't even think I know his real name. I doubt it's Tango. I'm sure the ID he showed me was fake, just like mine. That should be a rule or something. *I'm making it an official rule right now.* I will not sleep in a bed with a man unless I know his real name. There.

I sit up, realizing I forgot to brush my teeth and take my pills, and I clamber out of the bed, searching around in the dark for my bag. When my hand sweeps over it, I pull it up to my chest and bring it into the bathroom. After I manage to close the door behind me, I flip the light on. The mirror in front of me has a huge shard missing and a crack running through the center. Someone must have gotten pissed and punched it. That's what it looks like, anyway.

When I face my dreaded reflection, I come to terms with how horrible I look. My hair is still damp from the rain, and it's knotted into a mess—a disaster at best. My mascara has left streaks down my cheeks, and I have bags under my eyes. It's clear I have to sleep tonight. I unzip the bag and immediately notice it's not mine. I want to pull the two ends shut, trying to be respectful, but I can't help seeing his phone light up in the bag. I also can't help that I see the words, *love you* flash across the screen. I pull the bag back open wider and take his phone into my hand. I press the power button, hoping the text message reappears, just to confirm I'm not crazy, but it doesn't. It asks for the password. God dammit. He's in a fucking relationship and he's sharing a bed with me, not to mention the other flirtatious exchanges between us, especially coming from his end.

I dart back out of the bathroom and drop his bag on the floor. "Grabbed the wrong bag," I say, as if I need to explain.

He chuckles and says, "Yeah, they're both black and it's dark in here. It happens."

"I think you might have gotten a text. I felt your bag vibrate." Or I saw your phone light up with the words, *love you*. Same thing.

He doesn't say anything, but he climbs out from under the sheets and stumbles over to where I dropped his bag. He fumbles through it, but I realize I no longer have a reason for standing here watching him. I pick up my bag and bring it into the bathroom. I swallow hard and suddenly realize I have fucking feelings for him. Otherwise, I wouldn't feel a pit growing in my stomach at the thought of him having a girlfriend or worse, a wife. He isn't wearing a ring, but he's a bodyguard so he probably can't wear one. I should have just asked for a replacement guard when I had the chance. I knew this was not going to end well.

I shove my hand into my bag and wrap my fingers around the pill bottle. I twist the cap off and drop a couple into my palm. I throw them back into my throat and lean over to hang my mouth under the running faucet. I breathe in slowly, convincing myself that this shouldn't bother me. There's no reason for me to be upset. He wasn't sent to me to be my knight in shining armor. He was sent to keep me alive, and he's doing that, while also trying to keep himself alive.

I flip the light off and squeeze back out through the small opening of the bathroom door. I drop my bag against the wall and then slide under the covers on my side of the bed. I will not ask him about the text message. I will not let him think I care. I do not care. I do not care.

I *so* do care.

CHAPTER THIRTEEN

TANGO

BIPOLAR MIGHT BE a logical explanation. This chick shifts her mood more often than I can keep up with. Maybe I'm safer keeping to myself until she warms up to me a bit more. Although, I swear I can sense the anger radiating off of her back. We're both trying hard to stay on our own sides of the bed, but this thing is tiny and not meant for two people. I'm on my side with my arms tucked awkwardly under my body. But I know if my hand so much as sweeps near her, I'll be reminded of the 'no touching' rule, except it might not be so friendly while she's trying to sleep.

My phone lights up on the night table, reminding me I have an unread message. I look at the display and the normal pain in my chest grows and then subsides just as quickly. I want to respond. I want to tell her I'm okay and I love her too, but it will just make it harder on her. Frustration sweeps over me like it does every night at this time.

* * *

I've been tossing and turning for an hour. She's sound asleep and I wish I was too. I should be tired. I am tired. So why am I staring at the curves under her shoulder blades and the tattoo wrapped around the back of her arm? Her skin is so smooth, flawless. And the scent of her hair is pungent in my nose—flowers or some girly shit. Whatever it is will make lying like this all night a little easier, or harder I suppose. I want to wrap my arm around her small waist and pull her into me and stay like that until morning. Then I remember the fist print I'll likely wake up with. This girl is making *me* feel bipolar.

CALI

It's as if there's a wall between us—I didn't shift an inch all night, afraid of what would happen if we touched. It's clear now that I can't let anything like that happen. He's with someone. I wonder what she's like. I wonder if she's pretty or anything like me. I wonder if I'm his type, or if he's really just using me to save his own life.

As soon as my lids fully accept the morning glow, I roll out of the bed. I lift my bag from the floor and bring it into the bathroom. I crank on the shower faucet and let it heat up before stepping in, desperately hoping for hot water.

Thank God. There is one decent feature about this motel room—the water pressure and heat. I suck in as much steam as my lungs will hold. I hold it in until I feel the comforting stretch across my ribcage, and when I blow it out, the relief is instant. This whole text message deal was just a wakeup call. I know damn well I shouldn't have been looking at him the way I was. I know damn well I shouldn't have almost trusted him. He keeps breaking my barrier down, and I almost let him in. I have to be stronger than this.

I *am* stronger than this.

I pull the thin towel off the rack outside of the shower and wrap it around myself tightly, taking the comfort I desperately need.

I manage to dress in the small space between the toilet and the door and pull my hair up into a ponytail on top of my head. I zip together my bag and step out of the bathroom. Tango is standing in front of the window, stretching his arm behind his neck. The view of his half-naked body forces the numbness within me to resurface. And the thought of wanting what I can't have drives into my head like a nail.

He turns around to face me. His short hair is spiked in different directions. It's a mess, a hot mess. His skin has a glow, giving the appearance of a good night's sleep. "All set in the bathroom?" he asks, his voice croaks, an after-sleep sound that shouldn't be turning me on.

I nod my head and plop down at the edge of the bed to pull my boots on. He walks past me but stops at the corner where the wall meets the bathroom. "Everything okay? You seem kind of quiet."

"Just not a morning person." But I am the type of person who falls for the wrong people.

TAG

"There's a shock," he laughs. With that, the bathroom door closes and the water squeals through the pipes. He's in there . . . naked, and it's all I can think about. I'm fucked.

I whip my phone out and shoot Sasha a text:

We'll be driving through Western Texas. Let's meet. I'll call you when I'm close. I think I've fallen for my bodyguard. I know. It's a long story, and I think he has a girlfriend. I need you to slap me.

XO - Cali

I see the little dots flickering under the message I sent, telling me she's responding. Her response is taking forever, considering how nimble those little fingers of hers are on a keypad.

OMG, Cali. I am going to slap you. You just made my day. Can't wait to see your stupid ass.

Luv Ya - Sasha

The bathroom door opens and Tango comes out, dragging the scent of some amazing man shampoo. His hair is wet and glistening under the dull orange light above. I need that slap now. And hard.

"Ready to hit the road?" he asks.

"Yup." I pull my elastic out of my damp hair, hoping to let it dry before I lean on it in the truck. I can see my falling black waves catch his attention as his mouth parts slightly and his chest pauses between constrictions. He has a girlfriend. He shouldn't be looking at me like that.

He clears his throat and grabs both of our bags.

"I can grab mine," I say, taking my bag from his hand. I walk ahead of him, leading the way back to the front office. The office is locked, being so early in the morning, so Tango drops the key in the mail slot.

Once in the truck I prop my feet up and pull my sunglasses down over my eyes, which has become my now normal position. It annoys him, I think. But I'm not sure I really care about that right now.

Before putting the truck in drive, I can see Tango looking at me from the corner of his eyes. He slaps his hand over my knee and says, "Get your feet down. You're scratching up the dash."

I turn my head to the side before moving. I give him an unfazed, emotionless look. "Sorry," I mumble.

"I know what will cheer you up," he says. I refocus my attention out the windshield. No, you don't. Well, unless you tell me you don't really have a girlfriend texting you, telling you she loves you. Or I'd settle for the truth—being that you're using me to find my dad as a way of saving your life. Besides that, nothing will cheer me up right now. "Let's grab a coffee before we hit the road."

I guess that does make me a little happy. Why can't I just be in a relationship with coffee? Coffee doesn't bring drama.

"Oh, by the way, since we're moving onto what could be a death mission, I want to stop in Pecos on the way," I say.

"What's in Pecos?" he asks.

"A friend I haven't seen in a while."

"Hmm. A boyfriend?" He looks a bit taken aback as he clears his throat, seeming nervous for a response, which is ridiculous since he likely has a girlfriend.

"No. *She* is my childhood friend."

His voice rises into a higher pitch, "Oh nice. That sounds like a good idea. We'll be around that area at about six-thirtyish tomorrow night according to the GPS on my phone." There is a large amount of pavement we have to hit before then. I better wait on giving her a time until we're closer.

"Would you care if it had been a boyfriend?" Why did I just say that?

He pauses for a moment, obviously putting some thoughts together. "It's a free country," he says with an impish grin.

He pulls off into a gas station to refill the tank and I jump out and head for the bathroom. When I return, he's leaning up against the truck as a faint smirk plays across his face as he reads something on his phone. I can guess who he's talking to—although his expression doesn't change when he notices me coming closer.

As I reach for the door handle, he gently grabs me by the back of my arm and turns me around. "What's the matter with you?" Hmm. You've been hitting on me for the past week and I just found out you have a girlfriend.

"Absolutely nothing. I just didn't want to interrupt your conversation with whoever you were talking to."

TAG 113

"I wasn't talking to anyone. I was reading something funny on Twitter."

"Mmhm," I say. "Can I just climb into the truck, please?" He backs up and lets me by.

I whip the door open and slam it after I'm in. "Hey, easy on the door," he says through the cracked opening of the window. "These mood swings of yours are kind of giving me a headache. Did I do something to piss you off?" he asks.

"Let me just make something clear, Tango: I'm not a home wrecker. So whatever this is, was—" I point back and forth between us. "It needs to stop."

He looks bemused by my comment, but I try to avoid his face altogether. The flirting games are just games with him. I might look tough from the outside, but my insides are weaker than tissue paper. It wouldn't take much to tear me in half.

I feel the truck shake around as he screws the gas cap back on the tank. He rips the receipt from the pump and hops into the truck. He slides his key into the ignition but doesn't turn it. Instead, he turns to look at me. "I understand if I've come on too strong, and I apologize from the bottom of my heart if I've acted inappropriately in any way with you. But, I'm not sure what your home wrecker comment meant?"

Oh fuck. I shouldn't have said anything. Now we can sit awkwardly and uncomfortable for the next however many hours we have to be caged together like this. "I'm sure you have a girlfriend or something, so I don't understand why you're saying nice things and acting all friendly to me."

He doesn't respond, he just faces forward and turns the key. We slowly pull out of the gas station and back onto the country road that leads to the highway, and it doesn't take long before the silence becomes overwhelming. This is my fault. I should have just kept my mouth shut. I reach my hand out to turn up the volume on the radio and he places his fingers over mine. The feeling is electrifying and cruel. It's warm but cold. It makes my heart swell, and it makes my heart hurt. I have feelings for him, but I hate that he's made me feel anything at all.

"If you saw my text message last night, you should have just asked me about it," he says.

So now this is my fault? If I had confronted him sooner, I wouldn't have to admit that he's the same as every other asshole in this world. Like everyone else, it seems he thinks it's okay to hurt people. Maybe he didn't kill my sister, but he made me feel something, and I haven't felt a goddamn thing in so long—so fuck him.

I lean over and pull my headphones out of my bag and shove the adapter into my phone. I search for the loudest and heaviest music I can find and press play. The sound consumes me. It vibrates through my body and it makes my head numb inside. It's too loud to think, and it's too loud to feel anything other than the bass.

CHAPTER FOURTEEN

TANGO

A GIRLFRIEND? A wife? I laugh silently at the thought. I had a feeling she looked at my phone last night. That would explain her bipolar mood a little more. If I had a girlfriend, I would have been laid at some point over the past four years. Being in the desert for so long makes you realize how lucky you are to experience those moments with a woman. Before I left for my first tour, I'd sleep with any chick who approached me, which was a lot. But I'm over that. I just want to feel something that lasts for more than a few minutes, and she makes me feel something when I'm not even touching her. It also doesn't help that she's so beautiful when she's mad.

However, if she wants to play this silence game, I can play it too. She's waiting for me to admit something that she made up in her head, so I'm putting the ball in her court, because her assumptions couldn't be further from the truth. She has to break at some point.

CALI

We drove straight through lunch, and I know it's because he's waiting for me to say something to him. But I refuse to say anything. I can skip a meal if he's waiting for me to tell him I'm hungry. Besides, silence is a brutal force. That and it's my only tactic right now. I know muteness can drive a sane person crazy, although I do feel the slightest twinge of guilt for playing this game with a sick man.

Another hour has passed, and it's nearly four. I think the silence is finally getting to him. An exaggerated sigh escapes from the corner of his mouth. He's definitely breaking. I feel the truck shift and turn as he pulls off to the side of the flat and barren highway. Dirt sprays along the outside of the truck as we come to a complete stop, and he throws the shifter into park while slamming his head back against the seat. He takes a breath and his lips part slightly. He releases a loud painful sounding cough and opens his window. Sweat beads up on his forehead and he wrings his hand around the back of his neck. I can feel a struggle within his movements and guilt is hitting me with full force. I consider breaking the silence, but his eyes close and then so do his lips. He blows his pent up air out of his nose and looks over at me. His eyes widen, giving me a look like he wants me to say something. But even if I were to talk, I don't think I have anything to say. "This silence is killing me. There, I lose. You win. Now what?"

I shrug my shoulders, which makes him angrier. I want to make this better, but I don't know how. He was lying to me and I can't just forget that because he's sick. He knew how much trouble I have trusting anyone, and he played me like a fool. He doesn't push for me to say anything, though. Instead, he shifts the truck into drive and shoots us back onto the highway.

TANGO

I consider telling her. It would break through this uncomfortable silence. I haven't quite felt ready to tell anyone why I don't have a family right now. The vivid memories I seem to relive way too often are enough to kill me. But my time's running out, and if she doesn't already hate me after assuming I have a girlfriend, she'll probably hate me when she finds out what I put my family through.

And with that thought, maybe I should hold off a little longer. I can't stand the thought of making this any worse.

CALI

We have gone almost an entire day and a half without speaking much. We checked ourselves into separate hotel rooms last night, but they adjoined of course, since I need to be babysat and all. We've been living off of gas station junk food, but I'm not weakening. I can keep going like this. It'll make it easier anyway, not talking, not growing more attracted to him—definitely not hearing his voice or another compliment come out of those perfect lips.

The only thing I am thankful for is that we just passed a sign that says forty-five miles to Pecos. I pull out my phone to send Sasha a text:

> *Where do you want to meet?*
>
> *-Cali*

> *Churro grill, which is off the highway, hidden from non-locals. Should be a safe zone.*
>
> *-Sasha*

> *We'll be there around seven, seven-thirty.*
>
> *-Cali*

Now I have to figure out how to communicate this without speaking. There still appears to be steam spouting from Tango's ears and I can't quite understand what he has to be mad about. He's the one who caused this awkwardness. I never came onto him. I didn't comment on his good looks. And although I haven't admitted my deepest thoughts to him, I think he's the most attractive man I've ever laid eyes on, and I would do anything to touch him. But that's not a possibility. I will not be a home wrecker. Sick or not, he's an asshole if the thought even crossed his mind.

The road we're on is leading up a steep mountainous landscape overlooking hundreds of miles of farm and greenery. Nothing else. Wherever we are seems so peaceful and subdued, and it reminds me of a home I once knew when I was a child and had nothing to do but run around and be free. I would do anything to have a piece of that back.

The truck swerves off the road once again into another cloud of dust. We're stopped on the side of a lookout point at the edge of the cliff, and for some reason, I'm thinking he hasn't stopped to check out the view. Maybe he'll finally admit to having this girlfriend of his. Maybe the guilt finally broke him.

Before I have another second to think, my door swings open and he reaches over me and unclips my seatbelt. I'm pulled from the truck, and I don't fight him. I'm too tired to keep this game up.

He lets me down on the small patch of grass near the ledge. His hands find my shoulders and he bends over a bit, lowering his head to my level. His eyes are steady on mine. I won't blink. I won't let him think he's getting in my head, even though he has taken over almost every one of my thoughts during the past week and a half. It's been less than two weeks and this asshole has mind-fucked me. Clearly, he is my match, because normally, I'm the one causing the mind-fuck.

One of his hands releases from my shoulder and he reaches down into my back pocket. He pulls my phone out and throws it through the truck's open passenger window.

"What the hell is wrong with you?" I grunt.

"No phones. No nothing. Just us. You and me."

"Just do whatever you're about to fucking do. Throw me over the ledge if that's what you want. Don't drag this out. I've had enough."

He takes his phone out of his pocket and throws it into the truck too. "The text message you saw last night was from my sister, Chelsea."

"You said you *had* a sister, not have." What the hell? "So, when were you lying, then or now?"

"Neither." He turns away from me, sucking in every bit of fresh mountain air his disintegrating lungs can consume. His hands grip into his hips, and he turns back to face me. "We've all seen our fair amount of shit, Carolina. I've seen so much of it and somehow survived it. So you want my fucked up story? Here it is: I was discharged from the Marines—the only thing I've ever been good at. I was given two months-ish to live, as I told you. Rather than returning home to large celebrations, only to die two months later, I decided to have my family notified that I had died in the field. It was a really shitty decision. But it's not something I can undo. If they found out I was lying, I could land a lot of people in trouble. Luckily, I'm assuming it won't be an issue in a few weeks. I will be dead, and they won't know the difference. I wanted them to think I died a hero, rather than as a sick man. But I don't feel like a fucking hero. I just feel like a sick man. Everything I may have done overseas doesn't matter now."

I feel like I should be surprised by this, but it makes total sense to me. "This is why you're a mercenary?" I confirm for my own benefit.

"It's the only job I was allowed to have. I didn't want to sit around waiting to die. You know?" A crazed look swims through his eyes and he places his hands behind his neck. "Anyway, my family buried an empty coffin. I watched fifty people cry harder than I've ever thought possible. I watched my father shovel dirt and pour it over the coffin he thought my body was in. I watched my sister pass out from hyperventilating while standing over a six-foot-hole. I watched as my mother had to be held up by two people just so she could say her final good-byes to me. I watched this from a car in the shadow of my supposed death." He swallows hard. He's swallowing his pain. And I'm swallowing his pain with him. He sighs heavily up toward the sky. "The only thing that was in that coffin was my identity. I'm not allowed to go back to Michigan or any of the surrounding states for the rest of my life." Michigan? He said he was from Missouri. I guess that isn't important. "The only good thing that came out of that was hearing the words spoken in front of my gravesite. I was loved, Carolina. God dammit, I was loved so fucking much. I was able to hear those words. I know what I meant to my family. And I can die knowing my life wasn't in vain. Whether I died in a hospital bed from cancer or an IED blew me to smithereens, I was their hero. I was their fucking hero. But I was selfish for claiming to have died in Afghanistan, especially when I watched so many of my brothers die in action. It was a stupid decision that I made two days after finding out I was dying, and ironically, now I have to live with it until I actually do die. So if that's the reason you want to give me the silent treatment—that, I can live with. That I deserve. But thinking I was trying to make you a home wrecker—that, I can't live with."

TAG 121

I'm trying not to cry, and I'm trying to put all of these mixed up pieces together in my head. "Your sister knows you're alive?" I ask.

"She was on some trip with her friends. It was fate, I think. I literarily ran into her in Nashville a couple of weeks ago. I was state hopping, enjoying what little time I had left. There are things I wanted to do before I die, ya know? But running into her in a bar, it was too random to be random, so I have to think a higher power wanted us to find each other again." He bends over and picks up a rock from the sandy gravel. He smoothes it between his hands, squeezing it, holding it, crushing it. "I kept all information at a minimum, and I made her promise to never tell a soul. She was angry with me at first, but I told her there were reasons for this that I just couldn't explain. She used to hear that kind of stuff from me all the time, so she at least pretended to understand. Chelsea and I were so close growing up. There's only an eleven-month age difference between us. We had all the same friends and because my birthday was in September and hers was in August, we were in the same grade, the same classes. She begged me not to leave her that day we ran into each other. The only compromise I could make was to buy a pre-paid phone and give her the number." He looks over to his truck. "She sends me a message every night, telling me she misses me and loves me." He looks back over to me. "I never respond. I'm trying to save her from the pain she'll deal with when I'm actually gone in a few weeks. But knowing that someone still loves me has gotten me through these past couple of weeks." His eyes glaze over with a blank look. I can see he feels similar pain to me, and I think he realized this days ago. "So no, Cali, I don't have a girlfriend or a wife."

I feel like my gut was just pulled out of my stomach and thrown over the ledge behind us. I haven't hurt so much for someone else other than Mom and Krissy. I don't know what that means, but I can't just ignore the way I'm feeling. "I'm done giving you the silent treatment, Tango. You didn't deserve that from me."

Even though I'm done giving him the cold shoulder, I have no words to respond to everything he just said—to everything I'm trying to digest and understand.

When I finally lift my gaze from the red dirt beneath my feet, my eyes find his. My eyes find a comrade of agony. "I'm sorry you thought

I'd make you a home wrecker," he says as a tiny smile creeps over his lips.

"I was only upset, because . . . I—" My gaze angles toward the dirt again, but his finger slides under my chin, forcing me to look back up at him.

"I know why you were upset. I would have been upset too. It's why I asked you if your friend was a boyfriend."

His hands slowly and cautiously reach around my back and I can feel every part of his hands caress me. My skin craves to connect through the thin layers of fabric separating our bodies. He pulls me in closer, and I can feel the heat radiating off his chest. I can smell a hint of detergent in his shirt and the salty sweat beading up on his arms.

With his eyes locked on mine, waiting for a reaction, waiting for me to maybe stop him, his hand reaches down around my butt and he pulls me up to his waist where my legs loop around his body. His other hand slides up my side until it finds my cheek. My eyes close in response. His hand feels protective, reassuring, and I know how badly I need and want this.

"Open your eyes," he whispers. "Look at me." As if my eyes are obeying his words, they open without a thought. His face is only inches from mine. Being this close, I can see a teal ring surrounding the jade hue of his irises, and I can see tiny freckles making a straight line down the bridge of his nose. His breath tickles and teases my lips. The sweet scent mixed with the fresh air pulls me in. "I want to make you smile, Cali."

I bite down on my bottom lip to suppress my nerves. I want to smile too. I want to be happy more than anything in this whole fucked up world. I want someone to like me, to love me, to care about me. I want someone I can trust.

The fury building within him is clear. His thirst needs to be quenched, and so does mine. He moves in painfully slow and stops just before his lips touch mine. My heart pounds so hard and my breath feels as if it's been sucked completely out of my lungs. A sexy grin stretches across his lips. The seconds pass, the wanting in my body making it feel like forever. He finally closes the space between us, lightly pressing his lips against mine. All of his edges are so rough and raw, but his lips are soft and warm. His mouth explores mine, gentle at first before pulling away. His smile is replaced with a serious expression. I think he's gauging my reaction.

TAG   123

I don't know what my face looks like right now, but if I can't touch his lips again, it's going to look destroyed. "Kiss me," I beg.

His mouth quickly covers mine again, and his lips part as his tongue begins to pursue mine, allowing me to taste him, letting me breathe his breath. His hands move around my back, pressing me against him with what seems like all his strength. My fingers find their way to the back of his neck and into the nape of his hair. The slight touch of his buzzed stubble tickles my palms, forcing me to press harder until the prickles turn soft.

When air stops flowing, our lips part, and my eyes search between his, knowing words and explanations aren't necessary. We feel the same way. We need each other with the same desire. And I haven't ever felt this way about any other person. It's only been days, but this connection feels as though it's been here forever. If he can believe in fate, so can I.

The tip of his thumb finds my bottom lip and presses gently. "You're smiling," he whispers.

His words make me realize how unfamiliar the feeling is. I know how to fake a good smile when I have to, but I haven't grinned like this since before Mom and Krissy died. I haven't felt like it's been okay to really smile with my heart. And now that I can, it feels incredible. "I can't help it."

He leans in again and pecks my lips. "I can." He smiles in return as he places me back down on my feet. His arms wrap around me, and he holds me against him. With my ear up against his chest, I can hear the orchestra of his heart racing and his erratic breaths, along with wheezing and a struggle in his lungs.

I hope I didn't steal too many of his last breaths.

I believe everything he said, and I think I might even trust him.

I'm sorry, Mom, but I think I do.

He releases an arm and places one last kiss on the top of my head. "We better get back on the road." His hand drops into mine, and he pulls me toward the truck. I don't want to leave this spot, the place that will always hold an amazing memory.

*   *   *

It takes minutes before I acknowledge what just happened. I want to relive that moment over and over again.

The tips of my fingers keep finding their way to my lips, recalling the sensation of his mouth. I don't even know where we go from here. Do I pretend like he's not supposed to die in the next few weeks? Or do I just forget that he's sick—maybe I could just be his for whatever time he has left. I know what pain will come at the end of that road, but am I crazy to think the pain would be worth it in the end?

"Did you want to see your friend still?" His words sway me from my contemplation when he brings up Sasha. I almost forgot we were supposed to meet her. "We'll be in Pecos in about an hour."

"She named some place called Churro Grill."

He hands me his phone and says, "Open the GPS and type it in. It should come up."

The address pops up, along with a list of directions. "All set." I hold up the phone to show him. "Stay on this highway for another forty miles, then it's about ten miles from there."

"Must be off the beaten path. That's a good thing," he says, adjusting the rearview mirror. "She knows a lot about you?"

"Minimal information," I respond curtly.

"Good. She can't know where we're going."

"Tango, I know this."

"I know. I just felt better saying it out loud."

"So, if you buried your identity, does that mean . . . your real name isn't actually Tango? My thoughts come out in blunt words, but I want to know. I've wanted to know. I can tell he's searching for an answer. I can tell he's been trying to erase that part of his life, to forget who he was. But who he was made him who he is, and I want to know. This is the first time I've seen a nervous look appear on his face. "I won't tell anyone, and I won't call you by it. I just want to know who you were before you became no one."

He looks at me and grinds his jaw back and forth. After a heavy sigh, he says, "Tyler Wright."

A warm feeling tugs at my heart. "I like it." I place my hand over his. "But Tango suits you." I squeeze his hand gently. "Ooh! I know. You could call me Charlie," I laugh a little at my own militaristic joke.

"Impressive. You know the military alphabet?"

"Common knowledge in my household."

"Well, maybe I'll just call you Tango's Alpha Girl, TAG," he laughs, and his eyes gleam, making him look healthier and happier than I've seen him since we met.

I'll ignore that he just called me an alpha girl and focus on the fact that he just referred to me as *his girl*. "Your girl?" I ask with a raised brow.

"Maybe. The position is available and you're a suitable candidate."

I press my finger up to my lip, pondering the idea. "Hmm. What do I have to do to fill this position?" I can only imagine the typical man answers running through his head.

"I'll come up with a job description. Give me a little time." His smile keeps growing larger, and I want to kiss every inch of it.

TANGO

How many times can I lick my lips before I don't taste her anymore? Holy fucking shit. I can't believe I just did that. It was like my mind just stopped working. It did stop working. I stopped thinking and just reacted. Maybe it's because I haven't felt lips on mine or held a woman that closely to me in so long. I don't know what she's done to me. I don't know how she captured my heart the way she has, but she's raising the stakes, making me want to fight for this happy ending—actually for no ending at all.

I have to make it through these canyons. I have to survive for her. Now that I've drunk her, sipped her, savored her, and combed my fingers through her silken hair, how the hell can I just let my lungs take everything away from me? I don't know how I'll be able to focus on anything but her now. Although, I do know I'm going to end up hurting her very badly if this doesn't work out the way I'm hoping. I'm selfish. I am so fucking selfish. I have to beat this. For her.

CHAPTER FIFTEEN

CALI

WE PULL INTO a dirt lot filled with beat up cars, a couple of bikes, and a handful of eighteen-wheelers. Looks like a pit stop. The place is rundown, decked out with white Christmas lights and a deteriorating deck hanging off the front entrance. The confused look on his face matches how I feel, wondering why Sasha would direct us here. He doesn't even know she's a cute little blond girl probably sitting in the middle of way too many lonely truck drivers.

"I'm going to go in and scope the place out. What does she look like?" he asks.

I don't argue. Something feels a little off about this place. "She's a tiny little thing. Long curly blond hair, big blue eyes, and usually wears a lot of pink. If she's in there, you won't miss her." I try not to laugh at my description. I used to call Sasha Miss Piggy because of the amount of pink she wore. She's a little obsessed. As we grew older, it became apparent how much our personalities clashed. Nevertheless, when you grow up as close as we grew up, it doesn't matter what changes either of us went through, we still love each other for who we have always been. Acceptance and tolerance have never been questioned.

"Good to know we won't be drawing attention to ourselves here," he jokes.

"Who knows, maybe she's toned it down. But I'd have to say, I doubt it."

He casually makes his way inside of the shack-looking restaurant. I swear I just saw a rat squirm out through the hatch doors on the side of the building, and I think I've just lost my appetite.

It takes Tango less than a minute to observe and pop his head back out. He nods his head toward the front entrance, confirming it's okay to come in. I'm excited to see Sasha. It's been over a year, and our last encounter wasn't on the greatest terms. It was right after Krissy was murdered.

I can remember the call as if it happened yesterday. I called from the hospital room I was in, alone, after I was shot. Reaper escaped and was already on the run. There wasn't even a trace of his existence left for the police to find. I was in shock and in a lot of pain; especially finding out the bullet he shot me with would become a new accessory inside of my body. I was so alone. I wanted to pour alcohol into my eyes just to destroy the image of Krissy's neck being slashed. I couldn't figure out how I'd survive without her. I didn't want to. Our lives weren't supposed to end up like this. We had big plans. We were going to go with our friends, Chloe and Alex, to live in Paris for a year and then we were going to travel the world. We were going to forget about the lives we were left to deal with, and I was going to help her forget about the rape she was forced to survive through. It was a good solid plan. All she had to do was finish her last two years of college, but that night was the ending to our dream. It was the ending to everything I had left, and I had intended it to be my ending too.

I saw my bloody bag of clothes on a table across the room. I pulled myself out of the bed, pain stricken and weak, but grabbed the bag. I sifted through it until I found my jeans pocket where I had a small knife. I took it out and didn't waste any time. I made a slash across my wrist, but what I didn't know was that there was a proper way to end my life, and I did it the wrong way. I was just bleeding, not losing my life.

That's when I called Sasha, hysterical, explaining minute-by-minute the past three hours of my life. She's a strong girl, but she couldn't speak. She couldn't help me with this one. She just cried with me. We cried until a nurse found me bleeding with a bloody knife in my hand.

It only got worse from there.

Once I was released from the hospital and intense psychiatric care, I told Sasha she wasn't safe. Reaper knew her and if he killed Krissy for information, I wouldn't put it past him to go through her next. I had already told the police I didn't know who the murderer was. Part of me was scared to tell them the truth; the other part of me was as crazy as I still am today, wanting to kill him myself.

TAG

I pull on the flimsy door handle of the restaurant and inhale the scent of tortilla chips and refried beans. I look past the smoke clouding over the bar and I see her waving furiously at me. She jumps out of the booth and smothers me, kissing my cheeks, squeezing the air out of my lungs, loving me how my sister would have loved me if she were still here. The moment of affection nips at my heart.

When she peels herself away from me, she wraps her hand around mine and pulls me to the table. Our encounter doesn't disturb anyone and not a person has given us a second look. I now know why she's chosen this location.

Tango slides in against the window and I sit down next to him. She slides in across from me, her eyes never leaving my face. "Look at you, Cali-girl," she says with a cheeky smile. "You look beautiful. Happy, even."

Out of the corner of my eye, I can see Tango biting down on his bottom lip, probably knowing he is the reason for *my* stupid grin. Sasha's focus moves from Tango's face to mine, back to Tango's, and back to mine again. "You two are together, aren't you?" I can't believe she just asked me that after the texts I sent her last night.

"Sasha?" I groan.

"I know what you said, Cali, but—" she says.

"Wait. You told her about me?" Tango asks while wrapping an arm around me, which totally answers Sasha's accusatory question.

I throw my head back against the seat and kick her in the shin. I can feel my cheeks redden as I look over at Tango. It's clear my face is showing embarrassment, and by the look of his deepening dimples, he's nothing less than amused.

"I told her you were an asshole," I say to Tango. Seeing the slight arch in his brow and the smallest tug on the corner of his lip, I can tell he's calling my bluff.

"Actually, that's not what she said," Sasha outs me. "But he is pretty hot, Cali." She says, fanning herself. Who does that right in front of the person we're talking about? Sasha, of course. I now want to climb under the table.

Tango straightens the collar of his shirt and lifts his brows. "I know, right?" he laughs along with Sasha.

"Shall I leave you two alone here?" I grumble.

"Oh stop it. I'm just playing with you, Cali."

I huff; blowing the loose strands of hair off my forehead, lean back, and cross my arms over my chest. "So I guess I don't have to introduce you two."

"Sasha and I became insta-friends, don't worry," Tango says.

"Fantastic," I say. I should have known better than to introduce this smoldering hot marine to my best friend.

"I missed you, Cali-girl." She's staring at me, trying to read my mind like she always does. I can't help but wonder what she speculates about my life. I imagine she has a good idea of what's usually happening, but then again, no one could possibly guess the shit that I'm faced with on a normal basis. All I do know is, I wish I could tell her everything. "I ordered you fajitas and tequila, your fave." The memory of the last time she ordered me those two menu items swishes through me with a wave of nausea. Spring break, senior year of high school—it tasted great going down, not so much coming back up.

"Thanks, Sash," I smirk.

"Kidding. I ordered you quesadillas and a shot of tequila."

"And that is why we became insta-friends. This girl is awesome," he says about Sasha.

Sasha's expression becomes serious as she looks Tango directly in the eyes. "Hey, you have a girl at home?" I'm going to kill her, and I think the look on my face resonates with that thought.

"Nah, Carolina and I just settled this confusion."

"See, Cali, he's single. Free rein." She wraps her lips around her straw and winks at me. This girl loves to push my buttons, and she is the only one who gets away with it. When she pulls the straw from her mouth, she looks directly at Tango, seeming as if she's contemplating her next thought more carefully than she would normally look before spouting off embarrassing information. "This girl is like my sister, and I will go to the ends of the earth to protect her. If you hurt her, I'll kill you. Kapeesh?" I drop my head into my hands and remind myself again that I should have known better than to tell her about him.

Tango seems unfazed by her threat. "It's all good, Sasha. I'm sort of falling for this crazy chick." He squeezes me with the arm that's still resting around the back of my neck and places a quick kiss on the top of my head.

TAG   131

Everything. He. Does. Makes. Me. Melt.

"Aww! We're all a big happy family now." Her voice is shrill and piercing and punctures my heart. This *big happy family* will be broken up in about an hour.

My eyes fall to my hands, and I know she sees the look on my face, as I try to avoid her eye contact.

"I know you're not staying, Cali, but let's just enjoy the time we have together." I look up, and she's glancing between Tango and me then shoots down her shot of tequila, slams it to the table and says, "I think we need one more round."

Tango slams his hands down on the table and shouts, "Damn straight."

"You want one too, Tango?" Sasha asks.

"We have a long drive ahead of us. You two need it, though." His hand shoots up in the air, and a short Mexican man with a sombrero dances over to us. "Two more shots of Jose."

"Si, senor. Uno momento, por favor." The man dances away, singing words to a song in Spanish. He yells our order over to the bartender and I hear two shot glasses clap down against the bar top. I turn around and watch the clear liquid fill the two glasses, and then they're swiped from the counter and rushed back over to us. The glasses are placed down on the table, and I watch the liquid slosh around. This is such a bad idea.

Two more shots, two more margaritas, and a lot of memories make the hour slip by in a blur. The tequila deadens my overactive mind, and now I want to sleep. Sasha's arms are wrapped around my neck, and her lips are plastered on my cheek. "Love you, Cali-girl." She pulls away and looks me in the eyes. "Always, no matter what. You understand that?"

I don't respond, I just nod my head and place my forehead on her shoulder. I squeeze her harder and I feel pain in my chest. I feel sobs clambering their way up through my throat. I break away from her, and without turning back, I run out of the restaurant and back to the truck. I sit heavily on the parking curb in front where no one can see me, and the tears pour from my eyes.

After a couple of minutes, I hear a car door close, and headlights shine through the trees beside me. I can't see in through the windshield because of the glare, but I know it's Sasha in there. I know she can see me, sitting here, crying my eyes out. So I blow her a kiss. And I know she's blowing me one back. The cab I now see her in, blows by me and she's waving at me through the back window.

Two hands rest on my shoulders and I look up at Tango who is hovering over me. I glance back down and wipe my eyes over the sleeve of my sweatshirt, embarrassed to be seen crying. While my hand is up by my face, he grabs it and pulls me up off the curb. He leans back against the hood of his truck, drawing me into him. He sweeps my hair off my shoulders and wraps the loose strands behind my ears. He doesn't say anything. He just stares at me as he smoothes his thumbs across my cheeks and under my eyes, blotting away my falling tears.

When the tears stop, he loops one arm completely around me and with his other hand presses the back of my head until my forehead meets his rigid chest. This place over his heart is consoling. It's warm, and the rhythm of the beat is soothing to my broken soul.

I sniffle and suck in a deep breath. "I'm okay. We better start moving." I pull my face away from his chest and look up at him. He appears distraught.

"I know how bad this hurts, and I know you only just met me, but I'm here, and you're not alone. I miss my family too." His thumb sweeps over my cheek once more and his lips press against my forehead. "Let's go." I wait for him to release me first, and when his arms drop to his sides, I make my way back into the truck. I pull the seatbelt over my lap and lean my head back to stop the swaying motion in front of me.

Fucking tequila.

We drive just past midnight and pull up to a long line of cars waiting to go through customs. Who would have thought this many people would be trying to cross the border at one in the morning. "Pull out your passport," he says.

I reach down into my bag and pull out the blue book he handed me yesterday. I open it and study the picture under the glow of the streetlights. I don't know where or when he acquired this picture, but it's as old as my fake ID picture. Dad must have sent it to him just in case we needed a quick escape route out of the country.

We sit in the line for an hour, waiting for our turn. "Don't say anything unless they ask you specific questions," he warns.

When we pull up to the booth and the official asks for our passports, Tango takes mine from my hands and hands them to the man.

"Reason for travel?" the man asks.

"Pleasure," Tango responds.

"Length of stay?"

"Five days, sir."

The man hands the passports back to Tango and motions for us to continue. The open road leads us past a large sign welcoming us to Mexico.

"I wanted to do this now rather than in the morning. You don't even want to know what that line would have looked like in a few hours." I can believe it if we just waited an hour at this time of night. "I'll find us a decent hotel to crash in until the morning. We're still about ten hours away from Copper Canyon."

* * *

We pull off the road and into the parking lot of a motel. "Decent. Right?" He laughs.

"It's fine." I couldn't care less right now. I just want to pass out on something soft—or muscular.

We enter into the lobby that surprisingly looks a lot nicer than the last two hotels we stayed at. The blue tiled floor reflects off the mosaic glass windows on each corner and the open space offers serenity and comfort. The woman behind the counter is standing erect with a smile and welcomes us. "Hola, amigos," she says warmly.

"Do you want your own room tonight?" Tango asks under his breath. "I'm sure they have connecting rooms if you do." Last night, I didn't want to be near him. Tonight . . . is a little different.

"Sure," I say, really meaning no. But after today, it's probably best if we sleep in our own beds.

I can see the disappointment in his eyes, so I can't understand why he suggested our own rooms. I suppose it could be a respect thing, but I'm too tired to read into it right now. He asks the lady if she has two adjoining rooms, and she nods emphatically with a smile, approving of our appropriate decision, likely based on our two different last names.

She hands us each a key and points to the elevator on the side of the lobby.

The elevator is small and hardly looks as if it can hold both of our duffle bags and us. Regardless, we squeeze inside. Tango hits the button for the fourth floor, and the floor beneath us shakes and vibrates the entire way up. The doors open and reveal a narrow hallway with more tiled flooring and yellow stucco painted walls. Each door is wooden with a blue glass plate, etched with the room number.

He opens his door, and I open up mine. I step into a clean room with a full-sized bed, vibrant colored paintings on each side and a large window overlooking a pool.

I hear another door unlock and Tango appears through the connecting opening between our rooms. "Is it okay if I keep this open? I still need to keep you safe." Last night he opened the connecting door between our rooms and walked away as if it wouldn't matter to me. Although, I guess it didn't then. Now, everything matters.

I nod my head in agreement as I kick off my boots and fall backwards onto the bed. I hear him fumbling through things in his room and then he reappears in front of the doorway, half-naked with a playful smile. I have to force myself to turn away from the temptation, because every aching inch of my body wants to push him down onto his bed.

My eyes close quickly, and I try to shut my thoughts off, but my nerves reignite when I feel Tango's lips on my temple. I turn over and curl my hand around his bicep, tugging at him, wanting him to join me in this bed. Maybe it's the remnants of the tequila making me feel this way, but I know I had these feelings before the tequila too. Regardless, he pulls away with a seductive gaze—his lips parted slightly and his eyes half-lidded.

"I will do very bad things if I lie in this bed with you tonight," he says, sounding pained. "I just want to say goodnight."

"Well, for the record, I think I'd be okay with the bad things," I say.

He hovers down over me, leaning one fist into the side of my pillow while the fingers of his other hand trace a line across my collar bone and down between my breasts. His touch is so light; it causes a ripple of goose bumps to rise up on every inch of my body. He continues to graze his fingers down my body until he reaches the hem of my shorts. One fingertip slips underneath, but only far enough to torture me. He's not even inside of me and my back arches up toward his hand, begging for more. But he pulls his hand away and places it down on the other side of my pillow. He leans down, drawing his lips into my ear as he whispers, "Let today be the day of our first kiss." He moves to my lips, pressing his lightly into mine and lingers there until he nips at my bottom lip. "Goodnight, beautiful."

Damn him.

CHAPTER SIXTEEN

CALI

HER HAND is getting colder, but I try to keep it warm. Her skin is gray—almost translucent, and the color in her eyes is becoming dull against her pale skin. It's hard to remember the woman who once wouldn't leave the house without spending almost an hour getting dressed and carefully applying just the right amount of makeup. A smile still shows on her face though, and I don't know what has made her so strong. I would be crying, panicked, and terrified of the black hole that I would soon seep into.

Her lips are dry, and I've been watching her tongue press her cheek outward a number of times. The nurse says it means she's thirsty when she does that. I pull the small plastic cup of water off of the rolling cart and press the straw between her lips.

The effort of sucking the liquid from the straw is almost too much for her, but she tugs her hand out from beneath mine and touches my cheek, looking carefully into my eyes.

She releases the straw from her lips, and I pull the cup away from her and place it back down on the table. She clears her throat a few times before she can say anything. "Carolina, don't ever forget what I've taught you." She breathes heavily in between each word, showing me the effort it takes for her to speak at all.

"Know everyone . . . trust no one. I know, Mom. Don't worry. I won't forget."

"Good girl," her voice crackles. Her chest heaves in and out, struggling against the cancer that's fighting for the remaining breaths left in her body. "I love you, girls." She takes time to look at both of us for a few seconds. As her smile becomes a struggle, I wrap my hand back around hers, trying my hardest not to miss a second of any warmth left within her. "Take care of each other. Always."

And with that, the beeps of her heart monitor slow down. Her eyelids close slowly, and her hand goes limp, feeling heavy, considering the slenderness of her ninety-pound body. Krissy's cries ring loudly in my ear, and I want to fall to my knees and let go of all my pent up pain, but I won't let go. I'll watch her follow her light. I'll watch her find peace.

I watch as the nurses roll her out of the room. And I let go. I grab Krissy, and we pull each other to the ground. We rock back and forth in each other's arms, crying all of our pain out, trying to figure out what being gone for forever really means. We'll never see her again. Ever. How does one comprehend forever? It didn't matter how long we prepared for this moment. There is no moment like the one when you lose your mom.

* * *

I think I'm still dreaming and hearing Mom's heart monitor ringing out a long beep, until I realize I'm awake in the present, and there are sirens outside the hotel. Tango stumbles in, shoving his feet into each of his boots. "Cali, come on. Come on." He lifts my bags from the ground and throws them over his shoulder. He runs to the bed and pulls me out faster than I can even comprehend what's happening. "We have to leave." I can't even put together a logical thought. My head feels fuzzy and nausea is settling in, but I know I have to move. He hasn't overreacted since I've known him. And I haven't seen him panic yet. But I can sense the panic right now, so I follow in his footsteps.

We're running down the fire escape and out the emergency door. I can see the lights above the sirens flashing, but I'm still none the wiser as to why we are running. I don't ask questions, possibly because I can't quite form a question yet. As we reach the truck, he slows down a bit, and I can't figure out what changed.

He pulls out of the lot at a normal speed, and leans his head back against his seat. With a loud exhale, he says, "I'm sorry."

"What happened?" I ask.

"The alarm." He sighs again. " Cali, I've only been home from Afghanistan for a month. When I hear an alarm, I jump to attention. I find cover. I'm not used to it being a fire drill. We didn't have drills—just the real thing."

I place my hand over his arm. "It's okay. We needed to head out anyway." I'm starting to wonder how much he actually suffers within his head. I can't imagine what he lived through over the past few years. I mean, I've heard the stories, and I've seen the news, but trying to understand what it's like to live in a combat zone probably isn't something I can comprehend. He has this lost look on his face, and it's mixed with embarrassment. "Tango, you don't have to be embarrassed."

"What?" he asks as if he didn't hear what I said.

"It's nothing. Don't worry." I look back out the window, giving him the little time he seems to need.

TANGO

Jesus. This place reminds me of my first tour in Iraq. It's fucking with my head. A cool sweat drapes over my skin and a dark funnel surrounds me. I can smell the sweat, the sweet thick air and blood.

I fall to the ground with him, purposely trying to confuse them and cover my body as I reach for his weapon. No time to aim, I squeeze the trigger as soon as my hand grips the gun, raising a dotted line of lead starting with the first man's knees, up to the second man's stomach, and finally the third man's head.

Fighting the urge to think about how that just happened one handed, or the fact that the magazine was conveniently loaded, I jump up and quickly finish the first two men off. The third was dead on impact.

It's quiet again, except this time with the ever so familiar dull piercing of the ring in my head. I've always hated the sound of machine guns. With the street empty, I now see a stairway in the far side of the room. Was that there before? Doesn't matter, I reach the top and come out onto an open rooftop. The sun is hot, accentuating the accustomed smell of burning trash mixed with dust. Looking around some more, I stop. I hear it. The chops are too fast and offset to be just one. Are those helos I hear?

I look down into the face of the man I just murdered. His eyes are open, staring back at me. Was he born a bad person? Was he just following orders to protect his family? None of this mattered to me. It was him or me. I lift the shemagh scarf out of a pool of blood and drape it over his face, concealing the eyes that won't stop looking at me, begging me to take it back. I shake the image from my head, and it disappears quickly, but it's replaced by a growing shadow behind me. I can see the outline of an AK47 pointed at the shadow of my body. I suck in one breath, spin around, lock my foot behind his knee, jam my elbow into his face, feeling his skull morph around my bones, and watch him fall to the ground, moaning. I lift my blood-covered boot and smash it into the center of his face. This battle is never fucking ending.

I can't even remember what I'm fighting for. Is it for my survival or my country? Where is my country? Do they even know I'm here, having guns shadow over my head, watching children sacrificed in place of their parents? Do they know what kind of world I'm being faced with, while they're watching little snippets of sandstorms on TV? Do they think that's war?

* * *

A cool hand rests against my hot skin and it pulls me out of my flashback and back to the road. Shit. I can't be doing this while I'm driving. Fuck. "You okay?" she asks softly. "You just pounded on the gas." No, I crushed the skull of another asshole trying to kill me.

"I'm good. I'm good." Dammit. This shit has to stop. I need to pull over. I have to collect myself. I'm fucking sweating like a pig. I must look crazed and insane. This can't be a comforting feeling to the person I promised to protect.

CALI

It's clear we don't look like we belong here. We aren't in a tourist area, and the locals have us pegged. I can tell what they're all thinking, and I'm sure they've seen it millions of times before. *I wonder who they are, and who they're running from?* I step out of the truck to stretch my legs at the gas station. The ladies sitting on the bench in front of the small shop look like they are whispering about us, and the two men on the corner of one of the pumps are shoving each other, snickering and staring at us. I kind of want to go ask them what their problem is, but I don't speak Spanish.

I'm standing beside Tango, leaning my back up against the truck. It feels so good to stand after being in the truck for so long. I shuffle my toe around in the dirt, admiring the blush of each grain. Red dirt is prettier than brown dirt—my analysis for the day.

I hear gravel crunching beneath shoes and a shadow growing behind the pump. One of the elderly ladies who I'd seen whispering from the bench is approaching us. Her hair is white as snow, and her skin is as tan as leather—the wrinkles on her face tell me she's spent most of her days in the sun.

Her long bright pink and purple floral dress blows with the slight breeze as her arm reaches out to me. Her short and crooked fingers, which look worked to the bone, curl around my shoulder. "You go back home. No run away. Bad girl. Bad. Go home." Her broken English flows out in a raspy voice, and I can't understand her concern. She has no idea what she's talking about. Maybe they *don't* see as many runaways as I figured.

I force a smile and place my hand gently over hers. "Gracias, Senora."

A toothy grin stretches across her cheeks, so I'm guessing she thinks she changed my mind about the direction I was heading. She pats me tenderly on the cheek, and with her hand being so close, I can smell cooking flour and hot spices. "Good girl. Good." She turns her head toward Tango and points her finger at him. Her grin morphs into a scowl as she shouts, "¡qué vergüenza." She blows the loose strands of hair out of her squinty eyes and spits at his shoes before turning and walking back toward the bench.

I look at Tango and furrow my brows, mouthing, "What did she just say?"

He laughs a little. "She said, 'shame on you.'"

"Well," I purse my lips. "You are kind of a *bad* boy, teasing me like that last night."

The hose unclips under his hand and the gas cap falls from his other hand and bounces to the ground. He stumbles one foot backwards when he realizes he lost control of everything in his hands. Guess I have quite the effect on him. Good to know.

"Hey." He nods his head and sighs. "Get back in the truck." He grabs my ass and squeezes, making me yelp. As I slide into my seat, I see the old lady slap her hand over her mouth, apparently disgusted with our behavior.

When Tango finishes pumping the gas, he climbs back into the truck and places his hand down over the shifter. "Cali, I have something important to tell you."

"What's the matter?" I ask. What else is there left to say?

He looks at me grimly and it makes me worry. "I'm sorry but—" he sighs again, totally dragging this out. "Holy shit. Cali . . . you have a nice ass."

I slap him. "Bastard. You scared me." After steadying my racing heart, I ask, "Wait . . . does this mean the 'no touching' rule is gone?"

"You're the one who made that rule in the first place," he reminds me. "Plus, I think we kind of broke through that rule yesterday, a couple of times," he laughs. I love his laugh.

"Hmm, very true. I also made the fattening food rule," I add. "We've kept our word on that one at least."

His hand moves from the shifter over to my leg, and then he continues moving it slowly up my thigh, high enough to where his little finger sweeps against my most sensitive area, causing warmth to gush through me. "The 'no touching' rule. Should we reinstate it or—" he asks, pressing his finger into me a little harder, making me want to beg for more. "Get rid of it?"

"What rule?" I mutter. "I don't remember a rule about no touching?"

A game winning smile pulls at his lips and he replaces his hand over the shifter. "Good," he says, pulling out of the gas station, leaving me ravenous for his hands to find their way back up my thigh.

CHAPTER SEVENTEEN

CALI

I HOPE HE HAS a plan. This place is monstrous—canyons for miles. It's all I can see. Dad could be in any crater, nook or under any rock for all I know. I hate to even think where he's getting his source of food from, or where we're going to acquire ours from.

"We have nothing to camp with. Are we just going to wing it?" I ask, knowing I sound a bit apprehensive about surviving in the wilderness for an indefinite amount of time.

He ignores my question and unlatches the top cover from the bed of the truck. "I slept in the sands of Iraq and Afghanistan with explosions in the wind for about eighteen months each time. We'll be fine." He pulls two large packs out and sets them both on the ground in front of me. "Take whatever contents you might need from your personal bag and evenly distribute them in this." He leans over and sets my pack upright, lifting it as if it weighed less than a pound. He rips the zipper open and pulls the seams apart. "Go ahead."

I don't have much in my personal bag as it is, which is good since there's not much room in the pack he gave me. I pull a change of clothes out, my cosmetics bag, my pills and running shoes.

I toss my personal bag back into the truck and turn back to see him prepping my pack with something else. "What's that?"

"Camelbak. Water. You really haven't been camping before?"

"Not really. My dad wasn't around, and the only outdoors Mom enjoyed was the beach."

He walks over to where I'm standing and kneels down in front of me. I look down at him and give him a cutting look, feeling foolish as he unties the laces of my boots and yanks the top cross as tightly as possible. He pulls the loose lace until there's enough slack left to tie around my ankle twice. My circulation feels borderline cut off, but I assume he knows what he's doing. He moves over to the next boot and does the same thing. "You need to support your ankles when hiking through here. There's no time to twist or sprain anything."

He moves back over to his pack and retrieves a few more items. He returns to me with a holster and a handgun. "Wildlife, and maybe assholes."

"Hmm. You better watch yourself then," I say, inspecting the pistol.

He narrows his eyes at me, and takes my hand into his. "Carolina Tate. You might have scared a lot of people off during the course of your life, but being scared of you is like being afraid of a spider weaving a web. No one likes a nasty spider, but the web it builds can turn out to be one of the most spectacular wonders of the world. And like the spider, I know you are capable of much more than terrorizing people." I think it's funny or ironic that I was scared about getting tangled up in his web, and now he's calling me a spider. Seems like another case of fate.

I'm not sure he was expecting me to say anything, and I'm not sure how to respond. He continues organizing his pack and finally pulls it over his shoulders. I follow his lead and lift mine from the ground. Uh? This thing weighs like eighty pounds. I can see him trying not to laugh at my struggle as he walks over to me, carrying his pack as if it weighs no more than an empty bag. He pulls the straps from the side of my pack and clips them over the top of my chest, and then another set around my waist. He tightens them and I feel the weight distribute more evenly over my hips. I guess this isn't as bad now. I readjust my posture and stretch my neck to each side. "I guess I'm ready."

"You'll get used to it. I promise," he says.

Yeah. Before or after I croak?

Each step through the rocky terrain stretches the muscles in the back of my calves, and it feels good after sitting in the truck for so long. Although, the sun's heat is another story. Thankfully, it's later in the afternoon, and I can see the glare dipping beneath some of the higher canyons, eliminating part of the direct blaze. I imagine it must be brutal here in the mornings—something to look forward to tomorrow, I assume. I push forward, keeping up with his pace, careful not to appear as the weak link. Although, we both know he's been trained for this, and I have not.

We find an arched cave-like boulder blocking a bit of sun. Tango drops his pack to the ground and tugs at the waterspout on his Camelbak. "You need to drink more than what you've been drinking," he says, breathing heavily.

He crouches down into a dip against the wall and pours some of his water over his head. "God damn, it's hot." So. Are. You. I have to stop myself from biting on my lip. I look eager and hungry. Which I am, but still. "You sure you're all right? You're a little flushed," he says. As he's clearly worrying about me, he pulls out an inhaler. I'm not sure why I keep forgetting where this is all leading. He's sick. He's dying. And I'm starting to have real feelings for him.

"Are you in pain?" I ask.

"It's getting worse, yeah." He sucks in the medication, puffing his chest out and holding it briefly. He purses his lips and slowly blows the remaining medication back out of his mouth. "It feels like there's a fire burning in my lungs," he sighs. He presses the heel of his palm into the center of his chest as I've seen him do a few times and rubs it in a circular motion before releasing a dry painful sounding cough.

I wrap my tired arms around him and place my head against his chest, listening to his struggle. I can't understand his pain, and I can't feel it, but I can hear it. It sounds like someone trying to suck a lot of air through a little straw. I don't know how he's going to survive this hike. "Why don't we sit down for a few minutes so you can catch your breath," I suggest

"I'm good," he lets out a wheezy laugh. "You're the one who looks like hell." His sarcasm might just be my favorite thing about him.

"Gee, thanks. I'm really fine, though."

I'm dying. So fucking hot. I peel a layer off, noticing his eyes watching my every move as I pull my shirt over my head and drop my pants to my ankles, revealing my last layer: running shorts and a tight black tank top. When I pull my shirt off over my head, he stands up and walks over to me. He places the tip of his finger gently down over the curved line of the tattoo on my shoulder, and I flinch away from his touch. My skin is sensitive in that area, still painful most of the time. "Sorry." I'm not sure why I'm apologizing for being in pain.

"Don't be. Does it hurt when I touch it?" I nod my head and lean down to shove my shirt and pants into my bag. "I'm sorry they couldn't remove the bullet," he says.

"It's fine." Not really, but I hate talking about this damn scar.

"Does this tattoo really mean death?"

It's as if showing him the entire tattoo unveiled another dimension of my persona. "Yes." That, I have no problem talking about. "What does *that* mean?" I ask, pointing to one of his tattoos poking out on his neck above the back of his shirt. It depicts a skull within a spade stretched across a playing card. I tug on the bottom of his shirt and lift it up to see. I find four more of the exact same tattoo—five skulls on spades.

I release his shirt as he turns around and glances up at me with a dark look in his eyes. His pupils dilate as he appears to stare right through me. His voice sounds robotic when the word *death* escapes his mouth. His tattoo means death as well. We're so alike in so many different ways.

Acknowledging that this conversation clearly just hit a wall, I lift my pack and throw it back over my shoulders. "Ready?"

The eagerness in his eyes agrees with my thoughts. "Yeah, let's go."

The burning rays are becoming weaker and the heat isn't permeating my pale flesh as much. I glance down at my freckled arms, and I notice the subtle pink glow I had a couple of hours ago has turned into lobster red. I slathered on sunscreen before we left, but it seems ineffective here.

The path we've been on seems to be spiraling us up toward the peak of a high canyon and it feels endless. "Have you checked that tracking information against a map recently? I think we're walking in circles," I say breathlessly.

"We are. We need to find a place to camp tonight, but I'd like to climb a little higher before we stop."

I'm not cut out for this shit.

* * *

The peak appears to be getting closer, but my legs are becoming stiff and numb. Tango reaches his hand back to me, and I don't hesitate before grabbing a hold of it. His hand is covered in red dirt—it's hot and strong. Putting aside the sensation I feel every time this man touches me, I remind myself this isn't for romance. This is to survive the rest of this hike. Although, I should probably be the one pulling him up. His lungs hate him, and I don't know where his stamina is coming from.

TAG 147

* * *

The view forgives all pain and sweat. The sun's glare is now teasing the plateau of canyons on the horizon. The glow of the red clay meshes with the yellow hue of the fire in the sky, creating the most exquisite sunset I've ever seen. I can understand why some people would hike up just for this view. It's unfortunate I hiked up in hopes of finding the man who put me on this earth, and in turn saving the man I don't want to leave this earth.

No one else is up here right now. It's just us. We're alone, staring down at the world beneath. My eyes couldn't possibly focus on every detail below me, but I could spend every second of my life trying. I miss the times where I would have tried to paint this scene. I would have tried to study the shadow in each pit and nook on every canyon below me and the hues of each grain of dirt. I've been taught to take a closer look. To always notice every detail. And I do. Every. Single. Detail. Ugly or beautiful, I see it all.

I shove my hands into my back pockets and suck in the freshest air I've ever breathed. I hear Tango's pack drop to the ground behind me, and I turn around to find a tent already pitched. He's inside and the dimming sunlight is illuminating his shadow, along with every arch and bend of his perfect body. I force myself to turn back around and I find a rock to perch on. I pull my knees into my chest and wrap my arms tightly around them. My focus drifts up into the large gingered sky, staring through the forever, wondering if Mom and Krissy are looking back at me.

Tango's shadow hovers over me and he sits down on the rock beside me. "I think my buddies are up there staring back at me too."

I look over at him, wondering how he knew what I was thinking, but maybe it's how everyone thinks when they lose someone close.

"How many friends did you lose over there?" I might be stepping on unchartered territory, but it's just us up here and my question is just one of an endless list.

"Which tour?" he asks. My face responds to his question. Probably the same look he gets when he tells anyone this. "The first tour, we lost five guys. I was pretty close with one of them. The second tour, we lost one. He was a good guy. We weren't too close, but we were all closer than just friends. I was actually the one who had to greet his parents when we arrived home. The third tour was the worst, though. We lost twelve men. Three of them were part of my company, and we were closer than any people could be without being related by blood. Camaraderie and friendship is a given when you don't know when you're going to take your last breath."

I sadly understand way more than I should. I didn't volunteer to protect my country. I didn't even volunteer to protect my friends and family. I was forced to. He's a better person than I am. He's worked for the greater good. I have not.

"You hungry?" he asks, nudging his shoulder into my side.

"Yes, starved." We haven't eaten all day, and I haven't asked since I was figuring we'd be hunting our food down tonight. If that *is* his idea, I might go on an eating fast. He turns around and digs through his pack for a minute before he pops back up and tosses me a green air suctioned bag with the letters *MRE* written across the front. "What is it? Not that I'm complaining, obviously."

He takes it back out of my hand and studies the back of the package. "This one is chicken and rice." He lifts up his other hand with another green package and reads the contents on that one as well. "And this one is beefsteak." He hands them both to me. "Choose which one you'd prefer. They're meals ready to eat, MRE's. I lived off these things when I was overseas."

"I'll have the chicken and rice." He drops the bag back on my lap and I inspect it, looking for a way to open it. He hands me a knife.

"Can I trust you with this?" His brows arch, and I'm almost waiting for him to crack a smile, but I'm also thinking I seriously pissed him off with my knife threat the other day. I wasn't going to do anything to him—just trying to make a point, but he might not know that.

"I wasn't really going to hurt you the other night." I curl my fingers around the bottom of the knife and carefully take it from his hand. "I'm sorry."

"I understand. It's an automatic response to someone invading your space." He sits down next to me and stretches his legs out in front of him. "I know a little something about that. I have pretty bad post-traumatic-stress syndrome, and since I'm supposedly dead, no one can really help me. I can't talk to anyone about what's in my head, and I can't escape my own mind—not even for a second."

I keep my focus on his eyes, watching his gaze become lost in the caverns over the horizon. I try to extract information from people's minds and he's trying to extract memories out of his own mind. Maybe there's a reason we did find each other. "You can talk to me," I say.

I flip open the knife and drag its blade against the coarse plastic. The pouch opens and I expect a scent to pour out, but all I smell is more plastic. I flip the knife shut and hand it over to him, but he's already slicing his bag open with another knife. I peek inside, trying to figure out what I'm looking at since this meal looks like it should come with instructions. So I pour the contents onto my lap and place all of the items in front of me—lots of thick brown bags with black text written across each, an empty bag and a small bag filled with condiments.

"Put those two into the clear bag and add water. The bag will heat it up. Season to perfection, and eat when it's hot. Top it off with a little pound cake, and you'll think you're eating at a five-star restaurant." His smile is playful, and his excitement to eat this crap is a little baffling, but I'll go with it.

After preparing my meal for a few minutes, I shove the plastic fork into the bag and pull out a mouthful. When the food douses my tongue, I realize I didn't add the seasoning. The corners of my lips pull down, but I try to force them back up. He brought food, regardless of its less than desirable taste.

He laughs through his nose and hands me the salt and pepper. "Want mine too?"

I wouldn't ask my worst enemy to eat this food without seasoning. I'll deal with the one packet of each. "No, thank you. I'm sure you need it."

"You learn to forget about seasonings when you're under fire. You eat to survive, not to taste."

"It's fine. Thank you." I don't want to look like a bigger weakling than I already do.

After I added the salt and pepper, it was manageable. I've had about ten bites and my stomach has stopped rumbling, so I think I should be good now. I place the fork down on my lap and down some water. "No. You need to finish that. Five thousand calories will keep you going through this trek. Plus, it's another rule you made. Nothing but fattening foods. Right?" he asks, emphatically pointing his fork at me while he talks. "Not to scare you, but we haven't endured anything yet. Tomorrow's going to be harder." He empties the remaining contents from his bag into his mouth and then crumples the bag up into his hand. "We just need some sleep and food, and we'll be fine. We should be able to reach him by nightfall tomorrow." If tomorrow is going to be harder and he had trouble today, I'm worried about what his health is going to do.

I dig the fork back into the bag and pull out larger mouthfuls, hoping to swallow more and taste less. "How do you know my dad hasn't moved since he sent you the original coordinates?"

He pauses for a minute, probably pondering my question. "I don't. But I have to trust that since he gave me the first set of coordinates, he'd follow up with new ones, as well. He said they were for an emergency." He looks away from me, seemingly ashamed. "This isn't quite an emergency, so if he is where he says he is, I'm the one who's not trustworthy. Not him."

"This *is* an emergency, Tango. You're dying."

"Cali, there are a group of assistants your dad worked with in China who are after him. I can assume they've been offered a lot of money to return what he has to them. Along with those assistants, the private organization he stole from is after him as well, obviously. This shit your dad has is a big deal. If it can cure cancer, and he's hiding out with it, what do you think is going to happen when he's found?"

Reaper was after me for this exact reason. He wanted to use me as bait for Dad. For a split second, the thought makes me wonder if Tango has been lying to me and he's working with one of those two groups of people. What if I'm just the bait, as always? What if Tango isn't really sick? Maybe he doesn't need the drug to survive. Maybe he's just after it like the others. Maybe he's making me fall for him, so I weaken and trust him.

The echo of Mom's voice rings loudly in my head. I shouldn't trust him, or anyone. What have I done?

CHAPTER EIGHTEEN

TANGO

SUNSETS IN IRAQ looked the same. It was the only time of day where I would consider the place to be beautiful. Although that moment sometimes only lasted for a second until I heard shots fired in the distance. Sad as it may be, I wouldn't be surprised to hear the same sound here in these apparently calm and quiet canyons. Too many people are after Eli. Too many people know what he has. Too many people want the reward for returning it.

I can't help but wonder how long Cali can keep up this *alpha girl* act. I don't care who you are, if you aren't physically trained to survive in these conditions, complaints should accompany the flushed look on her cheeks, the sweat soaking up all of the material on her shirt, and the darkening sunburn on her arms and neck. Yet, not one complaint, moan, whine, whimper—nothing. She hasn't said a word. She just keeps trudging on. In truth, I find this extremely sexy. Although at the moment, she looks like something just bit her ass. She looks pissed again, and I'm guessing I'm in for another mood swing. "Something wrong?" I ask, worried to hear a response.

"Are you really sick?" she asks. The question quakes through me. She thinks I'm Reaper. She thinks I'm here to screw her over.

"I'm not sure how to prove it besides coughing up more blood. Maybe when I drop dead you'll believe me then." I know I just pissed her off, but I'm a little shocked she just questioned my motives. I've been honest with her. I've told her everything, things I shouldn't have even told her, and she still doesn't believe me. What else am I supposed to do to prove myself?

CALI

Tango stands up and brushes the dirt off his backside. "Grab your Camelbak. We need to go find water," he says coldly.

I nod my head and follow his lead. I wouldn't survive in the wilderness myself. We've been walking for twenty minutes and if Tango disappeared, I would have no clue how to make it back to our campsite. At least I hear running water, and the fresh smell permeates my nose. As we walk closer, a slight mist developing in the warm air prickles against my hot skin, causing tiny bumps to rise in response to the temperature distinction. The sound of cascading water thunders louder and the white noise soothes my recent internal tension.

When we come to a clearing in the rocky terrain where trees are sprouted along the curvature of a sudden drop, I see the spray of the falls colliding against the gorges, inviting us to peek over the edge. The drop from the top is about fifteen feet, but the rocks look suitable for descending lower.

Tango lowers himself down the first few rocks and looks at me. He doesn't reach his hand out, but the expression on his face is questioning if I need help coming down. I don't. If those hands touch me again . . . ugh. This is hopeless. I've already let this go too far.

I turn around and carefully lower myself down to the first flat rock. The sharp edges scrape against my skin, but I ignore it. I watch as he lowers himself down another rock and I notice his body doesn't skim along the side of the edge like mine just did. I'm not sure I'm strong enough to hold my weight off the rock like he is. I lower myself down again, but this time my foot slips from one of the lips in the crag. My leg falls against the coarse edges once more, and a sting burns up my leg.

"Quit being so stubborn and give me your hand," he shouts at me from below. "Dammit, Cali, you're bleeding." I glance down at my leg and see a trickling red teardrop cascading down my skin. I slide my hand into Tango's and his other hand wraps around my waist, pulling me down from the rock I'm hanging from.

We're only a few small boulders away from water and he helps me down the remaining steps. "Sit," he demands.

He pulls a green rag out of his back pocket and dips it into the water, all while never taking his eyes off me. If he is playing me, he's damn good at what he does.

I feel the damp rag drape over the gash. He presses firmly, applying enough pressure that I scoot backward a few inches. He pulls the rag off to inspect the injured area and his hands wrap around my leg, elevating it off the rock. "Good one. Probably could use a few stitches." Obviously, that's not happening here. He pulls another rag out of his back pocket. It looks like a piece of torn cloth, a T-shirt maybe. He twists the material around his hands and wraps it tightly around my leg, securing it with a knot. The material feels as though it's cutting off my circulation, but I trust—no, I don't. I hope he knows what he's doing.

I inspect my hands for further damage, and I think they're only superficial scratches. I lean down beside the rock and swish my hands through the water, watching the spiral cloud of floating moss swirl around my fingers. Tango pulls the Camelbak off from around my shoulders and dunks the plastic bag into the water. "Is this water safe to drink?" I ask.

"No." He shoves his hand into his left cargo pocket and pulls out a small tablet. "Iodine will clean the water and make it suitable to drink." He drops the tablet into the water pouch and shakes it around. "It takes about thirty minutes." He hands my bag over to me and repeats the process again for his water. After dropping the tablet in, he looks over at me with irritation darkening his eyes. "Just for your information, I do in fact have cancer. I am dying. I don't want to die, and like I said, I'm fucking scared as hell. I'm not just using you to reach your dad. You're the one who suggested finding him for the treatment, remember? I'm not the bad guy, Cali."

"I want to trust you, but I'd be lying if I said I did. And when there is no trust, paranoia can seep in through even the thickest skin. You say certain things that make me question everything, especially if I should really be here. I know this was my idea, but—" I sigh, frustrated with where this has gone and where it's going. "Look, we're complicating things—you know, pretending like there's something more than sexual tension between us. I've known you for a week, Tango. You're hot. You say the right things at the right times and you know how to make a girl swoon, but none of that proves your honest motives for being here. I'm sorry."

He looks at me for a minute, taking in my words, maybe thinking of a suitable response. "No, Carolina, *I'm* sorry if I haven't proven enough to you. I don't know what else to do to make you trust—no, sorry—have a little faith in me."

His words lead to silence, accentuating the screams of my internal battle. I feel like I'm gambling with my safety and the anxiety is driving me mad. It's not like I can just convince myself that I'm not in this situation, and I can't exactly control how I feel about this, about him. This is why I don't involve myself with people. This is why I promised not to fall for anyone again. I can't even fucking trust myself to do the right thing.

I'm the one who can't be trusted.

Deciding which direction I should continue on with, I close my eyes to listen to the sound of leaves brushing against each other from the slight breath of the wind. My heart has stopped hammering against my ribcage and I feel it's safe to open my eyes. I feel it's safe to go with my gut on this one.

"Tango . . . "

"I don't like the way you just said my name, Carolina."

"Look . . . I'm not sure I'm ever going to be able to believe you, and while I wanted that kiss to last a whole hell of a lot longer than it did, I know I shouldn't be getting involved with you, or anyone for that matter. I don't want to be hurt again." If what I'm saying is true, why is my heart punching me from the inside. My throat feels tight, as if it's trying to stop me from saying what I'm saying. I'm so fucking lonely, and I'm so quick to push anyone and everyone away.

"I—wow. I shouldn't have assumed. I'm sorry. I shouldn't have kissed you. You're right. The trust needs to be there before anything should ever happen between us. I was being impulsive and I shouldn't have been. I read you wrong, and that's a hard one for me to admit. I wish you would have said something sooner."

He didn't read me wrong. I'm an asshole, but I still believe every word Mom said to me. I lower my head to avoid any contact with his moonlit glowing eyes. I have nothing to say in return—nothing can make this less awkward or easier.

"I'm going to rinse off real quick. I need to clear my mind for a minute. You mind?" he asks.

I shake my head, still holding my attention to the rock below my feet. I see his shadow stand tall beside me, and his arms lift over his head. The scent of his shirt, which is a combination of man and sunscreen, swooshes into my face as the material drops down next to me. I hear the metal clink of his belt buckle release, which allows me to imagine what he looks like while taking it off. The clamor of his shorts hitting the rock forces oxygen to constrict in my lungs.

The shadow quickly disappears into the water and my eyes are unwillingly drawn out to him. He's facing away from me, probably admiring the waterfall, and I'm ogling the shadows of his half naked body.

The water cuts his body off at the middle of his waist, making me wonder what his clothes have been hiding. He lifts his arms and combs his fingertips through the short spikes on the top of his head. His biceps must be larger than my thigh. They flex with such a simple movement, showcasing what he's capable of.

I'm going to regret this. I just told him this was basically over and now . . . I'm changing my mind.

I stand up and pull my tank top over my head. The coolness of the musky air chills my skin, forcing a mist of goose bumps over my stomach. I drop my shorts down to the rocks, revealing more than I thought I'd ever allow someone to see again, and I kick off my boots while unwrapping the fabric from my leg. The bleeding has stopped, and I'm taking that as a sign that I should continue. I place the scrap of fabric over my clothes and dive into the water.

When I resurface, I rake my fingers through my hair to clear it out of my face and I open my eyes to see Tango staring at me. Getting a better glimpse of the front of him without a shirt convinces me that I was the biggest moron in the world a few minutes ago. The darkness in the hotel room last night didn't do his body any justice. He's so fucking hot. I can't just coexist on this trek with him and not touch him again. And I don't care if he thinks I'm crazy. I don't care about what I just said to him. All I care about is the way his hands feel over my skin.

Without an idea of what to say, I pinch my lip between my teeth again. It happens without a thought. It's my body reacting to his flawlessness. His eyes are having trouble focusing and his chest is heaving in and out at a much faster rate than it was a second ago.

His lips part and I can't take it. I tread through the water faster than I thought I could, and I wrap my arms tightly around his neck as I slam my lips into his and suck all the breath out of him. His hands loop around my waist and he lifts me up with ease, allowing my legs to wrap around his narrow hips. He's forgiving me for everything I've said and doesn't question my change of mind.

I feel his bulge press into me, and my body responds instantly. His hands slide down over the thin material of my panties as a growl hums from the depths of his throat. His grip tightens and his teeth clamp down over my bottom lip. My body presses against his as our skin blends smoothly from the water acting as a lubricant between us. There is no resistance, only a relentless desire. He treads us backwards toward the falls and pulls me under until we're being showered by the solid thick sheen of falling water. We continue to move in stride until we're up against a rock wall. "I'm not going any further until I know you believe me. I don't want to hurt you. I want to be with you. I haven't lied to you about anything, and I trust you, Cali. You don't have to trust me, but I need you to believe me," he says loud enough so I can hear him over the rushing water.

I can see truth in his eyes. It's something I didn't see in Reaper's. He looks at me in a lot of ways Reaper never looked at me. I look him in the eyes and let the truth roll off my tongue. "I believe you."

"Don't just say that to get in my pants," he laughs softly.

I slap his chest playfully. "No, I do believe you. And . . . you're not exactly wearing pants." I could hardly find the right words. It's been so long since I've felt anything like this.

He lifts me up a bit higher until my head is above his, giving his hand easy access to cup around my breast. He pushes it up and wraps his lips around my nipple, using the tip of his tongue to draw small pleasurable circles. The sensation causes my breaths to increase and my fingers to press firmly into his shoulders. Obviously he knows how to use his tongue, and that thought turns me on even more. Just as I think I can't take much more, his hand travels down my side and onto my thigh, lowering me until our eyes meet again. But it's only until his starved mouth finds the spot on my neck that makes my body tighten around his. He continues sucking and biting the spot until I let out a soft moan. I'm becoming weak in his hands and he definitely knows it. His hand finally slides under the hem of my panties and his finger slips inside of me briefly, but he pulls it out much quicker than I want. His hands instantly clamp around my sides and he drags me under the water with him, leaving me breathless and terrified. My body is too weak to struggle against his hold, and my eyes remain clenched shut, imagining my worst nightmare, knowing I shouldn't have fucking trusted anyone.

CHAPTER NINETEEN

CALI

TANGO'S BELOW THE WATER with me. He's pointing frantically at something, but I don't understand. As the remaining oxygen seeps out of my body, Tango's hands grip around my waist and he thrusts me up above the water. His hand slaps over my mouth and his other arm wraps around my stomach as he drags me up to the nearest rock. He puts his face in front of mine and mouths the words, "Stay here." The purposeful look in his eyes screams danger and my eyes dart around looking for the source. But I don't see anything. How could he have seen anything, but darkness or the water that was barricading us?

He wades over to the rock we jumped from, grabs our clothes and water, and holds it above his head as he makes his way back to where I'm sitting. "Get dressed, quickly."

I struggle to pull my shorts up over my soaked legs, and before I have them settled over my hips, Tango is pulling my tank top over my head. He places my boots next to each of my feet and I shove them in without tying up the laces. I toss my water pouch back over my shoulders just as he reaches for my hand from the above rock. He nearly catapults me upward and repeats this three more times until we're back on solid land.

He pulls me over into a nook of a rock formation and squats down, pulling me with him. "He's here," he whispers into my ear.

Those two words hold all the meaning in the world. I know exactly who *he* is and why Tango almost just drowned me. "Reaper?" I confirm. The name tastes dirty on my tongue.

"I'm assuming it's him. He's been tracking us, I'm sure. I saw a man with an assault rifle on one of the higher boulders. Moron was standing right in the glow of the moonlight." His eyes shift wildly behind me, searching through the darkness. "We have to lose him or whoever it is so he doesn't find our campsite." Tango hovers over me and begins to lace my boots up.

"I can do it," I say, brushing his hand away from my foot as I continue to lace them up, quickly and tightly. He steps into his shorts, pulling them up over his soaked boxers, and pulls his T-shirt over his head.

"This way," he whispers, nodding his head in the opposite direction than where we came from.

The slight sound of our feet crunching against the moss-covered dirt is loud enough to overload my ears, and I'm fearful whoever is after us can hear the same thing. But my fear disappears as my memory jogs back to the moment I watched Reaper murder Krissy. If it is him who's following us, I want to go after him.

I continue following in Tango's footsteps, noticing the maze he's created in the woods. I know how to throw a tracker off. I remember Dad telling me about it. You walk in different directions, leaving your footprints where you want the tracker to go. That's what we're doing.

By the descending angle of this trail, I believe we're heading back down the canyon, far away from our tent. Tango has his pack, but I don't have mine. I want to see inside of his mind right now and find out what his plan is, but I don't want my voice or whisper to carry through the breeze.

We've been walking for over an hour in what seems like circles. Tango releases his pack from his shoulders and hovers over to pull something out. He retrieves a pair of binoculars, which I don't know how he'll use within the darkness and cluster of trees surrounding us. He looks up at me and the confused look I'm giving him, then he hands me the binoculars, placing them over my eyes. Everything is green, and I can see through the murk. "Night vision goggles," he says softly. I nod my head with understanding and hand them back to him. He uses them to search around the vicinity, taking his time to look in every single direction. "Let's head back. We lost him for now."

For now.

It must be the middle of the night by the time we return to our campsite. Everything appears unscathed and unnoticed, but Tango isn't comfortable with assuming that to be the case. "Grab your stuff and follow me."

He folds up the tent enough to move it and tucks it under his arm as he looks back at me. He jerks his head for me to follow him, and I do. We find a small shallow cave and Tango shoves the tent inside. However, the cave isn't large enough for the tent to be opened. I don't think he intended to open it anyway. I can assume a tent is a clear indicator of our location, which is precisely what we're trying to avoid.

He pulls a large sleeping bag from his pack, and I open mine to follow suit. He lays his down inside of the cave and I lay mine next to his. The space is so tight we'll hardly be able to move once inside, but this is necessary. Once my sleeping bag is laid out, he tells me to climb in, and he follows. Being caught in a vulnerable situation by what was likely my ex—my sister's murderer—is too much to digest and I'm trying to avoid the thought. But I can see it's all he's thinking about as he pulls both of our packs toward us so they're blocking the opening to the cave.

"No one will see us in here now," he says.

Before settling into his sleeping bag, Tango removes his shirt and drapes it over his pack, but leaves his shorts on, which are likely still wet. And I leave mine on as well since there doesn't look to be enough space to change in here.

He places a small flashlight in the corner, giving us a bit of light so we can see one another. The slight glow is comforting and we both lie in silence, listening to each other's breaths, feeling the heat build around us from the locked in moisture.

We've been lying in silence for a bit, but a clap of thunder rumbles in the distance, and the break in the quiet is welcoming. Pellets of water ping against the rock we're beneath, one by one, until the rain turns into a steady stream. The cave is elevated on a short mound, which I'm now thankful for since the drainage isn't seeping in below us.

"How long were you with him?" he asks in a dour voice.

"Reaper?"

"Yes."

"A few months. Enough time to make me fall for him and trust him," I reply. "I wish I saw warning signs. She'd still be alive. But without sounding too cocky, I think he lost track of what his plan was. I think he might have accidentally fallen for me too. It felt like a normal relationship and I don't know how someone could fake that, but he must have

TAG   161

realized it had gone too far at some point—the point where he ended everything."

"I'm sure he did fall for you. It would be hard not to." He turns over onto his side to face me. "But even if there were hints, what would you consider to be warning signs?"

I know he's looking at me, but I can't look back at him. I can't look at anyone while talking about Reaper. "I suppose he tried a little too hard to spoil me. And I guess the compliments were overly abundant. And the gifts he bought me were too much. Thinking about it now, he was pretty ostentatious. But he was my first real relationship and I didn't know better. He told me he loved me after only a few weeks, and I fell for it. I fell for him. He never inquired about my parents, so I didn't have a reason to worry. I asked him about his family and he didn't retaliate with any questions about mine. He hadn't told me where he went to college or if he was in the military. That part was always a little fuzzy. He changed the subject a lot, and now I know why. But he didn't make me think I couldn't trust him until the night he killed Krissy. That was the night I learned that nothing I trusted was real." I feel myself breathing heavier, fearful of these emotions resurfacing. I've tried hard to keep them in the back of my mind, but nothing can keep them away for that long.

"Then what happened?" He swallows hard, and I can sense the story is making him angry.

"He came over to my house that night, brought my bodyguard his favorite beer to keep him quiet as he did most nights, and made his way upstairs to my bedroom. He sat down on the edge of my bed and said, 'I need to know where your dad is.' This was obviously a trigger for me. I was raised never to ask where my dad was or to give anyone any information on where I thought he might be. I told him I didn't know. I even laughed a little at his question. It was out of character the way he asked. It was also out of character the way he shoved me down onto my bed and wrapped his hands around my throat and yelled, 'Tell me where he is, Cali.' I choked out that I really didn't know. Because if I did know, I probably would have told him out of fear. He released his hands from around my neck and I bounced off the bed and out the door. When I ran downstairs, I saw a box of empty beer bottles, but my bodyguard was gone. I had run out the door and down the street before

I realized I had left Krissy home alone with him. I went back for her. But they were both gone." My chest is heaving in and out, trying to hold down the sobs—the pain from retelling this story.

Tango wraps his arms around me, and the comfort makes the tears start. "Is that when it happened?"

"He knew I was looking for him. He left me a note on her bed, telling me where he was taking her. I think he would have killed both of us that night if he had the opportunity, and I think that was his plan. I called the police and said someone took my sister. I told them where the note told me he'd be. But the police were too late. I had already been cornered and Krissy was already dead, and he ran off at the sound of the siren." I nod my head, reliving the moment. "My mom told me not to trust anyone. I should have listened."

"You don't know what it's going to take for me to not hunt him down and murder that son of a bitch, Cali. You did not and do not deserve that." He pulls me against his body and my head finds the curve between his chest muscles, the place where I can connect with his heart. "I understand why you can't trust me." His words are whispered into my ear, and it's the most comforting thing anyone has ever said to me. Being understood is something I have only wished for.

"I don't want the emotion of trust to end up in our way. I want you, Tango," I say, immediately wondering why I'm saying this? I'm nearly begging for him, and I sound desperate. Not what I should sound like right now after spilling my past miseries.

"You don't have to trust me, Cali, but you can trust that I will not let you down. You can trust that I will make you feel things you've never felt, because I'm real. We're real, and that makes all the difference . . ." I can see the corner of his lip curl up slightly. "If you want me, I will show you what real feels like." His words are driving a wild sensation from my heart to the most vulnerable place between my legs. My body is responding to his words alone—I want him right now, in the middle of these god-forsaken woods, under a rock, covered in sweat, and placed in the middle of a potential danger zone.

"Make me forget where we are right now. Make me forget what pain feels like."

"Tell me again that you want me, Cali," he whispers wantonly.

"I want you, please."

TAG   163

"Good," he whispers. The growl in his voice drives shivers through my stomach. His arms wrap around me, pulling me against him. "Because, I want you so fucking bad." He turns me over so I'm spooned in the curve of his body. His fingers skate along my skin, leaving a trail of prickles behind. His mouth presses into my neck as his hand wanders down past my shorts, finding my ass and clutching it while pulling me into his hardness. His fingers explore around to the front, dipping down into my wet shorts and under my panties. He enters me slowly, one finger at first, then another, continuing what he started earlier. This time he doesn't stop. This time I realize what those fingers are capable of.

"Still want me?" he asks.

I moan in response. It's the only type of sound I'm capable of right now. He flips me over on to my back and climbs over me, moving down, down, down until he's between my legs. He pulls my shorts and panties off, furiously pushing them down to my ankles. His hands grip around my thighs and his tongue fills the space his fingers were just occupying. He's slow at first, then fast, then slow again. Everything inside of me is throbbing, and I'm not sure how much longer I can last. His groans vibrate through me, causing me to cry his name out. "I'm going to—"

"Not yet," he says. He climbs back up my body and I pull at his belt, tearing it apart as fast as I can. I kick his shorts and boxers down, reaching my hand around his impressively large size. "Hold on. I'm not done with you yet." He reaches over to his bag and pulls out a condom.

"I'm on the pill," I whisper, breathlessly.

He tosses the condom back in his bag and I can feel his smile grow across my neck as he kisses me harder. He lifts his head and gives me a look that makes me think he wants me to beg him not to stop. And I'll beg and plead if that's what it'll take.

"Please, I need you," I say, offering him what I think he wants to hear. It works. He lowers himself inside of me while his hands continue to explore every inch of my skin—warming me, comforting me, making me need more of his touch. More of everything.

"How's this?" he asks, keeping his movements slow and gentle. I melt into him as he rocks me back and forth, his grip gradually tightening at a pace that's becoming too slow.

I dig the tips of my fingers into his chest and use my feet to increase the momentum. "Harder," I breathe. His breathing becomes shallow as his thrusts become more intense. Each movement feels like a welcoming rush of warmth inside. The intensity is making my limbs tingle, tighten, and contort to his.

The buildup is becoming too much. His growls are becoming louder and my breaths are becoming quicker. "I'm close," I cry. He nuzzles his nose behind my ear, peppering kisses in circles until he reaches my earlobe. He bites down gently, and that's all it takes. The sensation shoots through me.

"Me too," he utters. A feeling of overwhelming heat burns from within and my body succumbs to numbness. My breaths turn to moans as he pushes into me harder and faster. My moans become louder until his mouth suffocates the noise coming from mine. I can taste myself on his tongue, and it's nearly erotic.

With a final plunge of warmth, our bodies stop moving, but the rush continues torturing my insides as an aftershock. Our chests heave in and out against each other. Our eyes lock in an endless stare.

"Wow," he breathes.

"Yeah. Wow," I respond.

"I think we're kind of good together, Cali. I've never—that hasn't felt like . . . *that* before."

"I guess that's what *real* feels like." Soft laughter escapes my throat at the lack of conversation we're able to have. I'm speechless, I'm helpless, and I'm softening up to him. Trust or no trust, he's amazing.

CHAPTER TWENTY

TANGO

NOTHING LIKE the first time. The first time in four years. The first time with intense emotional feelings, and the first time with that amount of desire. Holy hell, I might have just become addicted to her—her smell, her taste and her body—it could heal me. I won't ever come back from that in one piece. And I might be okay with that.

I didn't think sleep would be possible tonight, but with her by my side, I can actually die a happy man now. She doesn't give a shit that I don't have a real name anymore. She doesn't give a shit that I'm dead according to everyone who knew me. She knows I might be dead within a matter of days or weeks, but she's accepted it. It's so clear how alike we are. I'm broken. She's broken.

Maybe our two broken souls can fit together and make us whole again.

CALI

I fell asleep within Tango's arms, feeling as secure as I possibly can here in the middle of nowhere, all while knowing Reaper or whoever could be creeping around any corner. But now I'm awake. It's still the middle of the night, and I have to pee. I shimmy out from beneath Tango's heavy arm and slide the concealing packs off to the side. I pull myself out of the cave and wait for my eyes to adjust to the darkness, trying to spot a tree to hide behind in case Tango wakes up and comes looking for me—I'm not quite ready to pee in front of him yet. I quietly walk to the nearest tree and stand behind it, reaching from the top of my shorts as a weird sensation overwhelms me. My gut is twisting, but I try to push the feeling away. I can't help feeling as though I'm being watched, but darkness usually seems to do that to me.

I relieve myself quickly and tug my shorts back up over my hips, but as I turn to head back to the rocks, a hand slaps over my mouth. It smells like sweat and feels grime-covered. I try to scream, but the hand is tightly cupped over my nose as well, prohibiting any sound or air to go in or out. My heart doesn't know what to do. I think I'm in shock, frozen.

Adrenaline courses through me and I loop my arms around the back of the person's neck and squeeze with every bit of strength I have. I nip at the person's finger since I can't manage a full bite. But an arm, a familiar arm is wrapped around my stomach, lifting me off my feet. I'm powerless. I flail, I swing and I kick, but it's all worthless.

I'm dragged for minutes before I'm slammed against a tree. My hands are tied around the back, the rough bark scraping against my skin. There's more than one person. They aren't in front of me or to the sides of me. They're behind me, and I can't twist my neck far enough to see.

"I know it's fucking you, Reaper," I seethe through my clenched jaw.

His outline steps out from behind the tree—even in the darkness I can see those menacing blue eyes. I kissed those perfect lips, and I told that beautiful face I fucking loved it. Now, I'm tied to a goddamn tree while the man I'm falling for—the one who's broken through my trust barrier and has made me feel something truly incredible for the first time—is none the wiser.

A light flashes in my face before it moves to illuminate my worst nightmare. "Hey, baby-doll. Long time no see. I don't like that you call me Reaper," he says, tracing a line down my cheek with the tip of his finger. This isn't what I planned. I planned to have *him* tied up. I planned to have all the control. "Where's Daddy now?" His voice is childish, comedic almost.

"I'm calling you what you are, and if I knew where he was, I wouldn't be tied up." I spit at his face.

He stands up and throws his head back, releasing a scathing chuckle. "Well, we're going to find him together. I just hope your new boyfriend doesn't mind that I'm borrowing you for a little while."

"He'll kill you," is my automatic response.

"And he," he points to the man standing beside him, "will kill *you*." The man looks like a linebacker. He is more muscle than body, and his face looks too small for his neck. He's actually kind of gross to look at. It's probably all steroids. Neither of them is dressed appropriately for hunting people down in the woods. They're both wearing jeans and t-shirts, which don't look too clean anymore.

I have to outsmart him. I have to manipulate his head, and I'm prepared to do that. I've trained myself for this. The opportunity is here and I will not let it best me or pass me.

Reaper pulls out a phone from his back pocket. He holds it up to my face and a flash blinds me. "There. Such a pretty picture," he squeaks, admiring the photo on his phone. "This can be bait for Daddy. I'm sending him a text message right now."

He stares at me with an evasive simper for minutes until his phone buzzes. He looks down at the screen and back up at me. "Daddy doesn't want you, princess." He lifts the phone up to my face, allowing me to read:

> *I will not give you my location for any amount of bait. Tell Cali, I'm sorry.*

"He's totally not sorry," he teases. I know it's not real. He doesn't have Dad's number. "I guess it's true, Cali. No one has ever loved you, not even your sister, Krissy. Wait, was that her name?" His eyes search the sky for an answer he knows. "Yeah, Krissy. She said she hated you for pulling her down into the trash you dragged yourself into." He squats back down again. "And that mom of yours, she would have left you with someone a little more reliable than your dad if she really loved you. Don't you think?"

The sobs are flooding my throat, threatening to erupt, but I tell myself this isn't true. It isn't true. They loved me. I loved them.

I struggle to maintain a straight face. I will not give him that power again. "You were always one with your words, Reaper."

"It's my strong suit in life. And when I acquire that treatment your father's guarding with his life and yours, I will be so fucking rich and powerful. I will be known for supplying the world with cancer's cure. How many people can say that?" he laughs.

"So now what? You have me and you still don't have his location."

"First things first, baby-cakes." He nudges his head toward the other man. "Jorge, go take care of the man she was with. Tango? Is that his name?" He gives me a questioning look with a wrathful grin still teasing across his cheeks. "I heard you moaning his name in your little love cave earlier tonight."

I swallow hard, silently refusing to respond. Tango's smarter than this. He's been through worse. He'll survive this.

Although, maybe if I yell, he might hear me.

But if I yell, I might make this worse on myself.

TANGO

When my eyes fight through the darkness, realization sets in . . . she's gone. I want to assume she's just looking for a tree to squat behind, but why am I having trouble convincing myself of that? I pull myself out from beneath the hovering rocks and squint my eyes through the darkness. She wouldn't have gone that far. Shit. Shit. Shit.

I rip my pack out of the rocks and secure it over my shoulders. I fucking knew it. I should have told her to wake me up if she had to go to the bathroom. This is all my fault. After searching around every surrounding tree, I still don't see a trace of anything or anyone. The memory of the assault rifle pointing at us earlier washes through me, sparking my nerves into realization. It's Reaper and he must have her. It has to be him. I throw my pack down and pull out my night-vision goggles to search the area again. It's several minutes before I find three sets of footsteps. This is getting worse by the minute.

After following these erratic footsteps for several minutes, I don't feel any closer but I hear a faint hint of leaves crunching in the distance. I pull out my knife and continue toward the growing sound. The fighter in me takes over, and I'm focusing on the target as I push myself up against the tree, waiting for this asshole to show his face. With only the thought of someone putting their hands on Cali, the rage firing through me will end this situation quickly.

CHAPTER TWENTY-ONE

CALI

WITH JORGE on the hunt for Tango, Reaper and I are left alone. Face to face. "How did it feel when the knife went through my sister's throat?" I ask him, swallowing the rising bile.

His eyes widen with excitement. "Mmm. Not as good as fucking her right before."

My toes curl, my teeth grind against each other, shooting pain into the roof of my mouth. Hearing a detail I would have been better off not knowing forces more heat to rage through me. I have to pretend he's lying. "All along you thought you had the upper hand, didn't you? You were sure you were using me as bait—using me to find my dad. But you know what's funny, Reaper? I knew the whole time. I knew you were my dad's assistant in China. When I told him about you, he told me to keep you *occupied* for as long as possible. Well clearly, I did what I had to do." I can't help the psychotic laugher pouring from my throat—it's pure adrenaline. "I made you fall in love with me." He didn't have to tell me he loved me three weeks after we started dating. He could have strung me along with all the other niceties. "You can deny it, but when a person's cheeks flush and their heart races while trying to speak those intimate words, it's pretty obvious the feelings are true. You stuttered those three dreadful words to me. You stuttered because you meant them." I look past him, remembering how sincere he was. He looked me right in the eyes. Actually, he was searching my eyes, probably wondering if I'd respond the way his racing heart wanted me to. I could see his pulse stammering along the side of his neck. "You must have been pretty torn between sacrificing me for money and power." I sigh heavily. "I think the best part though, was an hour ago when you were probably forced to hear the girl you fell in love with fucking another man, moaning his name, letting him feel all the parts of me that you once claimed to be yours. He was so good, Reaper. So much better than anything you ever gave me."

His lip twists between his teeth, his mind likely gnawing at a memory. This is why I study people. This is why I know every little thing about the people I'm around. I didn't know what his true intentions were, but I know he loved me.

"Every time you 'made love to me' I was faking it. Truth is, I never did care much for you. I was bored and trying to help my dad. I mean, I was hoping to get something out of it, hoping you'd *fill* that need I had. I guess . . . you tried, but I know no man can really control the size of his dick, so I forgive you for that. You couldn't even turn me on. So it's no wonder you need power. How else would you impress a woman?" I laugh, a real laugh, because I'm starting to believe every word coming out of my mouth. "Your words, your gifts, and your lying promises—they meant nothing to me." I laugh a little more, just to drive my lying points home. "Actually, since we're being honest. I was cheating on you the entire time. You were really *my* bait. You kept my bodyguard at bay while I snuck around behind your backs and fucked the other guy. You're such an idiot."

His eyes narrow at me and he stands up, brushing the dirt off his knees. "You're a cunt."

"Truth hurts, Reaper," I grin.

"Quit calling me that shit." He kicks the dirt below his feet and shoves his hands into his pockets, turning away to hide the look on his face. I've found his weakness. It was me. "Your parents ever ask you what happened to me? Did you tell them you were trying to use me to find my dad, but instead ended up falling in love with me like an idiot? I mean, really. Who does that? Did you tell them you murdered a nineteen-year-old girl? A girl who had already been raped and tortured the very same year by a different man? Does any one girl really deserve something so horrible in her life? Maybe your parents don't know that you have a one-way ticket to hell, but they'll know some day. They'll know about everything. Then you'll be a nothing to them too."

With one step, he's hovering over me again. His hand rests on the tree bark above my head, and his fingertip is pressed against my nose before his hand wallops my cheek. The pain sears through my head but increases my rage even more. A trickle of blood drips over my lip and I lick it for effect. I know I'm in his head, and I'm not done.

"Did I make you sad? Did I make you regret, Reaper? Have I made you wish you were dead yet? Because, if I haven't, I'm not fucking done yet."

Reaper places two fingers against his temple and presses firmly. His eyes bulge and he leans toward me. "You think you can get in *my* head?" The luminous complexion of his face is turning dark, highlighting the shadows of the veins protruding from his forehead.

I smile presumptuously and laugh. "Reaper, I have already gotten in your head. As a matter-of-fact, I'm making you do everything you're doing right now."

"You're a goddamn psycho. You know that?" he croons.

"What if I told you . . ." I pause. "Actually, I probably shouldn't." I can tell my smile is sickening him. It's sucking the control right out of his head.

"Tell me what, you little bitch?"

I pull my smile even tighter across my cheeks. "What if I told you, *you* were the one being set up right now? I mean here, in the canyons. You think you're after my dad? My dad is after you, Reaper." It sounds like it could be true, even though Reaper is probably the least of Dad's worries. "You can go kill Tango." The thought plagues my heart, but my words are only for effect. "But my dad will find you. He has you trapped up here. You aren't coming out of this alive." God, I hope what I'm saying is the truth. "In a matter of seconds, a group of men my dad works with are going to poke their heads up from the surrounding rocks and shine their flashlights into your face." I rub my wrists up and down against the tree, trying to weaken the rope holding me in place. His focus is darting from tree to tree, from rock to rock. To the sky and to the ground. He's losing it.

"You're lying," he says softer, his voice weakening under my control.

"Maybe. But I might not be." I continue tugging at the rope. My wrists are burning against the coarse fibers, but I have to push through it.

I stand up, pulling myself away from the tree, trying to catch the rope against the bark to weaken the fibers more. The rope is thick; this could take hours. "You hear that?" I say dramatically, nudging my ear toward the sky. I don't hear a thing. But I bet he does. He scouts every opening to the clearing we're in, paranoia sensationalizing his perceptual awareness. "I think they know we're here. You should run." I move my hands up and down against the tree faster and faster. I feel sprigs of the rope pulling away from each other, making me satisfied that the pain in my wrists is worth it.

Reaper sprints over to me, rips out a knife from his back pocket and slices the rope in half. His hand coils around my arm, and he pulls me behind him. My skin is so raw from the rope I might be able to leave traces of blood behind me. As we move past a broken branch, I swipe my wrist over the serrated edge. I can feel the warm trickle dripping down my hand. The drop beads at my fingertip and falls. I squeeze my hand together tightly, holding my grip for a few seconds, and release. More drops of blood follow.

After being dragged in what seems like circles for a half hour, we come to a ledge. He shoves me to the ground and walks away with his hands clutching the back of his neck. He's pacing in circles.

A gunshot sounds in the distance, and the sound pierces my heart. The thought of it being Tango works my mind into a frenzy. Forget about the fact that my feelings have quadrupled for him over night, if he's gone, I'm alone here in the middle of these canyons with no survival skills.

I look over my shoulder at Reaper. His focus is lost in the surrounding wooded area. I suck up my fears and continue to push forward. "They're coming for you."

His massive body is barreling toward me again, and I'm probably going over this ledge this time. I have nothing to back myself up against. I can't stand, because he'll knock me right off the side. Instead, I look him straight on. Seconds feel like minutes with his eyes burning into mine. He pounces on top of me, knocking my head into the rock below. The pain is numbing, and the trees above me are swirling. He's screaming at me, but I can't understand what he's saying. His eyes are bloodshot; his mouth is stretched in both corners as a muffled sound shrieks from his lips. I should close my eyes and shut everything out. But if I do, I'm giving up. And I will not give up. I will not lose this battle. It's him or me again. And this time, it's going to be him.

Clarity starts to wash over me. The numbness in my head fades and pain replaces it. A throbbing rattles through my ears, making me feel as though there's an earthquake inside my head.

"Tell me where he is," I hear the words still screaming from his crazed mouth. "I've invested the last two years of my life into finding him. You're not worth giving up this fight."

Oh, yes I am.

I push the tears out, and I force fake sobs up through my throat. "I'm sorry—" I should call him by his actual name so he thinks I'm sincere. "Reagan." I sniffle a bit. "I did love you. I wasn't cheating on you. You did bring me pleasure. A lot of it, but—you just hurt me so fucking bad and then you took my sister." The tears are starting to feel real as the truth pours out of me.

But the truth ends here.

"For the life of me, I can't understand why you did what you did, but I still love you. I do. I'll help you do what you need to do. I'll go with you to find my dad. I just want you to love me. Make me yours again. Forgiveness is trivial in the shadow of love. Reagan, you were my one and only. My forever." I lift my hand toward him, hoping he takes it.

I see the weakness develop in his eyes as his hands loop around the back of his neck, and he squeezes tightly. "Fuck, Cali. I do fucking love you. I always have—never stopped. I'm so sorry for everything I did." Yeah, but sorry can't bring my sister back. He actually thinks forgiveness for murdering my sister could come so easily? "And I didn't rape her before—you know. I was just saying that to piss you off."

"You didn't?" my voice shakes. "Let me help you find my dad. We'll do this together, and then you'll have your power and success, and we can live a happy life together." I smile lustfully. "What do you think?"

He takes a couple of steps over to me and takes my hand, pulling me up to my feet. Ugh. My head swirls and pounds from pain, but I push it to the side. He takes a couple of steps away from me before pacing in small circles. "Cali, you deserve more than me." Yeah, um. I know.

"No. You and I are meant to be together," I cry.

He turns to look at me, hope swirling through his eyes. He opens his arms, waiting for me to jump into them and claim him as mine again.

I run toward him, my arms open wide. I wrap my arms around his neck and press my lips into his, pushing hard. Harder. And harder. Walking him backwards as he loses himself within our kiss. I pull away and look him in the eyes once more. "Reaper, I—I—" I shove him once. I shove him less than three inches, and I watch as he topples off the ledge, screaming like a girl. "I never fucking loved you, asshole!" I shout.

The moment gets to me. The release of adrenaline in my body makes me weak and causes my knees to give out. I fall backwards and hit my head against a sharp corner of a rock, forcing more swirls and swishes to float in front of my eyes. The memory of his body falling off the cliff disappears, and I feel like I hear faint screams in the distance. But I'm sure the sounds are from within my head. The screams soften almost completely . . . and then the noise stops. I hear nothing—nothing but silence among the grasshoppers singing against the soothing winds whisking through the greens.

He's gone.

I killed Reaper.

CHAPTER TWENTY-TWO

CALI

I'M SCARED to close my eyes. I'm scared of becoming unconscious here in the dark. The pain in my head is radiating through my entire body, and I'm stiff, lying here gazing up into the millions of stars. Some twinkle, saying hello. Others just stare with curiosity. I wish I could send them an S.O.S, but no one would respond.

The place between heaven and earth is a one-way mirror that separates those who've moved on from those who are still on earth. They can peek in on us; see how we're doing, and rest knowing we're okay. But those of us down here, who are wondering the same about them, have to live with the unknown.

Footsteps sound in the distance, but I don't care. I have no desire to know what's next. I fulfilled my promise to Krissy. There's nothing left on my to-do list.

A cold sweat and darkness washes over me. I see Tango's smile. I think about how we were here to save him, and now I'm the one who needs to be saved. God, I hope he's okay.

* * *

As the footsteps quicken into a run from whoever is nearing me, I notice the subtle glow from the sun sneaking up over the horizon, telling me I made it through the night. My fingers curl into each other by my side. I have no energy to fight. If it's Jorge, he can just push me over the edge, and I'll follow the path Reaper took.

The noises are muffled again, but the ground vibrates next to me, and a hand swoops under my head as I hear the word, "Shit," yelled loudly. "Cali?" I think I hear. An arm curls under my back and another around my legs. Why is my head still spinning? Why can't I see who's holding me?"

I feel something pressed against the back of my head as I'm set down on a spongy surface. My hands rest by my sides and the sensation of grass tickles my palms. Tango appears in my sight, clambering on top of me. His lips are moving, but I can't make out what he's saying. It's the ringing noise in my ears that is blocking out all softer tones. I feel his lips on my forehead. My cheek. My chin. My lips. The sensation lingers there.

Tango slides behind me and carefully lifts my head to rest on his lap. He strokes his fingers through my hair and into my scalp. The sensation makes me weak and I succumb to more sleep.

TANGO

I have to assume she's the reason he isn't here anymore. He wouldn't have left her. He would have either finished her off or taken her with him. There's no blood, just a slight bump on her head. I'm sure she has a concussion, and I'm worried since she's asleep. But she's breathing and her heart is beating normally. I continue to comb my fingers through her hair—I love wrapping the strands around my fingertips and watching them slightly bounce away when I let go. She's so beautiful, and I've come to love staring at her like this, when she's unaware of my lingering gaze. I press my lips against her forehead, hoping it will pull her from her sleep. I need her to wake up. My worry for her injury is growing by the second, and it's only been twenty minutes since she fell back asleep. But I know how important it is for people with head injuries to stay awake.

I feather my fingertips over her cheek, trying to rouse her again. Her body responds to my touch this time. She flinches a bit, and I'm relieved she's at least reacting to me.

"Cali," I whisper softly into her ear. "You okay, baby?" Baby? Did I just call her baby? That's a new one for me, but it sort of feels natural. This girl has seriously done me in, and it's hardly been a week. She's made me feel things I've never felt for another woman. She's made me care in a way that I didn't think I had the ability to do anymore. Maybe that's what an undesired four-year abstinence does to a man. Knowing she could be the beginning to my supposed end is the answer to my last dying wish.

CALI

The hot sun nips at my skin as my tongue struggles to find moisture on the roof of my mouth. My eyelids feel heavy, but I force them open. Two large bright green eyes are looking back at me. "Cali?" The sound of his voice is crisp, and I vaguely remember I could only hear a ringing sound when I closed my eyes.

I try to respond, but my mouth is too dry. An achy noise grumbles in my throat to let him know I need water, and he gently places the mouthpiece to his water-pouch between my lips. My lips are cracked, and when I move them, they crack more. I feel warm air swish across the separated cuts on each lip. My tongue works hard to suck the water from the straw, but with the first drop, my mouth craves more and sucks harder. A steady stream of liquid cools my throat and fills my stomach. The satisfaction is almost instant.

"I'm going to try and lift you up and sit you against the tree." His hand presses beneath my shoulder blades and his other hand lifts under my arm. Slowly, he eases me up.

My head still feels like it's spinning a bit, but steadies after a moment. I think I'm okay. My lungs constrict when a flash of what happened last night trips my memory. I clutch my hand over my heart and twist the thin fabric of my shirt into a ball. "He's dead," I croak out.

"Who?" His hands melt into my shoulders as he lowers his face to my level.

"Reaper."

"You killed him?" Unease and wonder reels through his voice.

"Yes." I did kill him. I forced my way into his head then . . . "I pushed him." I point to the cliff.

Tango stands up from my side and approaches the ledge where he found me. He leans over, looking for the evidence, but I'm not sure what he'll find, and it doesn't matter. After a second, I notice whatever he sees causes him to recoil. "I'm going to recommend you don't look over this ledge. I've seen some shit in my day, and that's bad." He sits back down by my side and places his hand on the small of my back. "What happened before you pushed him?"

"I had gotten up to go to the bathroom last night. I only went behind the nearest tree. He captured me there and dragged me somewhere else that I don't remember. He sent someone after you: Jorge, I think his name was. He said he was going to kill you. But I knew—"

"I'd win," he interrupts me with a wry grin.

"Yes."

"I did," he says softly, tracing the pad of his thumb along my cheek, brushing off specks of dirt. "Then what?"

"I got in his head—like my dad always did to people. At one point, he became so angry he slammed my head into the ground, but I held onto my strength and kept feeding him what his mind wanted to hear." Tango intertwines his fingers with mine and kisses me on the forehead. "He's gone now. The promise I made to Krissy helped me to hang on."

* * *

It took a few hours for me to regain my bearings and for the dizziness to subside, but clarity is catching up to me. Now I just want to find Dad and help Tango. I push forward, throwing my pack over my shoulders and hold my stride tightly behind Tango. He spent some time studying the map against the coordinates this morning and said we're still hours away. I can't help but to think this could all be for nothing, and I'm sure Tango has already considered this as well. He talks about dying like it could happen tomorrow and doesn't mention a word of hope that all of this effort is for a purpose.

"Hold up," Tango stops short in his tracks. He pulls his phone out and turns on the GPS, pointing the device in each direction. "Shit."

"That sounded like a loaded—" I burst out laughing at my pun, realizing I'm likely getting dehydrated again. Jokes aren't my thing, but I guess they are when I'm losing my mind.

Tango stifles his laugh and quickly straightens his jaw. "Cali. Water. Now." He drops his phone back into his pocket. "We have to cross over that bridge." He points off to the end of an upcoming ledge.

"What bridge?"

He tugs on my wrist and pulls me closer to where he was pointing. The bridge is made of rope and loose planks of wood—definitely untrustworthy and not so secure. The rope is pale and brittle, and there are missing boards every few steps. I've already proven to be the weak link here, so I have to suck it up. I straighten my pack, pull back my shoulder blades and walk forward.

"Hold it!" he shouts. "I understand you want to take the lead, but are you going to check that thing out first?"

"I think I'll know within the first step," I say, giving him a *duh* look. He holds up his hands in defense. "Fine, be my guest."

I approach the start of the bridge, which is a foot below the ledge. I curl my fists tightly around the rope and lower my foot down, slowly applying pressure to check for sturdiness. My foot wobbles as if I were standing on a plastic swing. *This should be fun.*

I lower my other foot down and bare most of my weight throughout my hands. My knuckles are becoming pale, and the bones beneath my skin's surface are becoming more apparent. I glide my right hand along the rope, careful not to shift my weight. The sprigs of the rope scrape against my palm like fine needles and the sensation mixes with my sweat, making my skin itchy. I step over to the next board, which is a bit firmer. I twist my head to look back at Tango, putting on my bravest face. "Come on in, the water's fine," I say, grinning like an idiot.

"God, you really need more water," he shouts over.

With bravery acting as a sidekick, I move a little quicker over to the next board, which also feels firm. The next three boards are the same, and my confidence is at a high peak. *This isn't so bad.* With my foot dangling over the next pane, I feel a shift below me. The board slides backwards about an inch, but the inch feels like a mile as I'm hanging hundreds of feet over boulders protruding from a rapidly moving river. I continue forward, anxious to move from the wobbly plank. I make it over the remaining distance and hop over the last missing plank. My heart is hammering against my chest as I look back to see what I just crossed over.

Tango hasn't even left the ledge yet, which is best. I'm not sure this bridge could have held two people at once. He moves across, seamlessly, unafraid and unaffected. Everything he does makes me feel like I could never live up to his example. I've always been the most fearless person I've known until I met him. Compared to him, I look like a coward.

His chest is still rising and falling at an even pace, not even a bead of sweat more than when he left. He brushes the dirt from his hands and readjusts his pack. "Ready, princess?" His smirk tells me he knows what I'm thinking. He knows he's better than I am. He knows he makes me weak.

Bastard.

It's been two hours of an uphill trek, and my knees are starting to wobble. The sun is just as fierce and unforgiving as it's been and my skin is beginning to feel like leather on top of the relentless ache in my shoulder. "Hang on," I shout ahead.

I lower my pack and pull out the sunscreen and my bottle of painkillers—good thing I just refilled. I pop the pills into my mouth and then slather on the white cream, leaving it thick over the spots that burn the easiest. "How are you not getting burnt?" I ask him.

He shrugs while taking a closer look at his exposed arms. "I think my skin has seen its day in the sun—Iraq and Afghanistan's rays aren't too forgiving and we ran out of sunscreen early on." He reaches his hand out for the bottle, probably just to appease me. "It wasn't pretty for the first couple of weeks. A couple of the guys needed a medevac due to third-degree burns." He slathers a bit on his arms and his shoulders, then tosses the bottle back at me. *Men.* "Your shoulder bothering you?"

"I'm fine," I lie.

As I'm tucking the bottle back into the side pocket of my pack, I hear a couple of voices in the distance. I look over at Tango, who's already searching in every direction. He pulls himself up against a nearby tree and waves me over.

He presses on my bullet-less shoulder, pushing me to lean down. My focus meets an opening in the trees, and I see two men looking at a map. They're disheveled, covered in dirt, and have enough weaponry between the two of them to start World War III. I'm studying their mouths in hopes of determining what they're saying.

Tango grapples with the back of my shirt and pulls me away from the trees. He drags me a dozen more feet until I pull myself out of his grip. I know he wants to put some distance in between us and them so we can talk, but I'm capable of taking a hint.

We end up near a small waterfall, but it's loud enough to cover sound. "I don't know if they might be with Reaper or if they're with the Chinese Agency. There's too many people looking for your dad, and if they're after him, we won't make it past them." He pulls out his phone, looks at the screen and pulls out another device to plug into it.

"This is why your dad was constantly telling you to leave wherever you were. These two groups of people have been after him and essentially you, for three years."

"It wasn't too bad before Krissy died, but after that, it was like I just became a target. I have not stayed in any location for more than a few weeks in the past year. I've been alone, very, very alone." Alone doesn't even hint at how I've felt over the past twelve months. I feel like I've lost two-thirds of who I am, and walking around as a third of a person, just doesn't work." His eyes soften and he reaches for my hand, but I hold it down by my side. "Don't do that. Don't feel sorry for me."

He reaches down and snatches my hand up anyway. "Don't tell me how to feel. No one deserves that shit, Cali. And yes, I do feel sorry for you—whether you like it or not." He puts his phone up to his ear and waits for what I assume is someone to pick up the phone. "Sir, the job took me to the Copper Canyons. I'll send you coordinates. I need two backups, fully-loaded, ASAP."

Backup?

CHAPTER TWENTY-THREE

TANGO

THE BURN is catching up to me. It feels like there's a layer of sand caked up in my lungs. I try to cough it up, and while it feels like I'm coughing up sand, it's not sand. I sweep my arm across my mouth to clean up the spattering of mucus, and when I pull my arm away, I see another smeared red tinge. It's happening more frequently, just as warned. I realize I haven't taken my inhaler since yesterday, and maybe I can assume that's why. I pull out the inhaler and suck in as much of the medication as I can, hold it for as long as I can, and blow the shit out as hard as I can—hoping I'm blowing the cancer out too. I clean my arm off on my camo shorts, ridding myself of the bloody evidence since I don't need to deal with a concerned Cali on top of all this shit. I'm so close. So damn close.

As soon as these guys arrive, things are going to intensify. My boss promised me they're good men, but I don't trust mercenaries. They all have a story and they aren't always good ones. Although, they're probably saying the same thing about me right now. And my story is not a good one. I doubt they'd be too happy to hear I was dragging them here with the hope of saving my worthless life.

CALI

My head is pounding. I want real food. I want to take a real shower, and I want air conditioning. Tango is looking at his phone again, just as he has at least ten times in the past hour, tracking the backup.

He drops the phone into his pocket, stands and stretches his arms from side to side. He points his head toward the downward direction and starts walking. I follow closely behind. "They'll be here in two hours. They're probably being dropped from a helo."

We round a few more corners and find a gully to plant ourselves in. Tango unclips his pack and meticulously pulls various metal pieces out and lays them on the ground in perfect order. "More rifles?" Actually, I'm assuming he has a lot more than that in there.

"Check your pack. Bottom left. I assume you know how to put one of these together?" His lip pulls up into a snide grin.

"I think I can manage." I pull each piece of cold metal out and place it down on the ground before attaching the pieces in the order in which my dad taught me. The one thing he didn't fail at was teaching me about weapons, how to use them and how to protect myself with them. That might actually come in handy today. If only he wasn't the reason for it, I might feel a little prouder.

Tango stands up after he finishes putting his rifle together and watches me adjoin my final pieces. I think it's cute that he's looking at me with amazement, like he's proud. "That might just be the hottest thing I've ever seen," he says.

His words send a rush of heat through my cheeks, and I'm fighting against a smile, since we're supposed to be in a serious situation right now. "We should probably separate business from pleasure, Tango." I stand up and walk to him, then wrap my arm around his back, slowly lowering my hand to his ass, and I squeeze. "Glad to know you can maintain control at all times, Marine," I say softly into his ear.

His stiffness below responds to my words and he fists his hands into the material over my chest, pulling my body in firmly against his. "If you want to play rough," he says, his voice dour and gravelly, "save it for later." His teeth clamp down over my bottom lip, and it takes everything inside me not to make a noise. He's learned what those little nibbles do to me and he's totally taking advantage. But I need to show restraint for the sake of this situation. Business and pleasure. Business is pleasure. The lines are becoming blurred, and that's okay with me.

We hear a low buzz in the air and I know it's the helo arriving. The heat between us sizzles and we both regain a firmer grip over our weapons to appear ready and waiting for this backup. It goes without being said that from here on out, this has to be only business. No more pleasure.

Tango pulls out his phone and I can see some kind of navigational system display across his screen. "Let's go. They're over here."

We arrive at a small opening on a flat piece of land. Two men are descending with parachutes from a helo that has already disappeared. They make a soft landing, seeming as though they've had plenty of training in this area. Tango helps them with removing their parachutes, and they stand up to readjust their belongings.

The first one introduces himself to Tango. "Hey man—Seaver. Nice to meet you." He's tall, taller than Tango by about three inches. He's dressed from head to toe in desert camouflage—short blond Mohawk and same firm jaw and cheekbones as Tango. I'm guessing ex-marine. I'm thinking they all look the same. His diesel Oakley sunglasses cover his eyes, and the straight line across his mouth tells me he's here to accomplish this job, and that's it. "We hunting someone down?"

"Yeah. It's her dad. He has something vital to someone's health," Tango explains cautiously without stretching the truth too much.

"Say no more, man. We have your back."

"There's a couple of groups of people after him, and we think we ran into one of the groups earlier. Reason for my call."

"Sure. Got it," Seaver says.

The other man, clearly the weaker of the two, is still adjusting the straps of his bag and retying his boots. Definitely the follower. His hair is long for a military cut. It hangs low, sweeping over his eyes. The stubble along his chin looks groomed—on purpose, rather than a five o'clock shadow. In contrast to Seaver, he's wearing a black v-neck T-shirt, ripped jeans and combat boots. He extends his hand out to me first. "Kacen. Nice to meet you." His eyes stare into mine intently and then slowly and shamelessly gaze down to my chest. His lips and his eyebrows arch with an agreeable look. "Nice," he whispers.

Great. Another asshole.

Tango shoves his hand out to him, probably to distract him. "I'm Tango. Let's go, lover-boy."

Kacen's cheeks redden and he clears his throat. He turns around to lift his bag and swings it over one shoulder like a high school student. What an idiot.

Tango nods his head to Seaver. "What years were you in?"

"2003 to 2011. Operator. You?"

"2008 to 2014. NBC for the first two years, then an operator for the remaining time. I was recently discharged," he emphasizes with air quotes around the word discharged.

"Figured. Lack of information on your background gave that away," Seaver says.

Kacen jogs up to their side and plays into the conversation. "I was in from 2006-2010. Never deployed, though. Mostly office work."

"Yeah," Seaver grins. "We can tell." He laughs softly and it's the first time his lips have even twitched since they landed. "*Carolina* can probably tell."

"Cali," I chime in. "You can call me Cali."

"My apologies." He nods his head slightly. His attention redirects to Tango and matches his pace.

Since Seaver's interested in Tango's background, the two engage in a comparison conversation, which gives Kacen the opportunity to try and make more conversation with me. "You enjoying the canyons?" he asks.

I give him a look that clarifies my feelings on this situation.

He scratches the back of his neck with one eye squinted shut. "Where you from?" His fingers loop around the straps of his bag as he repositions it over his shoulder.

"The United States?" I quip. "Maybe you should put your bag over both shoulders. Less strain. Ya know?"

He shrugs his free shoulder and chuckles at my advice. "You have a boyfriend at home?" Well, that escalated quickly.

"Eight of them and two husbands." My sarcasm doesn't carry as much vigor as I hope, because he smiles. This one is going to get on my nerves. Quickly. "Why are you here, exactly?"

"Orders. Why are you here?"

"If you don't know why I'm here, you clearly weren't briefed. You're being used as a tool, huh?"

"You gotta mouth on you huh, girl?"

Beyond annoyed with the conversation, I speed up my pace to join Tango and Seaver. I can hear Kacen's footsteps behind me, following like a child. "Why did they send you with a broken wheel?" I ask Seaver.

"Wow, you're kind of a bitch, aren't you?" Kacen yells at me. "For your information I was the top ranked marksman in my company."

Tango stops dead in his tracks and turns around, placing himself directly in Kacen's path and about three inches from his face. He places his finger so close to the tip of his nose I'm wondering if he's actually touching him. "I don't give a shit if you can put a hole into something a mile away. Call her a bitch again, and I'm going to use you as a target to prove my marksman skills." He doesn't give Kacen an opportunity to respond. He turns back around and continues his conversation with Seaver. It's clear they've both dealt with people like Kacen before.

We've been hiking for a couple of hours. Everyone is silent and the only audible sound is the noise of dirt crunching below our feet. If I could smell danger, the fumes would have knocked me over by now. I know we're nearing the location where we spotted the two-armed men, but I can't imagine they would still be located in the same place. Tango takes a few longer strides ahead of the rest of us and nestles his back against a large tree. He curves his neck to look around the bend and immediately straightens his posture.

He points to his chest and then over his head, squeezing his rifle in the opposite hand. Seaver takes his place behind the tree as Tango pushes forward. Seaver directs Kacen to stay with me, but I wonder who would be protecting who if we were under attack. This idiot couldn't possibly be a top marksman.

"I gotcha, babe," Kacen says. He places the palms of his hands around the tree I'm leaning on, encasing me between his arms. Every part of me wants to jerk my knee into his crotch, but he'd scream, and that could put Tango and Seaver in danger.

"Get. Away," I fume through my clenched jaw.

"Just following orders, hon." The anger rushing through me is pulsating all over my body. He's reminding me of Reaper and I sort of want to push him off a cliff too.

"If you don't move your hands, I'm going to remove them in your sleep tonight. Okay?" I tap my hand against his cheek a couple of times to drive my point home. I think it works since he slides his hands down the tree and takes a couple of steps back. I hear a whistling noise in the distance, followed by three other similar noises. It's a call, and it's not from Tango or Seaver. We've been spotted. I skate my fingers over the base of my rifle, focusing on the increased rate of my heart. I can do this. I pull the rifle up to my shoulder and hold it in position. I swing around the tree, meeting up with Tango and Seaver.

"What are you doing, Cali?" Tango's face contorts with anguish when he spots me. "Get back. Go back with Kacen."

"He's going to cause us all to be fucking killed, Tango. I can handle this."

"You're right. I'm sorry. Stay with me, just keep your eyes open, and keep your ears alert. Try to sense where they're coming from." His eyes are locked on mine, and I can sense a hint of fear behind the blackness of his dilated pupils.

"I got it," I whisper. I suck in a lungful of air and blow it out slowly, easing my nerves. There's no room for nerves. I follow in their steps, sensing Kacen approaching me from behind. I can see the shadow of his head darting in every direction. Nerves will get you killed, and he's going down alone.

I spot a small patch of yellow in the distance. It's behind a tree, but it's moving subtly, as in, with each breath, I can see the slight rise of the fabric. I curl my fingers into Tango's pocket and tug him back with a gentle force. His head twists to look at me and I point my gun at the moving yellow target. The corner of his lip curls into a proud grin. He taps Seaver and points his rifle in the same direction. We all hover behind a nearby tree and Seaver drops to the ground. He pulls a scope out of his pack and twists it on to the end of his rifle.

"When this shot is made, all hell is going to break loose," Tango whispers in my ear. "Keep yourself covered at all times. If you become nervous, hide." He pinches his fingers around my chin and pulls my lips fiercely into his. He inhales my breath and pulls away just enough to look into my eyes. My cheeks briefly flush with embarrassment, knowing our secret is out. I doubt Seaver cares though, and I couldn't care less about Kacen. Maybe he'll back the hell off now. "Please keep yourself safe. I can't lose another one."

Tango's words bring on a wave of nausea. Nevertheless, I swallow the rising bitterness and straighten my posture against the tree. I have this. I have this. Holy shit. I hope I have this.

"Ready," Seaver whispers.

"Go," Tango responds. His voice is so soft it sounds like a short stiff breeze.

The shot is fired and a groaning shout follows. I see the patch of yellow fall to the ground. When it disappears from my sight, I know he's gone down, but more shouting commences. I try to decipher the number of voices, and I think I hear six, but it's becoming difficult to tell as they near us.

I position my rifle, focusing my eye on the crowd running toward us with a variety of weapons. Shots are firing around me and I use the tree as coverage.

Two shots. Two kills. Seaver and Tango took the rest down. Twenty seconds and six are dead. I guess we won't know whether they were after Dad or protecting him.

Seaver waves back at Tango as he crouches into the clearing where they all came from. Another shot is fired, and I hear *clear* yelled from the distance.

"Holy shit, Cali." Tango scoops me up and swings me around. "You fucking saved our asses."

I try to conceal my proud grin, knowing they did more than half the work. But it felt good to finally put my skills to use, regardless of what the skills caused. Lucky for me, death and sadness are a numbness I won't overcome. You know you've gone to a place you'll never come back from when you can stare death in the face while the rate of your beating heart remains steady. The emotional wiring in my head doesn't twitch, and I don't feel remorse. "You didn't do so bad yourself," I say, sliding myself out of his arms.

"Seaver and I are trained operators, Cali," he laughs. "There's something to be said about a chick who can accomplish two shots and two dead bodies in two seconds." Regardless of the growing desire in Tango's eyes, he shifts his attention over to Kacen. "You fall asleep, dude? Need some help with that thing?" He nudges his head toward the fully loaded rifle in his hands.

Embarrassment creeps over Kacen's face with a pink hue. "I didn't have the right shot. Didn't want to waste any ammo."

Tango arches an eyebrow. "Well, that's one thing you did a good job at: saving ammo." He throws his pack over his shoulders and looks back once more at Kacen. "Who knows, man, a huge bear might attack tonight. We'll all be thankful you have ammo then." The laughs continue as Tango wraps his arm back around my waist, pushing me forward with his stride.

"Were they after us, or were they just a roadblock?" I ask.

"Your dad probably has many roadblocks set up. It's hard to tell how many shit-storms we'll be going through before we reach him. We need to stay alert."

The energy is rushing through me, and I feel full of momentum. I want to shoot something else. I want to pave a path to what will save Tango.

* * *

Nightfall is upon us and my eyes are set on the sun bleeding into the canyons. I could almost consider this to be the most amazing place in the world, but in my life, where beauty lies, death follows.

Seaver has started a fire and Tango and I have pitched a couple of tents. Kacen is fumbling around on his phone, which he's been doing for the past two hours and I doubt it's for any legitimate reason.

"Hey," Tango whispers in my ear. I twist my head to find his lips only inches from my forehead. His eyes are hooded and peering into mine. "Follow me. We're getting . . . water."

Without a moment's hesitation, I follow him. I'm so wound up and speeding on adrenaline, I feel an extra hop in my step. How could I be happy in this situation? I don't even know if that's what this is . . . happy. We turn the corner into a mess of trees, and when we're out of site, I feel Tango's fingers slip in between mine. He pulls me harder, forcing me to jog instead of walk. I have to wonder how he knows *where* the water is. Maybe he smells it. Maybe he was trained to do that too.

We approach another pool with a lapping waterfall. It's smaller than the one last night. It's more private and secluded. The trees bow over the water, acting as a roof, and its darkness is mixed with the subtle glow of the sun's rays swirling with the shine of the rising moon. It's enough to cast a perfect shadow.

No second is wasted when we enter into the seclusion. His arms wrap around my waist, holding me so firmly against him it's as if I hold the last bit of air left in this canyon. His lips crash into mine and his tongue reaches into my mouth. My heart swells and my stomach tumbles around like a pinball.

He pulls away, his lips tracing a line from my ear down to my collarbone. "You were so fucking hot today. Watching you handle that rifle turned me on more than I could ever explain."

"Show me," I demand.

A shallow and soft growl rumbles in my ear and the sound electrifies my nerves. His hands reach down my sides and he grips the hem of my shirt, ripping it over my head. I tuck my hands under his shirt and skate them up his bare chest, pushing his shirt up to his neck. He pulls it off and then moves down to his belt. I unclasp it for him, slowly. But with his impatience growing, he nearly rips the button off my shorts, trying to yank them off quicker than they're cooperating. He scoops me up before running off the rock and catapulting us into a pool of cold water. With my legs wrapped around him, he treads us over to a shallower end where we can place our feet down over the glassy smooth rocks below. My body tenses against his, shaking uncontrollably from the mixture of temperatures. With our noses pressed against each other and our eyes locked in a gaze, the only thing I feel is desire.

His hands squeeze my breasts as his lips move hungrily around my chest. His fingers trace the coolness prickling my exposed skin . . . the sensation he drives through me is incredible. With his erection pressing against me, my mind has shut off and my body is focused solely on his cock and what it can do to me.

My panties are floating in the water beside us and his hands are sliding up and down my legs. His grip is tight and unforgiving but wonderful at the same time. He enters me, squeezing me tighter with each thrust. I slide my entire body up against him, letting my bare skin melt into his.

With his fullness filling me entirely, I can't stop the soft moans crying from my throat or the sounds that erupt when his teeth gently bite down on my shoulder. The sensation becomes overpowering, sending currents through my body. His fingertips grip harder around my thighs and he pushes himself in even farther.

"I'm . . . I . . . " Oh my God.

"Cali," he breathes. His eyes open and he's looking me straight on.

"Sit there," I point to the top of the rock that's flirting with the water line. He does as I say. I move between his legs and wrap my lips around his shaft while gazing up at him. My tongue traces up and down and in a circular motion. He tangles his hands into my wet hair, guiding my head down and causing him to breathe heavier. I suck him into the back of my throat and his hands slide down to my breasts as he teases my nipples with his fingertips. I pull my mouth upward, letting my teeth gently graze his length and then I go down once more. His warmth runs down the back of my throat and he groans with pleasure. I pull away and lick my lips, needing to lap up every bit of what he gave me.

"Holy shit," he says, pulling me up on his lap. He closes his lips over mine and wraps me in his arms. "You're fucking amazing."

We sit together, our bodies entwined in a knot as our erratic breaths blend beautifully with the sounds of the soft breeze. He pulls away slightly and looks down at me. "Carolina," he pauses.

"Yeah," I breathe, waiting for what he's about to say.

He continues looking between my eyes, almost as if he can't choose one to focus on. Then he slowly closes his lips back over mine. I prefer this to words. Spoken emotions aren't my strong suit. This I can handle— this I *love* . . .

CHAPTER TWENTY-FOUR

TANGO

ALL I WANT to say to her is: *Even if I die tomorrow, you have made my life worth living.*

CALI

"Hey man, can we talk for a minute?" Seaver looks at me with a straight line carved across his face. "Alone." We've only been back from *getting water* for a minute, and Seaver doesn't look too happy.

Tango gives me a subtle look with a slightly raised brow and briefly places his hand on the small of my back before walking over to the growing flame where Seaver's resting.

"Where were you two?" Kacen asks, walking up beside me and leaning his back against the same tree I'm leaning on. Too close.

I move to the side and cross my arms over my chest. "We went to grab water."

"Nah. You didn't. I mean, you brought back water, but you got something else too." His dark eyes are feeling me out as if I didn't make it clear enough earlier that he should keep his distance. "You giving handouts?" His eyebrows dance around his forehead and I catch on to his intended pun.

"Sure, Kacen." I wrap my fingers gently around his shoulder in a caressing manner. I look him in the eyes and jerk my knee up firmly into his balls. He drops to the ground and curls up into the fetal position, moaning and whining. "Would you settle for a hand . . . *up*?" I stretch my hand out to him. "Here, I'll help you up when you stop crying."

"What the fuck is wrong with you?" He curls his legs into his chest tighter. "You're a fucking psychopath. No wonder your dad is hiding out here. He's probably hiding from your demented ass." I press my boot down over his throat until he twists his head to the side, giving in to the pressure. His chest is heaving in and out, and I can see his mind searching for something to say, but the tightness around his throat won't allow words to sound. I move my boot, allowing him to move away from me.

It's at that moment when I've lost his attention that a hand slaps against my mouth and an arm wraps around my waist. I'm sure I've pissed Tango off, but I have a feeling if he were dealing with this asshole, he would have reacted the same way. He's dragging me away again, out of the main camp area. Maybe he hasn't had enough yet. Maybe this is all for fun. I let him continue dragging me, and I don't put up a fight.

The hand smells weird, though. Different. I can't see anything due to the tight grip, but I'm now wondering if this is actually Tango?

We stop in the center of a small patch of grass, and I whirl around, hoping to find Tango.

When my vision sends the proper signals to my brain, my mouth opens and my bottom lip drops. My eyes soften and my limbs feel like jelly. Maybe I'm hallucinating. I don't . . .

I reach over slowly, unsure if I want to confirm this sensation, or if I only want it to be a hallucination.

My fingertips brush against soft skin before I jerk my hand back against my body as if I just touched a flame. At this moment, my chest feels heavy and I've forgotten how to breathe and talk.

"Carolina," she says. Could I hear her if she wasn't real? My mind is twisting in every direction, contemplating if I'm dead, delusional, or maybe lost.

"Mom?" the word croaks from my throat.

"Hey, baby girl." Her arms wrap around my body firmly and she pulls me into her. I breathe her in, all of her scents resonating with my memories. I don't understand. I was there when she died. I watched them take her away. I was at the funeral. This isn't right. But then why am I not questioning it? The tears start and I don't know if they'll ever stop. The feeling of Mom's arms around me is more than I ever could have asked for in the past three years. But when reality sets in, I'm immediately questioning why she left me suffering in pain, missing her and Krissy. Is Krissy even dead? Oh God, what I would do to prove that wrong, too.

"How are you here?" I run my sleeve under my nose, wiping away the tears. "I watched you die, Mom."

"Honey," her hand drops into mine and she brings it to her chest. "I didn't die."

"But I watched you die?"

A small laugh sings from her throat. "It was definitely a close call, sweetheart."

"How, Mom? How? I was at your funeral. How?" The hardness that has encompassed my persona for the past few years is wilting with each second I stand in her presence.

"Your dad saved me," she says in a soft hush.

TAG

"How?" I know I keep asking the same question, but I feel like I'm mentally breaking down. But maybe that's exactly what this is. A breakdown. "How did he save you, Mom? Why haven't you told me you were alive?" I've felt the pain of someone dying—of losing someone. But I haven't felt the unfolding acceptance of realizing that when she told me not to trust anyone, she meant her, as well.

She takes my hand and leads me over to a nearby rock where she pulls me to sit down. She drops down next to me and curls her legs up into her chest. She seems so youthful, much younger than I ever remember seeing her.

"Are you really here? Or am I losing it?" I ask with much seriousness.

"Sweetheart, you know your father was part of the CIA for many years." She reaches out and cups her hand around my chin. Her scent floods my eyes, making the tears form again. "He was in China the year I was dying. He was in charge of protecting a drug patent— an unregulated treatment that hadn't been released to the public yet or even used in trials. The part of the CIA he was working with was responsible for protecting this privately owned company who was responsible for developing this drug."

"I don't understand where you're going with this." I pull my legs in against my chest too, for comfort. I wonder if Tango's looking for me. I'm not too far away, and he'll catch up. I don't know how this will go over or if he would understand—because I sure as hell don't. "Mom, they're going to find us out here."

"It's okay, sweetie. Let me finish explaining." Her eyes look past me, and I can tell she's trying to collect her thoughts. "He was protecting a treatment for cancer. He took the substance, Carolina." Her eyes are now set on mine. "He brought it to me. I would have died in moments if the drug hadn't worked so quickly, which doesn't usually happen. You know how many drugs those doctors pumped through me? Nothing worked. But this treatment, whatever it was, it worked. It could be huge, But it didn't belong do your dad. It belonged to a private company, which he stole from. They want to keep it a secret and they don't want anyone to have it, especially since they only have a couple of treatments. I guess it takes months to grow whatever plant extract was formulated into the drug. Whatever the case is, they're after him, honey. And if they find him, it won't end well."

I know I'm in shock. I know I should have something to say, but this is unreal. "So, you didn't die?"

"I didn't expect to wake up , but I did. The doctors didn't have an explanation for my recovery. It took me a few days to be well enough for the doctors to release me, but then they did, miraculously cancer free and tumor free."

"Mom, that's amazing. But, why . . .?" *Why the hell have you been hiding from me for the past three years?*

"I'm protecting your dad. He saved me, so the least I could do was stay by his side. It meant I had to disappear, Carolina."

"You left me alone when you must have known Krissy had been murdered? You knew, right?"

She looks down, ashamed. "Yes, I know." She looks up at me and places her hand down over my knee. "But I knew you were strong enough to carry on. You were always my strong one—a force to be reckoned with. If I had come back for you then, you would have been in even more danger than you were already in. I did what I thought was safest for you."

"Leaving me alone and on the run at nineteen was what was safest for me?"

"Carolina, I struggled with this decision for years and there isn't a day when I wake up and don't question what the hell I've done. Part of me wishes I died that day. It might have been better than living on the run. You have no idea where we've had to hide. People are always after us. They've been onto us since your dad paid people off at the hospital to create a death certificate for me. Obviously no one can be trusted, like I've told you." None of this is understandable to me. I've been on the run and I've been chased. I was never safe. "How did you know your dad was out here?"

"I don't think that's important right now," I say. "A better question might be: how long have you two been out here?" I look at her with purpose, almost anger-like, a look I wouldn't have given her before today.

"Only a couple of weeks. We're always on the move." Her face is full of shame and remorse and she's having trouble holding her focus on my eyes. "Your dad and I aren't running from you, but if you are planning to bring that man you're with to your dad, please remember what I always told you."

I'm guessing she knows how I found dad if she knows about Tango. "He's the exception to your rule, Mom," I snap back without thinking.

She places her hand on my cheek and smoothes her thumb over my ear. "He's a good looking guy. Is he good to you?"

"Uh—you saw him?" I ask.

"I'm pretty good at being aware of my surroundings. Your dad knows you're here too," she confirms with a straight-lined smile stretching across her face.

Oh God. I hope she doesn't see everything. Embarrassment washes through me with the thought of Mom bearing witness to my waterfall sexcapades. "He is a good guy," I say, trying to remove the humiliating thoughts from the front of my mind.

"Where is Dad?"

"Does that boy you're with have the coordinates your dad gave him?"

"Yes, but he said we would be within two miles of that location."

"Once you're there, you'll know where he is," she smiles.

I nod my head, knowing I have so many questions I want to ask her, but none of them seem like they'd result in a good answer. "Won't you help me, us?"

"I don't trust those other men you are with. I'm sure you can understand." I don't understand a fucking thing. All I understand is that I'm living in a world full of lies and deceit, and I hate questioning who I can believe. Will anyone ever be completely honest with me? I can't even trust my parents. What does that leave me with? "I have to go sweetie. I'll see you soon, I'm sure." I don't give her a hug. I don't say goodbye. I don't wish for a longer encounter. And yet, twenty minutes ago, I would have paid money; I would have gotten down on my hands and knees and begged to see Mom one more time. But now, I feel even more alone and more betrayed than I've ever felt in my entire life.

I turn around to wipe the tears streaming from my eyes, and when I turn back to face her, she's gone.

"You okay, babe?" Tango rounds the corner and I realize what I must look like right now—frazzled and pale. Did he not see her pull me away? "What are you doing over here? I've been looking for you. I thought you were in the tent at first, but then I heard you talking out here. You talking to yourself?" he laughs.

"I, ah. I just saw my mom." I point to the empty space beside me. "She was—she was right here."

"Your mom is dead, Cali." He sits down next to me, wraps his large hand around my cheek, and pulls my head into his lips. "You've been through a lot today. You need some rest."

"She told me the treatment my dad had stole, saved her. She is hiding with him. "Maybe she went to her funeral like you went to your funeral."

He doesn't say anything, which tells me he believes me. His arm stiffens around my shoulders and he holds me tightly against him. "Do you want us to turn back and leave?" he asks softly. "I'll do that for you." He looks worried for my response.

If I leave, Tango will die. If I leave, I won't see Dad or Mom again. If I leave, I will continue to be on the run for as long as they survive here.

If I stay, I can possibly save Tango.

"I'll stay."

"Do you know which direction your mom went? We can try to look for her. It's likely she knows where your dad is. What's her name?"

"Alice," I say.

TANGO

If she's not hallucinating, it worked. This might not be all for nothing. Her mother could be fucking alive. I could make it through this shit. So many things are firing through my mind right now, but mostly the hope of living past this week. Cali's parents must be a little too old to be living lives of drifters. It's hard to imagine either of them surviving out here or wherever they've spent most of the past three years hiding. We need to find them. We need more answers. I need answers.

"You really didn't see where she went?" I ask again, hoping for an answer this time.

"I literarily blinked and she was gone, Tango. If I knew, I'd tell you."

"We should definitely try to look." I lift her hand from her side and pull her along. It takes minutes of looking in each direction before I begin to question again whether this woman was actually sitting here talking to Cali. Maybe it was only in her head. Maybe her concussion is causing some kind of mirage. I know that can happen. There isn't a trace of this woman or anyone besides us in any direction. The dirt is particularly dry here and I have to believe I'd see at least a hint of a footprint somewhere along one of these paths, but I don't.

"Did she say anything else?" I ask carefully, trying my hardest not to push her or make it sound like I'm desperate for information.

"Not really. I told you almost everything that happened in that short three-minute span. Maybe you're right, though. Maybe I'm just seeing things. I think we should go back to the campsite. Sorry for worrying you," she says.

CALI

Kacen is sitting where I left him up against the tree. One leg is pulled into his chest, the other flat out in front of him. He's peeling a blade of grass apart with an evident scowl, hopefully from the swelling pain in his balls.

Seaver is seated on a log next to the fire and feeding branches and twigs slowly into the burning mouth, watching as the flames devour each fragment. I take a seat on one of the logs opposite Seaver. No one is speaking, which only accents the slight howl of the wind, blending with the cry of a coyote and the soothing crackling snaps of the fire. We haven't come across any wildlife here, but the clarity of the howls I'm now hearing remind me we are not alone. None of the guys seem concerned though, so I block out the unsettling noises.

Tango drops a packaged meal down on my lap and instructs me to eat the entire portion. I haven't complained about the food, but I haven't been finishing it either. Flavorless food really takes an acquired taste. Although with as much activity as we've had today, my stomach isn't arguing with him on this matter.

"Tomorrow is the capture," Seaver states. Tango's eye glints at me subtly, making me aware that Seaver doesn't know the real reason we're after Dad. It's clear he thinks it's for a different reason than curing Tango. Part of me is wondering if we should try to lose these two before we get close to Dad tomorrow. I don't know either of them well enough to trust them, and even if I did know them both better, I still wouldn't trust them. I still have a few doubts that Tango is who he says he is.

Tango clears his throat and responds with a short, "Yeah." He takes a bite of what looks to be some kind of beef stew and chews it for a moment before saying anything more. "He's supposedly about ten clicks from this location. We should be able to reach him within a couple hours tomorrow."

The end is in sight, and yet I have no idea what that will actually mean. We've come all this way in hopes of convincing Dad to forfeit this treatment and give it to Tango with a little hope of it working. He may not be so willing to share it. Although, I think with everything he's put me through, he owes me at least this favor.

TAG 203

Kacen scuffles over to the fire and sits down on one of the logs. He rests his elbows on his knees and keeps his head low. "Have any more of those," he asks without lifting his head.

"Dude, didn't you prepare?" Seaver quips. "At all?"

Kacen doesn't respond. It's the first time I've seen a hint of shame behind his eyes. There's more to his story I'm gathering. "No," he says simply. "I thought they'd give me the shit I needed."

"Dude, we're not *in* anymore." Seaver turns around and reaches into his pack, pulling out a meal. He tosses it over to Kacen, and it lands in front of his feet. "You need to take more initiative. You ever question why you sat behind a desk, instead of the wheel of a hummer?" I can tell Seaver isn't intending his words to sound like a dig—more like curiosity.

Kacen lifts his head, and the trouble stirring behind his eyes is clear to all of us. "I didn't need to question it." He pulls his knife out and shoves the blade into the plastic of his packaged food. There's one point for him on survival skills. "I enlisted as a promise. I never promised to go to war."

Tango and Seaver don't question him. "Who did you make a promise to?" I ask.

Kacen gives me a *how dare you ask me that* look. But I couldn't care less.

"Let me guess." I point my plastic fork at him. "One of your parents died in combat?"

His eyes narrow at me and I know I've hit the nail on the head. "My father made me promise to defend my country when I was old enough to enlist. He said it would make him proud. He left for the first Gulf War and never came home." He nods his head at me. "Happy?" He shoves a forkful of food into his mouth and keeps his focus set on the fire. "Didn't know this was a fucking psych retreat."

This would be the time where I'd expect a snicker from Tango or Seaver, but neither of them flinches. "You did a good thing, man. Every job needs a body in the military. Sorry for giving you shit," Seaver says. "Why did you come here, though? Obviously this isn't cupcakes and rainbows." And there's the dig.

Kacen looks directly at Seaver, then Tango, then at me. His eyes linger on me and a slight grin creeps up one side of his face, illuminating a deep dimple in the very corner of his mouth. "I know what we're after. I know why the world is after your dad. Actually, I know why each of us is here." The grin relaxes back into a straight line across his face. "I may not be a fucking war hero, but after I was discharged, I worked for a man named, Eli Tate. Anyone know him?" A dubious smile stretches across his cheeks as he takes the time to look at each one of us.

Blood is boiling in my face and scorching the tips of my ears, and I know I'm not the only one feeling this way. He's another Reaper. Seaver didn't even know this. Seaver didn't even know the real reason he was here. I can see that much written on his face. He's a war hero, being used as nothing more than a body in this situation. And Tango, he's being used as Kacen's bait, like I am. I can see the veins swelling over Tango's forehead and his neck. I'm waiting for an animalistic snarl to groan from his throat. Tango looks over at Seaver, and with one look, they both stand from their logs and prowl over to Kacen. But Kacen doesn't move, and he doesn't blink.

Seaver fists his hand around Kacen's shirt and lifts him to his feet. "You have one chance to tell us what you know."

The asshole laughs as if what Seaver said was a joke. "Or what, you're going to mind fuck me like Cali evidently does to people?"

That was all it took to push Tango over his mental cliff. Kacen's flat on the ground. Blood is spewing from his nose, and his legs are twitching below Tango's weight. Seaver stands guard, his arms crossed, admiring Tango's handiwork. I don't know if he's going to kill him. I wouldn't blame him if he did.

Kacen could be a roadblock for Tango acquiring his cure.

CHAPTER TWENTY-FIVE

CALI

KACEN'S ROPED to a thin tree. Seaver is lobbing pebbles at him, and Tango is zipping us up in our tent. The mixture of thoughts stirring in my head is making me dizzy. I need to keep everything straight somehow. Reaper and Kacen were both working with Dad. Dad stole this treatment he was protecting in China. He cured mom, saved her life, and then they ran to hide, knowing he'd be hunted for stealing this unpatented drug. Two groups of people—some being the team he used to work with, and some who just know of this drug—are after him to retrieve this shit he has. And as I've known, I've been left high and dry as bait or maybe a barrier in front of my parents. Why the fuck would they do this to me?

I prop my pack up behind me and slide my feet into the cushy sleeping bag. The soothing feeling of something soft on my feet comforts me after the tortures of this day.

Tango is nestling back against his pack and turns a small flashlight on and tilts it upward, illuminating the entire tent. His legs rest on top of the sleeping bag and he folds his arms behind his neck, keeping his eyes locked on my face. I can see thoughts forming behind his eyes.

"I know I don't need to warn you that things are going to be a little rough tomorrow." His voice is hoarse from coughing so much throughout the day. His symptoms are getting worse, but he's trying his hardest to hide it—to act like nothing's wrong. But every time I hear him cough, I know he's getting closer to his last breath and it's breaking me. Everything is breaking me.

I nod my head with understanding. This life isn't new to me. I am ready to move on one way or another, though. "I know."

I pull the elastic band out of my hair and rake my fingers through the snarls. While I'm tugging at one of the bigger knots, I see Tango's eyes drift over to my left wrist. "Tell me what happened here," he nods his head toward the scar.

"A knife slicing through my thin skin felt better than the pain in my heart." I pull my wrist down and cover it with my other hand.

"And the tattoo covering it?" He scoots over next to me and tugs my hand onto his lap. He turns my wrist over and traces the outline of the wings puckered up against a heart, and the touch of his fingertip sends shivers down my arm. His hand curls around my wrist, covering the tattoo. "Tell me," he pleads softly. He pulls my wrist up to his lips and the sensation of his mouth covering the numb spot on my skin is strange—but wonderful.

"When I realized how dumb I was to slice the knife across my wrist, I could hear my sister's voice telling me to live for both of us. I felt guilty, so I covered it up with the heart and wings—her free soul." I point to the initials KT scripted in tiny letters on the bottom of the heart. "Krissy Tate."

He lifts my other arm and inspects the artwork detailed over my skin. "And this?"

"My favorite painting," I respond quickly.

"Who's the artist?"

I look up at him and admit another truth about myself. "I am." I haven't told anyone how much painting means to me. "Painting was my escape. My feelings. My beliefs and dreams all on a blank canvas, forcing me to believe that everyone starts with a blank page and can fill it in however they want. Someday, I'm going to pour a bucket of white paint over my life and start over."

"You created this?" he asks. He lifts my arm closer to his face, inspecting every detail, letting his eyes decipher what he's looking at. "A girl curled up on a deserted island?" A non-artistic eye would see this as only a girl curled up on a deserted island.

"The girl is me. The girl is alone, deserted by the world around her, from love and happiness. The girl is tired. I am tired. The vines coiled around her limbs are the constrictions she lives within. The obscure low bearing clouds cause the shadows to hover over her life. And the dominating waves surround her are like a prison, keeping her where she will always be—alone, abandoned, and in the dark."

"What happens to this tattoo when someone saves you from this deserted island?"

"Maybe I'll consider adding him to my island," I smirk.

"Well," he skates his fingers along the tangled vines, "only if these vines are still holding you down. Otherwise, if I'm that guy . . . no deal." He laughs. I'm falling in love with his laugh. I might be falling in love with him.

He slides his feet into my sleeping bag and molds around me. Unsure of what's on his agenda, I'm surprised when he pulls my head over to his chest, curls his arm around my stomach, and closes his eyes. "Good-night, island-girl."

I reach my lips up and press them against his stubbly chin. "Good night, Tyler."

He reaches over and pinches my chin between his thumb and finger, then pulls my lips up to his. "Thank you for reminding me of who I am," he whispers into my mouth. He grabs the flashlight and shuts it off before replacing his arm around my waist, squeezing me tightly. His grip doesn't loosen until I hear his rigid sounding breaths elongate. My breaths soon follow. Sleep has never come so easily.

* * *

My body is stiff from sleeping so deeply. Birds are chirping from the overhanging trees, and the glow of the sun is seeping into the opaqueness of the forest green tent where we're still curled up. I roll onto my back and Tango is lying sideways, leaning on his elbow, staring at me. His finger twirls around a loose strand of hair and he tucks it behind my ear. "Want to go find some vines?" he asks, biting down on his bottom lip. I elbow him in his chest, making him groan and clutch the sore spot. "Geez, all you had to say was, *later*." I roll my eyes and pull myself up against my pack. I flip my head forward, twirling my hands around my hair to pull it up into a knot. I snap the elastic band into place, and Tango pulls me in, causing me to lose my balance and completely fall into him. "Everything you do turns me on, and I need to concentrate today." His fingers skate against the bare skin where my shirt is lifted partly away from my shorts. "You are so damn beautiful. I don't think I'll ever get tired of telling you that."

I turn around and press my hands into his shoulders, forcing him flat against the sleeping bag. I straddle his hips and pull his shirt up while speckling kisses from the slight trail of hair below his belly button up to his collarbone. I move my hands slowly up his chest until they reach his chin and I cup my palms around his cheeks. "You're pretty beautiful too." I cover my lips over his slowly, softly, causing a rush of tingles to tickle over my lips from the little hairs growing around his mouth.

His arms wrap around my back, pulling me into him, making it hard to breathe. "Damn you. Making this life-saving business impossible."

"Guys, you ready?" Seaver yells. "I'm unleashing the asshole from the tree in a minute if you're ready to head out."

"Damn you, Seaver," Tango whispers in my ear. "We need some vines anyway." He slaps my ass and sits us both up.

We dress quickly, hunched under the tent's top, throwing everything into our packs and unzipping the thin layer of fabric separating the cruel world from our makeshift love nest.

I pull my sunglasses from the small pocket on the side of my pack and slip them down over my nose. When my focus reaches Kacen, I notice one of his eyes is swollen shut. His perfect model-like nose is now crooked, and dried blood is stained over his cheeks. He moves forward with a limp and I wonder if Seaver pulled any information out of him. By the looks of it, I'm guessing he didn't.

Tango shoots a glance over to Seaver. "Anything?"

Seaver shakes his head, clearly pissed.

* * *

We walk in silence for an hour. Tango and Seaver have been comparing coordinates off and on, and I have this feeling we're coming closer. But with the base of the canyon cutting off our trail, I'm questioning whether or not we went the wrong way. Although, neither Tango nor Seaver look lost. They're looking up, searching for a method.

Crap. I already know where this is going. "We're going up, aren't we?" I ask.

Tango nods despairingly and they both drop their packs while simultaneously pulling out climbing gear. Tango loops his legs through a harness and clips himself together with various buckles. Once he's secured, he moves over to me and digs my climbing gear out of my pack. "You can do this, Cali." He holds two loops in front of me and I lift each leg and step into both sections. "Hmm. This could substitute as a vine." He looks up at me and shoots me a wink.

I purse my lips as I feel my cheeks redden. "Want me to fall down this canyon?"

"You're going to be fine." He tightens the straps over my legs, tucks his hand under the belt over my waist, and pulls on it. The sensation turns me on, and I'm wondering if it was his intention. The smirk on his face confirms my suspicion.

"If you don't stop, I am going to lose my grip," I remind him again, realizing my apprehension about ascending this canyon wall is growing by the second.

"I'll catch you," he says, placing a soft kiss on my cheek. He clips a rope between us, and tugs on it to show its security.

After a short informative introduction to rock climbing, we're scaling upward. It's not as bad as I thought it would be. I curl my fingertips around the lip of a rock and shove my toe into the crevice of a boulder below. I press upward and lift myself to the next resting place. We stop every few minutes to let our muscles relax since according to Tango, if our muscles lock up, that's when we'll cramp and lose our grip. Right now my arms and legs are trembling and my fingers are burning, and the top still looks far away. I twist my head over my shoulder and take in the distance from where I'm clinging to the base of the canyon. From this view, it looks like we've already climbed at least a quarter of a mile. How the hell did Dad make it up here?

Tango's hanging next to me, Seaver is at the next ledge, and Kacen is below, belaying us. I watch Seaver search the surrounding area above his head, and I watch as his head jerks to a stop. His eyes sift forward and then down to Tango. He points his forefinger and middle finger at his eyes and nudges his head up and to the left. I don't shift my head, but I shoot my focus up in that direction.

The sight of more men with guns, all staring directly at us nearly causes me to lose my grip on the rim of this rock. Losing my grip would only save them a bullet, though. So, I hang on.

"Carolina," Tango says between his breaths. "Don't move." Wouldn't that technically be keeping me in their sights as a good target?

Are these men working for Dad or against him? The lines are a little blurred and it's clear I'm in the wrong place. But I've been in the wrong place for the past couple of years.

I don't move, as Tango instructed. I clench my eyes, avoiding visual contact with the bullet that will likely be soaring at my head in a moment. I'm not sure I can survive another bullet wound—the memory of that red laser pointing at me as Reaper stood holding onto Krissy's hundred pound body is haunting me right now. I can feel the same fear—the type of fear one must feel when a gun is pointed at them. It's like my insides are all weak and useless. I would think my heart should be racing, but it's slow—it's chugging along to keep up with my panicking nerves. I'm not sure if I'm even breathing. I think I may have forgotten how to do that too. I'm staring directly at a man pointing his gun right toward me. I wish I knew what the chances of him hitting me from there were. There are about twenty-five feet in between us, and I feel like that gives him a good advantage. If it were me shooting that gun from twenty-five feet, I'd have a hole straight through his chest.

I hear the first shot. I swallow hard and squint my eyes. If I prayed, I'd do that now too, but I don't pray. I gave that up after Krissy was murdered. My fingers tremble and struggle to hold my weight up on this rock. I can't let go. I've made it this far. I can survive this. I can.

I hear a second shot. Fear accents the sound of each of my breaths. He still hasn't hit me and I'm hoping this means he's untrained in the firearms department. If I were good at ratios, I'd say if he didn't hit me the first two times, or even come close, then the next three times should clear by me as well.

Time feels as if it's lapsing over and swirling around my head as I hear a third shot. That one was closer. I could hear the buzz swoosh by my ear. It makes me swallow the dry heave in my throat. I open my eyes briefly to see what's coming next, and I see the man's arm stretched out in front of him while his finger is pressed over the trigger. I can see him looking through his sight as he closes his left eye.

With life zooming by in slow motion, I hear the gun's blow and feel the burn of lead stab through my leg.

CHAPTER TWENTY-SIX

TANGO

"DOWN! SHE'S DOWN!" I hear my voice screaming. How did I let this happen? *Again.* A bite swells on my arm and I look down to see a bullet grazed me too. *It's nothing.*

A white flash blinds me and the flashback of Iraq and Jake's body trembling against the sand rips my heart out. I promised to take a bullet for him if the opportunity arose. I'm his sergeant. I promised his mother I'd bring him home in one piece, alive. He's only eighteen. He promised his girl they were getting married as soon as we returned. Now I have to tell his mother I lied and I have to tell his girl I'm sorry for the loss, for what she thought was her future. It's all my fucking fault. How could I let this happen?

Jake's body is covered with dust from the sandstorm, and another white flash covers my eyes. Screams echo from the near distance and then they stop.

My eyes refocus and I'm still hanging from a fucking canyon and Cali is dangling beside me. Her eyes are wide and in disbelief. She's in shock. She's bleeding. She's been shot. And I told her not to move. I did it again.

I pull out a smoke grenade and toss it over to the ledge where the bullets were flying from, watching it hit the exact spot I was aiming for. The smoke forms a wall in-between us, giving us a way out—or up.

"You're covered," Seaver yells down from the ledge above. As the smoke dissipates and thins out, Seaver drops over the ledge and shoots the three men down. "Clear!" he yells.

Seaver makes his way back down toward Cali as I continue to look around, making sure the coast is really clear. When my focus drifts down to Kacen, who's holding the bottom rope, waiting to be pulled up last, I'm not the least bit surprised to see his mouth hanging open.

The only reason he's still willing to help us is because he wants to reach Eli as much as we do. He won't actually end up close enough, but for now, we'll use him like he was using us.

"I have her, man," Seaver shouts.

Anger is searing through me and my lungs are burning from breathing so heavily. This is the precise moment where I become weak and admit to myself how unfair this fucking world is. Maybe I should give up right now. Maybe I should call my time of death and cut my rope. It would be fast and it would be over. I've been fighting for my life for so long and I'm tired of fighting for something I think I deserve. Here's the part where I say, why me? But then I look up at Cali being reeled up to the top and I realize I would volunteer to die a slow death if it meant I had the opportunity to experience her—to have her in my life, even if it's only for a little while longer. Because if this plan fails, I don't know how much time I have left. The pain I was warned about is catching up. I don't know how painful it's supposed to get, but I'm getting to the point where I can't hide it anymore. I've been dizzy for days, weak, and struggling to push forward. I feel weak and useless, and all I've done is put the woman I care about in more danger than she's been in since her sister died. Survival doesn't seem like a viable option right now. My hope is almost completely gone. I've dragged us here on the notion that Eli has this drug in his physical possession, when in reality, I don't know if he does or not. If I didn't have Cali by my side, I'd say this could have all been for nothing, but even if I don't survive this, she was worth the fight.

CALI

The ground is bouncing below me. My toes scrape against the rocks and my body arches backwards as I'm pulled up to the top ledge. My head is placed against a bag on the ground. I'm tired and weak. The skin on my thigh burns brutally, and a throb pulsates from within. I look down at my leg. Blood spurts from a wound. And rather than feeling the pain, I feel nothing but anger and resentment. I'm not in the police force. I'm not in the military. I'm not in a gang. I'm not a convict. I haven't asked for shit. Yet, I've been shot twice in my lifetime. This isn't fair.

Tango kneels at my side. His hands are covered in blood, and I don't know if it's his, mine, or from one of the other two. "You okay?" I ask.

His eyes glimmer a bit in response to my question. "You've been shot, and you're asking me if *I'm* okay?"

"Are you?" I ask again.

"I'm fine. It's only a nick," he reassures me. I look back down at my leg. My face crumples with concern, scared to see the true damage. "Same for you."

"There's no bullet in my leg?" I ask for assurance.

"No, it's a superficial flesh wound." He pulls out a small first aid kit and unzips it. He pulls out a small bottle filled with clear liquid and pours it over the wound. I want to scream from the burning pain, but I grit my teeth instead. He leans his head down toward my leg and blows cool air over the painful area—relief is almost immediate. He places the bottle down and puts a decent sized bandage over the wound. He smoothes it over my leg and places a kiss on my thigh. "Out of sight, out of mind."

As I regain my bearings on what's going on around us, I look across the canyon from where we were being shot from. The three men are flattened to the ground, dead.

Kacen and Seaver are unscathed and waiting for me to pick myself up and keep moving.

"We're here, by the way," Tango says, reaching his hand out to help me up.

"Here?" I scan my eyes around, but I don't see much other than a deep hole in the ground.

Tango points at the hole to confirm my assumption. "Do you want to go in first?" he asks.

"First? You mean you're not coming in with me?"

"I think it might be best if he sees you first, knows your intentions—our intentions. If you don't agree, I will come with you."

I shouldn't be afraid of facing Dad alone. I should be somewhat happy to see him, but I'm not. I'm not that ten-year-old who can be bought with gifts and hugs anymore. I'm hurt by him and I'm not sure how to even act in his presence. Not to mention the shock of me entering into his territory—his hideout. I wonder if he'll even be pleased to see me. Part of me thinks he's hidden from me because I was a part of his life he wanted to forget about. If I ever had a child, I couldn't imagine picking up and leaving one day, and never looking back. "I'll be okay," I tell Tango.

"If he's not in there, come right back out. If something goes wrong, yell for me. I'll be down there in a matter of seconds."

For some reason, his words make me freeze. I'm supposed to lower myself into that hole—that trap, believing Dad and Mom are actually living in there? I'm supposed to just trust Tango's word.

Trust.

What if it's a trap? I look over at Kacen, knowing what has to be done first. I've kept my anger somewhat at bay with him, and I've wondered why Tango and Seaver haven't gotten rid of him yet. But my dad and possibly my mom are down there, and this is where Kacen goes away.

"Tango, can I speak to you privately for a minute?" I say.

He takes my elbow and leads me behind a couple of trees. "Do you not want to do this? I can go down there first if that would make you more comfortable."

I shake my head. "No, but . . . we need to rid Kacen from this situation. He's after my dad for the same reason Reaper was, and if he gets his way, you will not be getting that drug. I don't know how Seaver feels, and I don't know him well enough to determine whether he'd go along with this, but we have to—"

"Yes," he agrees simply. Tango takes his pistol out from his holster and bends his body around the trunk of the tree we're standing behind.

TAG 215

I'm observing as if I'm watching a movie. Kacen's on his phone, tapping on the keys, probably sending a message to someone telling them he found Dad's location. He's making this too easy. My eyes shift to Tango, and I watch him squint his eye, about to release the trigger. I can see the contemplation swimming through his darkening irises. I'm not actually sure I can watch this, and I don't know if he can either. Just thinking about how much he's seen, this is almost too much. Our thoughts must be in sync as he lowers his gun and looks at me before dropping his focus toward the ground. "I can't. We'll deal with him later. I won't let him near your dad."

"I understand. You don't need to explain yourself," I say.

"You sure you don't want me to go down there first?" he asks again.

"No. I have this," I say.

He pulls me back by my hand and twists me around to look at him. "You are still the coolest chick I know, Cali." He leans down, placing his lips by my ear. "I'm pretty damn lucky to have found you in this fucked up world we both coexist in." He pulls back and squeezes my good shoulder gently. "Your leg good? You'll make it down there okay, right?"

"I'm good." I force a smile. The look of the dark hole is anything but inviting, but I have to do this . . . for me. "You know, I'm starting to think you might be the exception to my rule— you know, where I trust no one." The words are harder to say than just thinking them, but I have to do this to prove Mom wrong—maybe among all of the untrustworthy people in this world, Tango's one-of-a-kind.

"It's kind of like the 'no touching' rule, you made quite the exception for that, as well," he winks.

I laugh softly and curl my arm around his neck, giving him one last kiss on the cheek. "Okay. I'm ready."

"I'm going down with her," Kacen says, walking up to my side.

"The hell you are. You are lucky we haven't killed you yet. And unless you'd like me to stop regretting that decision, I suggest you move away. Now." Tango pulls his pistol out, pointing it toward the ground, showing it as a warning.

"Fine, but when she's done, I'm going down there," Kacen says with a bit of hesitance.

Tango laughs and turns back toward me, ignoring Kacen's nearby proximity. "Come here," Tango says to me. He wraps a headlamp around my forehead and tests it one time to make sure it turns on. "It's going to be dark down there."

I walk toward the darkness, which grows larger with each step, and when I reach the ledge, I see a hanging ladder descending into the obscurity. *Great.*

I turn around to place my foot on the ladder and I see Tango swallowing hard, he's shuffling his weight from foot to foot gripping his pistol so tightly his knuckles are white. Seaver is squatting, drawing his fingertip through the dirt, and seeming unfazed by all of this. Then there's Kacen, who looks like an angry teenager leaning up against a nearby tree. I try to shut them all out as I lower myself down, feeling the claustrophobic space constrict around me. As the sun slowly shrinks above the hole, I reach up to click the headlamp on and then replace my hand on the ladder. I feel a space open up below me, accompanied with a slight breeze. My feet touch the dirt ground and a barrel is immediately pressed up against the back of my neck. Please be Dad. Please.

"It's me, Cali," I say, still pleading it's him at the other end of the weapon.

A dirt-covered hand is clamped around my bicep and I'm flung around and into a puffy chest—*Dad*. He squeezes me so tightly I'm having trouble breathing. "Carolina," his voice croaks out. He shoves me back with his palms and looks me in the eyes. His face is covered with red dirt, leaving only the whites of his eyes to recognize. The comfort of his arms around me is enough to make me break down again. "Carolina, sweetheart." I lift my gaze to his face. "How did you find me?" The reunion was short lived, as I knew it would be. He knows I wouldn't have found him on my own.

"Dad, so many people are after you. They all want whatever you have. I was escorted here by Tango—the bodyguard you hired to take care of me. You gave him your coordinates in case of an emergency."

He pulls me back in. "What is the emergency, Carolina. Are you okay? Are you not well?"

"Dad, it's Tango. He's dying. He said you have a trial drug that can . . . cure cancer? Whatever you stole from China to use on Mom . . . "

"I see," he says.

All I can do is look at him, trying to ignore the anger and resentment I have toward the two of them at this moment. "I ran into Mom yesterday, or she ran into me. I saw her. I know she's alive, and it's because of you."

"Honey," he calls out. But it's too dark down here to see if he's calling out to mom. I don't know how large the area we're standing in is, but I hear footsteps.

"I see you found him, sweetheart," my mother's voice sounds from a dark corner. I can't quite contain my anger any longer. I didn't think I'd have the opportunity to say what I want to say to the two of them, and I have to realize I may not have another opportunity to do so again.

"Before this reunion commences, I think there's something you both need to know. And that's . . . you should be ashamed of the life you've forced me to live for the past three years. Leaving Krissy and me to believe we were nearly parentless. You both left me to grieve her death, the death that one of your assistants caused, Dad. Reaper, I mean—Reagan, remember him?" I ask. His eyes show recognition, but he doesn't respond to me verbally. "Not only did he swoop in when you took off after Mom died, but he made me fall in love with him. And do you know what he did after that, Dad?" I shrug my shoulders, not even understanding why I should be informing him of the consequences of his thoughtless actions. "He tried to force your location out of me, but thankfully for you, I didn't know where you were . . . ever. And because of that, he decided to kill Krissy. Right in front of me. I watched him murder her. I watched her die. And where were you two? Living in a fucking cave somewhere?"

"Carolina," Mom interrupts me. "Honey."

"No. No, Mom. I've been grieving alone for you and Krissy for the past year, all while holding my steady pace on the run from the people who were trying to use me as bait to find Dad. I've been shot twice, and I still have the bullet in my shoulder—the bullet I wish would have flown through the center of my chest."

I have been suffering, feeling like a small child in the constraints of my own mind, wondering what I was supposed to do to carry on. Now here I am, at a crossroads, and I still don't know what I'm supposed to be doing. What the fuck am I even fighting for anymore?

But as quickly as the question enters my head, the answer catches up almost as fast. I have a reason now. I want to save Tango. I want to save the one person I've been able to trust and to feel something real for. To have known a person for only a few weeks and realize that they have been more honest with me than a lifetime of bloodline relationships, makes me realize I'm fighting against a brick wall with the two people who put me on this earth.

My mother's hands find their way to my shoulders and I want to squirm out of her grip, but for some reason I give her a chance to say what she has to say.

"Honey, what can we do to make this better?" Everything in me wants to laugh at this question. "I know we destroyed your life, and in a way your dad was selfish to save me and sacrifice you. But in the name of love, I have a feeling you might do something similar—kill, fight, and beg for the one who you care the most about. That is what your dad did for me. And it's what you're doing for that boy you are with."

Tango.

"You know what you can do for me? You can salvage the last person in this world who wants to be a part of my life. Tango is dying. He has maybe days left, if that. I want you to use whatever the hell you stole from China and cure him."

They both look at me with saddened eyes. "Carolina, if I do that . . . he will become the bait," Dad says, breathing heavily. "You were never the bait, Carolina, you were always the fish. Tango is the bait, and he can have it, because once he does, I'll be free."

CHAPTER TWENTY-SEVEN

TANGO

I SHOULDN'T HAVE let her go down there first. It's been five minutes, and I haven't heard a sound. I pull my pack over my shoulders and secure it around my chest. I'm going in.

"Dude, do you think her dad knows about you?" Seaver asks.

"Yes. He hired me to be her bodyguard."

The little amount of information Seaver has is pissing him off, and I can't say I blame him. But this is where we part ways. This is the part where I find out whether I will live or die.

I offer my hand to Seaver, and he reluctantly shakes it. "Wish me luck, man."

He nods his head. "Good luck with whatever, dude."

I remove my pack and lean it up against a nearby tree. I need to look non-combative when I go down there, so I hide my pistol under my shirt. I look down into the hole and I don't see anything but a faint glow of a flashlight. I close my eyes briefly and pull in a tight, sharp breath before lowering myself onto the ladder.

This is it.

CALI

"Carolina," Dad whispers through his heavy breaths. "I was trying to save your mother from dying." He places his hands over his wobbly knees and pushes himself upright. "I wanted to save my wife—the love of my life. I couldn't just let her die." He walks over to me and places his hands around my elbows. "As you apparently already know, I was protecting an unregulated drug which was being developed by some Chinese scientists to cure cancer." He pauses for a moment, swallowing hard enough that it sounds like sandpaper going down his throat. "My morals stopped working and my heart took its place. Whether the treatment was controlled, tested or unregulated, I didn't care. I wanted to try and save her, Carolina. I didn't want to leave you without a mother."

"Guess that was a lose-lose situation," I say, crossing my arms over my chest. "Instead of just losing my mother, I lost you and Krissy too." Dad buries his head into his hands, looking defeated—as he should. "Did you ever consider that Mom didn't want to be saved?"

"Carolina," she interrupts me in a scolding manor. "Your dad did what he thought was right."

He nods his head, saying no, and slowly backs away. "It was me who couldn't stand the thought of losing her. It was me who committed an international crime in order to try and save her. It was me who didn't give her the option."

"What exactly is this stuff you have? Is it down here with you?" Please tell me he has it. I walk closer to him. "Why are all these people after you? Why have people tried to kill me for this? Why are you hiding in a hole in the middle of a canyon in Mexico?"

Dad lifts his face slowly from his hands. They fall to his side and he walks back over to me, placing his soot-covered fingers over my shoulders. "I didn't think past the implications of saving your mom, Carolina."

He removes his hand from my shoulder again and drops it into the cargo pocket of his brown pants. His hand fishes around for a moment and then he pulls it out. A Ziploc bag with a syringe?

"Is that *it*?" I ask.

TAG   221

I hear thuds tapping against the ladder. I whip my head around toward the hole in the ceiling, watching the ladder clatter against the stone wall. When I see a pair of shoes appear within the dim light, I immediately know they belong to Tango. Dessert-sand colored boots, soles nearly worn flat, and laces so tight I've been wondering about the circulation in his toes. I don't speak his name. I'm not sure what his intentions are. I'm not quite sure what to expect at this moment.

Dad looks worried. Mom looks knowing.

"Do you know this man, Carolina?" Dad whispers as Tango's face glows under the light.

Tango's expression is inquisitive, and I'm sure he wants to know what I've heard without having to ask me. I'm sure he wants to know if everything is okay, and if he has a chance at survival.

"Yes, Dad. I know him," I confirm. "This is Tango, Dad. Mom, Tango," I point between the three of them.

"I can see why you like him, Carolina," Mom says exuberantly.

My face blushes. "Mom," I say, making an attempt to stop any further observations on Tango's looks.

Tango snickers in return, probably trying to work the light-hearted mood. "I've become quite fond of your daughter, sir, ma'am. " Tango approaches Dad without nerve and offers him his hand. "Sir, I apologize for showing up here, but I'm a desperate man. And as I'm sure you already know, desperate times call for desperate measures. I've been given a death sentence. I most likely don't have many more days left, and I've looked at this situation as a selfish opportunity for another chance." I want to call a timeout and tell Tango what Dad said about him becoming the bait, but I know he won't care about the repercussions.

Dad closes more of the space between him and Tango, careful not to move his icy stare from his face. Dad plunges his hand into the dangling Ziploc bag and pulls out the needle. He looks up at Tango, the half-foot tall gap between them making Tango's six-foot-two size prominent compared to Dad's five-foot-seven height. "Do you care about my daughter, son?"

The question catches all of us off guard. Dad has never asked anyone this question. He hasn't been around to meet anyone of any interest. Maybe if he had been, Krissy would still be with us.

Tango doesn't shift his body. He doesn't blink. He doesn't flinch. His stare lowers to Dad's eyes, and the look on his face is alarming.

Tango usually says exactly what's on his mind, and he never seems to plan out his words. But right now, he appears to be carefully thinking about a response. The pause is silent and is stressing me out.

"Dad, leave him alone." I place my hand on Dad's chest and try to push him away from Tango, trying to create a space I want between them. Maybe I'm only interrupting this because I don't want to hear the answer. I don't want to hear if he doesn't have an answer. I don't want to watch his face contort with sympathy when I find out he was only using me—that I shouldn't have trusted him.

Dad takes my hand away from his chest, removing me from this situation between him and Tango. "Do you care about my daughter or is this only for a cure?"

I watch Tango's Adam's apple dip into the crook of his neck and then bounce back up. "Yes, sir." Tango's eyes flash over to mine. They slowly gaze over my face, and his expression softens. "Sir, I care very deeply for your daughter, and yes, as I said, I'm sick."

"Well then, it gives me great honor to do this . . ." Dad takes the needle and grabs Tango's arm, pushes his sleeve up and looks him in the eyes once more. But as he's looking at Tango we all hear gunshots from above. We all freeze.

Seaver and Kacen?

The ladder descending from the hole above rattles against the wall. "Just do it," Tango demands, trying to ignore who might be coming down here.

Two Asian men drop from the middle of the ladder and stand before all of us. "Give it back, Eli," one of them says.

Dad doesn't look at either of the men. He keeps his focus on the injection spot. Dad quickly plunges the needle into Tango's arm as the men try to stop him. But I put myself in their way. I use myself as a shield even though I'm quickly thrown to the side. I hope it was enough time, though. I'm not sure if the substance transferred into his body completely. "Sorry men, I don't have the drug anymore," Dad says as one of the men snatches the needle from his hand.

The two Asian men are yelling something in a language I can't decipher, but I can tell how very angry they both are, and I can tell things are going to turn bad quickly.

TAG 223

I consider drawing my weapon as the men stop yelling. It almost sounds as if the two of them came up with an idea to settle their anger. And now I'm worried about what that idea might be.

Dad releases Tango's sleeve and pats him on the back. "Well, son, you are about to make my life a whole hell of a lot easier. It gives me great pleasure to say: tag. You are it." Dad looks over at the two men and places his hands in the air. "I'm not holding this drug anymore. You don't have a reason to be after me."

"You, come with us," one of the men says to Tango. "We'll need to find out for sure if the substance is really a viable cure."

"No need, men," dad says proudly. "You can leave knowing the treatment does in fact work. He points to Mom. "I used one of the two injections on my wife here three years ago. Look at her. Healthy as a horse."

The men look to each other, both smiling proudly. They say something to each other and turn back to us. "Good, you both come with us."

The words become real, instantly. This isn't going to end how I hoped. The two men draw their weapons and I try to pull mine, but before I can, a barrel is pointed directly at my face.

"Cali, don't," Tango says with desperation. "I'll go. And I want you to leave." I won't leave him. Not for anything.

"You will not take my wife," Dad says loudly, and the barrel turns toward his head instead.

"We will return them if they survive when we are done. Deal?" Each man offers my dad and I a hand to shake.

"Cali, do it," Tango says, gritting his teeth together.

"What do you mean if they survive?" I ask before I make any deals.

"We won't kill them ourselves. The cancer though, that can still kill," one of them says. "You two are the first people who have been inoculated and we need you for analysis. This drug was not ready for human testing, but since you've both nicely offered to be our guinea pigs, you can give us the data we need to prove whether or not this drug does in fact work properly."

"Cali, this could help other people too. If I make it through, I will find you. It's okay."

This is far from okay. How can I sit here and watch these two men take Mom and Tango, leaving us here to wonder whether they might kill them or not. I don't trust that they won't do that. I don't trust anything, certainly not the words from men with guns pointed up to our heads.

"Please let me have a minute," Tango says to the men. "I will come with you, but I want to say good-bye."

"Yes, me too," Mom says.

"We will be up there waiting. Two minutes, or we come back down." The two of them were true to their word and scale back up the ladder, leaving the four of us in shock and staring between one another.

Tango pulls me into a dark corner where neither of my parents can see us. "Listen to me," he says softly. "Your mom is still alive, which gives me good odds at surviving this. I've been through much worse, Cali, and I can take care of your mom and myself. If I make it through this, you better believe I will find you."

"Tango," I cry. "I want to come with you."

"We both know that's not going to happen, Cali. And if you try, they'll probably kill you. It isn't worth it. You need to live for Krissy. Remember?"

I nod in understanding, trying to stop the tears from pouring out of my eyes. Tango takes his thumb and clears away my tears. "You know what?" he whispers closely to my ear. "It's always about fate, Cali. We will be together, some way or another." I can hear the smile in his voice. The air between us disappears as his lips press over mine. He leaves them there for several seconds before his arms wrap tightly around me and he pulls his head back. "Take my phone out of my pack up there. It's against the first tree on the right. Call the emergency number to get you and Eli out of here." I nod in response, and even though he probably can't see me agreeing, he still tightens his arms around me and kisses my forehead once more. "Good, say good-bye to your mom. Love her like you did before she died, Cali. Don't hold grudges. Life's too short for that."

I don't want him to let go of me, so I clamp my hands around his wrists, bringing them to my chest, begging for a little more time. But I know he wasn't the one who set the timer. He slides his wrists out of mine and lowers his lips to my ear once more. "Thank you for saving my life. I don't want you ever to forget how much you mean to me," he says.

"Tango, I wouldn't piss them off, son," Dad says. "You both should go." I want to yell and scream. I want to say wait, I need more time. But I can't.

TAG 225

Mom finds me in the darkness and her arms wrap around my neck. "I guess this is good-bye again, sweetheart." The memories of our last good-bye sting my heart and force more tears.

"I think we both know it's never good-bye, Mom. It's always, see you later," I cry softly over her shoulder.

"You are right, dear. And I *will* see you later." I can tell she means that in a more ethereal way, whether later means from heaven or earth, but I'll take it.

They both leave, trailing up the ladder to God knows what. All of me wants to follow them and try to shoot the men down, but I don't know if there are more up there. And I'm smart enough to know Tango and Mom could be at the losing end of that battle. So I end my internal fight and fall to my knees and cry more. I cry for all the times I tried to be brave. For all the times I held it in to look strong. For all the times I thought there was no such thing as love, compassion, or trust in this world. Everything I believed in was wrong.

CHAPTER TWENTY-EIGHT

CALI

DAD MADE US wait an hour before we climbed out of the hole. I think he was scared to find the two of them dead when we came out. When we reached the surface, we were in fact faced with two dead bodies: Seaver and Kacen.

"Kacen?" Dad questions as he hovers over his dead body. "What the hell was he doing here?"

"He was after you, Dad," I say simply.

Completely unfazed by the dead bodies, he then looks over at Seaver. "They killed that guy too." I do feel sadness for Seaver. He was a good man with a good heart. And like Tango, he had been through way too fucking much to come here and be killed the way he was.

I retrieve Tango's pack from behind the tree and pull out his phone. Of course there's only one bar left. Shit. I press the emergency button on his phone, and I press it up to my ear, waiting, hoping. After a minute, the phone connects, and an English speaking man answers the line. "State your emergency?" he drones.

"We're in the middle of the Copper Canyons in Mexico. I don't have a location, but I found this phone and I'm lost here with my dad."

"We'll send you a rescue crew immediately. If you can start a fire, it will help us find you. Otherwise, keep an eye out and stay put."

"Thank you," I say, pushing the end button on the phone.

I drop the phone into my back pocket. "Everything is going to be okay. I need you to hang in there," Dad says.

Except nothing is okay. At all. I'm completely and utterly heartbroken. My insides feel shredded and torn apart. I feel helpless and alone again. Having Dad by my side doesn't give me the comfort it should, because I can assume he'll disappear the first chance he gets again. He's good at that. I'm refraining from asking where he's been my whole life and where he plans on going, but I'm smart enough to know he'll either make up a story or look me in the eyes and say he's sorry. That's the way it's been since my earliest memory.

An hour goes by and we started a small fire with the materials I took from Tango's pack. The smoke must have done the trick because it's only minutes before I hear the spiraling propellers pushing through the winds. We walk out into the clearing, and I pull a dirty red shirt out of my pack and wave it around, waiting for the helo to spot us. It only takes a couple of minutes before the thing is above us and a hanging ladder descends from the opening on the side. I take one last look around, wishing and hoping to see Tango and Mom running toward us. But they're both gone. So far gone.

Loss is and always will be my one and only reality. It's one constant I can rely on in my life.

An older man with salt and pepper colored hair makes his way down the ladder, which is swinging coarsely in the air. He reaches for my hand, and I give it to him. He pulls me up to the ladder and I place my feet firmly on the bottom rung. Once I'm inside, the man lowers himself back down the ladder to retrieve Dad. Once they're up, the ladder is pulled up into the helo and another man pulls me into the back.

The man has short, fire engine red hair, bright green eyes, and his face is covered with reddish freckles. His cheeks look as though they've been pinched, but there's only pink around his cheekbones.

"Was it your phone you called from?" the redhead asks.

"No, sir. I found it in a bag. Someone must have lost their belongings," I lie.

"We should send another search out for whoever's bag that is," the redhead says to the pilot.

"Copy that," the pilot says.

One of the men appears to be a medic, and he's checking Dad out. I can understand why they'd think he might need medical attention. He might have only been in the canyons for a couple of weeks, but he looks as if he's been living under a rock for two years and doesn't exactly scream the picture of health.

"You're lucky you found that phone," the man says. He picks up his radio and calls for a search unit to go in and find the missing person.

I can only wish they'd find Tango and Mom, but I'm sure they're long gone. "Oh," I interrupt the man on the radio. "I heard some fighting going on in the canyons. There may have even been gunshots. Not sure what was going on, but you might want to check it out." Just covering my bases.

Dad made it clear that we can't call the police or any type of official and report missing people. Information on the untested drug he gave Tango and Mom can't be public information, which I can understand. If the public knew there was a potentially simple cure for cancer floating around, riots would erupt and all hell would break loose. There's no possibility of that ending well for anyone.

"Where are you from, hon? And what is your name for the record?" The redhead asks.

"I'm from . . . Pecos, Texas. My name? It's Carolina Tate." Saying my name with confidence is a first. It's the first time I know I'm not being chased.

"Is there someone you want us to call for you?" he asks.

TANGO

I didn't cry at my own funeral. I didn't cry at any of my brothers' funerals. I sucked in the pain and held it strong, hiding it behind my heart. But right now, I feel like crying. I feel like crying like a little girl. This was all for nothing. I'm locked in a fucking room in some underground facility in China, I think. They kept us blindfolded when we departed the jet. Alice and I have been placed into two different rooms.

What's worse is the symptoms I have been living with have worsened. I can hear death knocking on my door with each struggle to take a small breath. I have come to the conclusion that I'm not scared of anything else in this world, except for dying. Moreover, I wouldn't wish dying with a broken heart on my worst enemy. I already miss her. She was in my life for three weeks, but those three weeks felt like forever. Leaving her and being strong while trying to do so has been my biggest challenge yet. The look on her face, the one I could barely make out in the dark, was enough to kill me and of itself. She weakened me and made me realize I can't be strong all of the time.

My lungs are burning so badly it feels as though I ran miles in near freezing temperatures. A knife slicing into my chest would be a more desirable sensation. Coughing is becoming my best way at sucking in enough air to survive, but with the coughing comes more blood. I'm only twenty-four, but I've used up more of my lungs than I was apparently allotted. All I wanted to do was protect and serve. I did. Then I end up with a death sentence and a bunch of realistic nightmares. Saying life isn't fair is such an easy way out. It's as if life takes some people by the neck, strangles the air out of them, kicks them in the face and throws them to the wolves. Is this karma? They didn't tell me karma would be the death of me. They told me I might not come back from war. They told me I would die with honor if that happened. But no one knew I'd make it back and have the rug ripped out below me and then die without honor.

This shit isn't working on me. I can feel my insides closing in, disintegrating and shutting down. If that's what's happening, I can only hope I die in my sleep. I slap my arm over my forehead to conceal the dim white light hanging over my head.

I suppose if it's going to happen, I'm ready now. I look up to the ceiling and close my eyes. "God take me to where the sun is always shining, to where love doesn't die, and to where war won't haunt my living memories."

CHAPTER TWENTY-NINE

CALI

SASHA'S ARMS around my neck cause me to burst into tears. We hold each other for what seems like an eternity as we stand in the middle of an empty dirt parking lot. The faint lights of a run-down burger shack flirt with the broken glass bottles that pepper the ground below. "Ready to go home, Cali-girl?"

If home is where the heart is, Tango should be there. But he won't be, so I'll probably never find my home again. I nod my head and she loops her fingers through mine, squeezing ever so tightly.

I clamber into her old beat up Cherokee and pull the seatbelt down over my lap. She starts the engine and the pop music immediately fills my ears. I must have flinched at the sound because she hits the volume button and shuts the music off. "Start talking, girly."

"Reaper is gone and Tango is gone." What else is there to say, that I actually could say?

"What happened to Tango?" She doesn't care about Reaper, and why should she? All anyone would need to know is that he's gone, and everyone should feel instantly safer knowing that asshole doesn't exist among us anymore. "Um. He was pretty sick it turned out. Didn't make it back." The words cause a tearing sensation to rip through the middle of my chest.

I feel the car jerk to the right side of the road, reminding me of when Tango did the same thing, when he wanted to kiss me. My lips won't ever know of something so wonderful again. I will not let them.

She keeps her hands wrapped around the steering wheel, assumedly contemplating what to say to me. She knew I was falling for him. She knows I don't fall for people, and now I'm telling her that he didn't make it back in a way that sounds like I'm telling her he went to go buy a cup of coffee and never returned.

"What do you mean he didn't make it back?" She finally looks at me with nothing but utter concern within her beautiful blue eyes. I shrug my shoulders and turn my head to look out the window, avoiding her sympathetic stare. Her warm hand covers mine and she tugs on my wrist to pull my attention away from the darkness outside.

"There really isn't much to say, Sash. He's gone." I bite on my top lip, hoping it will stop my chin from trembling. I've spent the last three hours being strong, and I can't just let it all go now. I have to maintain this super power of not showing my true emotions. Because right now, my true emotions are pulling me back to the same place where Krissy's death pushed me. I pull my hand out of Sasha's grip and turn my wrist over to admire the heart with wings—my reminder of why I'm supposed to want to live. I close my eyes and imagine Krissy telling me to be strong. I have to be strong for her. I have to continue on for both of us.

We've been driving for a while down a long dirt road. She really moved to the boonies, and I can't blame her. "You live pretty far out here, huh?"

"Yep." She rolls open her window a bit and looks over at me briefly. "Your dad okay?" She knows she shouldn't ask, but she also knows we're in a car in the middle of the fucking desert with no listening ears.

"My dad is fine." The second we landed, he told me had some stuff to do. I gave him Tango's phone number since I have his phone, but I know I won't hear from him anytime soon. It's nothing new. Dad was meant to be a man on the run. Who knows, maybe he's turning himself in. Maybe that's what he should do.

"Hmm," she responds.

My mother is alive too. I wish I could tell her that part—although, that might be a little harder to explain.

We pull into a dirt-covered driveway, which appears to be an extension from the dirt road. A small red ranch house residing in the middle of nowhere somehow looks to be the perfect spot for Sasha. This girl can make anything look beautiful. A dozen little lights line the dirt driveway all the way up to her front awning, which shadows over a tiny porch. Two wooden rocking chairs sit perfectly on each side of the white screen door. And the front door, which I can now see is a tattered wooden slab—is wide open. "You leave your door open while you're gone?"

She giggles a Sasha giggle. "No, silly, Landon must be home."

"Landon?"

"Oh gosh, I forgot to tell you—well, I guess technically I didn't forget to tell you. It all sort of happened over the past couple of weeks. Remember the guy I sort of told you about?" A couple of weeks? That is not the Sasha I know. "I think you'll like him." Her smile warms my cold heart.

I remove my pack from the back of her trunk and pull it over my shoulders. The thing feels so light now compared to the heaviness within my heart. I follow her into the house and the aroma of something delectable instantly overwhelms me. I smell spices—fresh garlic, rosemary, and basil. It smells like Mom's old kitchen.

A ginger-blushing lamp perched on a worn oak coffee table lights the living room. It is surrounded by a set of mismatched couches that all somehow complement each other perfectly. The room itself smells like fresh bread, the scent of a warm home. The scent of love. It calms my nerves and comforts me in a way I wasn't sure I could be comforted right now.

"I'm home!" Sasha shouts into the kitchen. "I have my girl back." She wraps her thin arm around my neck and squeezes tightly while placing a wet kiss on my temple. "Come meet Landon."

TANGO

A light above me flickers on, forcing me to squint from the harsh burn. I'm scared to open my eyes. I'm scared to acknowledge that what I wish is only a hanging bulb might be my light calling me from above. The pain in my chest isn't quite gone, but it's not as severe. Would I feel pain if I were dead? Maybe. What if the enemies whose lives I ended are waiting in front of me when I open my eyes? What if I'm surrounded by flames?

A frail soft-skinned hand is resting on my forehead, though, and I force my eyes open, avoiding my fear of seeing *the light*.

"What are you doing in here?" My voice comes out surprisingly strong considering the way I felt last night.

Her voice, so soft and pleasant—she speaks slowly. "They're letting me visit with you." When I look around, I see I'm still lying in the same place I fell asleep. With moments to focus on what's going on, I feel a stinging sensation on my left arm. I look down to see what the cause of the pain is, and I see a number of tubes and wires connecting me to machines.

"Testing," Alice says, acknowledging my confusion. She extends her arm out toward me and shows me a number of bandages covering her skin. "They want to keep us for eight months. And if we make it through that period of time, they'll release us. They said that's how long it will take to do all of the necessary testing. I've made it three years, so there's hope for you too." She sighs softly. "There is a bright side to this . . . if everything turns out the way they're hoping, they might be able to push this treatment to become regulated. And I'm sure you can understand what that might mean for the general public." She squeezes her hand around my wrist. "This isn't for nothing after all."

"Oh," is all I'm capable of saying.

"What did you do before you became ill, dear?"

"I was a Marine."

She sweeps her hand through my hair, and it reminds me of my own mother's touch. "You're a good man, Tango."

"No, I'm not. When I found out I was dying of cancer, I had my parents notified that I had died in the field. I'm actually quite the opposite of anything good."

"You were trying to save them from going through more pain?" she asks. She understands why I made that decision. I wasn't even sure I understood why I made that decision, or if it had any point to it.

"Yes, that's exactly what I was trying to prevent."

"In my book, that makes you a good man." She stands up from the edge of the bed I'm lying on and looks down at me with a smile. "They gave me a few minutes to come in and see how you were, but they asked me not to stay long. I promise I'll be back when I can."

CHAPTER THIRTY

CALI

IT'S BEEN TWO WEEKS. Sasha let me move into her spare room and I promised her I'd find a job as soon as possible so I could help with rent. I'm depressed and miserable. I think about him every second of the day, wondering if he's dead or alive, and Mom too. I keep his phone on the nightstand, wondering if he might ever call it. I keep it charged. I keep it alive, wishing *he* was that easy to keep alive. I pull the phone from the table and turn on the display. I just realized he took the password feature off of his phone at some point after I saw Chelsea's message to him. Not sure why I didn't think of it until now, but I'm thinking he did it so I'd trust him, which makes me hurt even more.

My thumb accidentally hit one of the apps and a notepad pops open, displaying a note addressed to Chelsea, his sister. Normally I wouldn't read something so personal, but I don't think he's coming back, and I don't really think he's even alive anymore.

The note reads:

> *Chelsea, I should have told you sooner, sis. I'm dying. Not from a bullet, or a hand-to-hand combat fight, not from an explosion or a knife. I'm dying from lung cancer. It came on suddenly and left me no time for intervention. It is the real reason why I've done what I've done.*

> *To everyone else, I died a couple of months ago, but you have been the only one to know the truth, and I'm sorry to put you through this twice. As it seems, life has had its plans for me. I ran from the bullets that were chasing me in the field. I fooled them. I fought hard and I cheated death while I watched others*

TAG

237

who weren't so lucky. But as it turns out, it wasn't the physical enemies I should have feared, it was the enemy within my body that would have the final shot.

Chels, I heard someone say something once that made me understand your situation. I want you_to live for both of us. I want you to be happy for both of us. I want you to find a good job, settle down, and give Mom and Dad lots of grandkids. Live the life we both should have lived.

I'm thinking today might be it for me. I love you for constantly thinking about me. Even though I couldn't respond to your text messages, I've always been thinking about you, Mom and Dad. I love you, and I miss you.

Love, Tyler

While wiping my tears then clinging my free hand to my chest, I scroll my finger over the text and click copy. I paste it into a new message with Chelsea's phone number attached. At the beginning of the message, I write:

Hi Chelsea--you don't know me, but I knew your brother. He had taken a job, which involved working with me. Unfortunately, I'm not sure where he is now, but he left his phone behind. I'm not sure if he's alive or—you know. But I found this message on his phone, and I think he would want you to have it.

I am so sorry for what you're going through. Your brother was an exceptional man and he loved you and your parents very much.

If you ever need anything, please feel free to call his number. I will do whatever I can to help you.

Best, Cali

My text message spreads across six different comment boxes because it is so long. I can't imagine the look on her face when she sees this number show up in her message box. I can't imagine the pain she will feel when she finds out he's either dying for real this time or worse, already dead. She is the only person on this earth who has had to experience the death of her big brother—twice.

Almost immediately, the phone rings. I stare at the caller ID for a second before I select *answer.* "Hello . . . "

Chelsea sniffles into the phone, crying so hard she can hardly speak. "Is this Cali?" she asks weakly.

"Yes, this is she."

"He just disappeared?" she asks.

"I don't think he wanted me to see him sick. I think he was embarrassed."

She laughs a little. "Yup, that sounds like Tyler. Always the hero." She sighs. "When I ran into him in Nashville a month ago, he wouldn't tell me much. He certainly didn't tell me he was sick. I didn't ask questions, though. I knew whatever he was doing was for a reason, and I've trusted him enough not to pry into his life. We were so close, Cali. So close. And then he had to go and join the Marines." She sniffles into the phone again. "You know it's funny, he told me he carried a picture frame around with him with my picture in it. I'm his stupid little sister, not a girlfriend. But he said he carried it around because he didn't want to leave me. We were best friends. He said I was his motivation to make it home." I hear her crying quietly into the phone, so I give her a minute. I remember seeing him look at a picture in his bag the first night we were in the apartment in Massachusetts. "I'm sorry, I think I'm kind of in shock right now," she says.

"I can understand. I know this was out of the blue, and maybe you would have never known . . . but I thought you should know. My sister was taken from me at nineteen, and we had a similar relationship to what you're describing." I'll spare her the details. "You're not alone. I feel your pain."

"Thank you for letting me know, and thank you for sending me his message."

"Absolutely. I'll hold on to his phone, so, feel free to call if you ever want to talk."

I hear her breathy sobs again. "Thanks again. I will." Then I hear a click.

Now that I've started my day off even more miserable than I have for the past couple of weeks, I sit up, noting the time. It's nine o'clock and an aroma is suddenly pulling me up from the bed. It smells so damn good in here again. Every morning, it's like a wake-up call. I pull my sweatshirt over my head and walk around the corner into the tiny kitchen.

"Hi," I say quietly, looking over his shoulder into the frying pan.

"Hungry?" he asks.

I nod my head, because even after my four-course dinner last night, I'm starved again. Landon and Sasha work at the same local restaurant. He's the chef, and she's the boisterous hostess. They aren't officially together, only friends as she says. Although I'm pretty sure he sleeps over every night. I haven't actually seen him arrive, but he's here making breakfast every morning, so I'm not sure who she's fooling. He's totally her type—on-purpose messy beach blond hair, dark eyes, soft-spoken and kind. He has a passion for cooking, or as it seems, an obsession. I won't complain about the food part of all this. But as always, with each bite of food I place into my mouth, a tinge of guilt washes through me when I think about Tango and Mom most definitely not eating the way I am.

I still regret letting them go. I shouldn't have left their sides. I should have fought for them. Having him in my life for such a short period of time made such an impact on me and now I have to realize how temporary he was, and how I need to move on from him. I'm supposed to be numb to heartache by now, but I did it to myself again.

"Morning, love bugs." Sasha meanders into the kitchen, stretching each arm slowly across her chest. Her hair is tousled into a curly mess, and I laugh a bit, noticing how little she cares about her appearance in front of Landon. Even if her hair was lying perfectly across her shoulders, she's still sporting purple flannel pajama bottoms and a stained university sweatshirt. Although, looking down at myself, she looks like she's ready for dinner and dancing compared to the way I appear—but I'm not trying to attract anyone here.

Sasha sits down in the chair beside me and allows her eyes to linger on Landon's backside as he flips the last round of bacon. Her elbow plops down on the table and her chin falls into her fist. "You're too good to me, Landon," she says.

He twists his head around and raises one eyebrow while giving her a slight smirk. "I know," he retorts. Landon's smirk is purposeful to get a reaction out of Sasha, and it makes my chest hurl with jealous pain.

Landon decorates a plate with a heaping spoonful of scrambled eggs, bacon, and homemade hash browns, and serves it to Sasha whose tongue is nearly hanging out of her mouth. Then he hands me a plate, as well.

"I think I understand this arrangement thing," I say. "You like to cook," I point my fork at Landon, "and you like to eat," I pucker my lips at Sasha.

"Precisely," she confirms.

"But you two are definitely sleeping together."

Sasha's eyes burn into mine as her cheeks explode with redness. This is exactly what she did to me when I introduced her to Tango. Payback is such a bitch.

Landon drops the frying pan into the sink then pulls a dishrag off the stove bar and cleans his hands off thoroughly. "On the contrary, we've been sleeping together every night for the past four weeks. You could probably just say that my cooking is the icing on the cake." He gives her a devilish grin and winks, making him look quite sultry for the innocent looking gentlemen I took him for only moments ago.

Sasha's head falls into her hands, hiding the spreading rosy warm color curling around the backside of her ears. "It's true," she mumbles into her muffled hands. "I mean, look at him." She removes one of her hands from around her face and gestures to Landon like a game show host.

"Well, that makes me happy. She needed to get laid. Bad," I rumble with forced laughter.

The motion of laughter causes my stomach to churn, forcing a nauseating feeling up through my esophagus. Ugh. What the hell? I curl over, clutching at my stomach and clamping my eyes shut, hoping to tune out the queasiness. And while the motion of losing my breakfast subsides, a strange numb feeling spirals up the side of my body and I'm not sure what to make of it. I want to ignore it, but the room is spinning in slow circles . . .

Everything is muted and numb . . .

Breaths are short, skin is cold, head is heavy, and . . .

CHAPTER THIRTY-ONE

CALI

OH SHIT. Oh Fuck. No. No. No.

White walls, white sheets, ammonia, machines, beeping, and a woman dressed in white. What am I doing here? Why am I in a hospital? Where's Sasha?

"Good morning," an overweight, mannish looking woman says in a very deep voice. "Have a nice nap?" She lifts my wrist between her fingers and checks for my pulse. "Don't worry, hon, you're going to be fine. We think you might have some kind of head trauma or possibly an ocular headache."

"A what?"

"It could be caused by a variety of things. Have you hit your head recently or done anything out of your normal routine? We found a pretty intense wound on your thigh as well," she says while pulling the clipboard out of a bin.

"I fell on a garden tool in the backyard last week. That's what the wound was from. But other than that, nope, work and home," I say.

"Hmm. Well then—" She taps the tip of the pen firmly down onto the clipboard, clicks it, and shoves it into her black web of hair. "The doctor will be in to speak with you soon."

"Can I leave?"

She snorts with laughter and says, "We wanted to rouse you before we started with the blood work and tests. Those have to be done first, and if everything checks out okay, you'll be free to go." She presses a couple of colorful buttons on the wall above my head and turns to leave. "Another nurse will be in shortly for the blood work and to take you for an MRI." And with that she is gone.

I have to find a way out of here. My eyes scan the room searching for my clothes, for anything that will conceal my ass from hanging out of this thin, pale blue gown. There is nothing by the bed or the window and I'm about to wrap this goddamn sheet around me and make a beeline for the front entrance.

I sit myself up and drop my hospital sock covered feet to the ground. I wrap the sheet around myself like a toga and walk over to the long dresser sitting beneath the window. I open each drawer, hoping to find something to wear, but all I find are portable toilet bowls, latex gloves, and a spare set of blankets. I slam the drawer shut with frustration as a hand presses down over my shoulder. It startles me and I turn around, hoping I didn't miss my opportunity to escape.

"Sasha? What happened? Why am I here?"

"Cali, you passed out cold at the kitchen table. Landon called 9-1-1. The ambulance came and took you away. I followed you to the hospital. I don't know anything more than that."

"I wish you wouldn't have let him call 9-1-1. I don't want to be here."

"Well, something made you pass out cold, Cali. It could be serious," she says, looking at me with large eyes.

"Please take me back to your house," I beg.

She tries to pull me back to the bed, and as I start walking, I notice a bag of my clothes on a table near the door. "You need to calm down. Everything is going to be fine. But I am worried about you and I'm not taking you home until they give you whatever blood tests they want you to have. I'm sorry."

I glare at her for a minute, completely pissed off. But she doesn't flinch. She crosses her arms over her chest. "I love you. And I'm taking care of you. Get back in that damn bed and stop acting like a brat."

I do as she says, not because she scares me, but because I have no energy to fight with her. I still don't feel great.

She sits in the chair next to my bed and flips through her phone for the next half hour while we wait for the doctors or nurses to come back.

* * *

It's been two hours since they've taken my blood. I've cooperated nicely, and I would really like some answers so I can get the hell out of here. With a knock at the door, I sit up in the bed and wait for someone to come in with some news. A nurse walks in with a clipboard and sits down to give me the facts.

"It's not as bad as it could have been," the nurse says with a smile.

CHAPTER THIRTY-TWO

CALI
EIGHT MONTHS LATER

I'VE PICKED UP the pieces to the best of my ability. I can't understand how someone can make such a large impact on my life after only three weeks and cause me so much pain and heartache for months to follow. Maybe it's because we weren't given a fair chance. But life clearly doesn't care about fairness. Although, one of the doctors who helped me in the hospital months back was finally able to remove the bullet from my shoulder. Life threw me a bone, I suppose. The doctor said it had worked its way closer to the surface and further away from my artery. They thought it could have been one of the reasons for the ocular headache they determined I had. But the headache could have been caused from a variety of other things too. Whatever the case, my bodily pain is now manageable and I'm off painkillers.

I've been working for a laborer placement company for the past seven months. Sasha's dad had a connection and helped me get into a human resources position here. They've put me through training and they're financially helping me work through the last few college courses I need in order to earn my degree. The pay is great and the benefits are fantastic. It's exactly where a girl my age should be. I want to forget about the last four years of my life, but that would mean closing the door on my entire family and Tango. And that door will always remain open.

I don't think Mom and Tango made it out of wherever they were. I'll never know if they were killed or died on their own. I sometimes think it's better off that I don't know the truth.

It's been quiet at the office today and I've had my personal email inbox open on my screen for the past couple of hours. Sasha and I send emails back and forth to each other throughout the day. It makes the day go by quicker I suppose. I clicked on all the spam mail and dumped them in the trash, leaving me with only one unread e-mail, which I've been staring at for the past ninety minutes.

Krissy's last e-mail that she sent to me the day she was killed.

When I see her email sitting there all alone, I normally click out of the screen, but today would have been her birthday, so for her, I'm opening it. As I click on the e-mail, my heart hammers against my ribcage so fast, I feel a bit dizzy. But I continue on, knowing I've already done the hardest part and clicked open.

> *Cali!!!*
>
> *I know you're at class right now, but I wanted to know if I could borrow your black sweater tomorrow night. I have a date. Squeeee! It's that guy I've been crushing on in my business economics class. His name is Landon and he's studying to be a restaurant owner. Mmm, imagine marrying someone who can cook. I think I could be the happiest girl on the planet. God, I'm getting ahead of myself, but I'm excited and I need to look perfect tomorrow night. Maybe after a few dates, we can join you and Reagan some time.*
>
> *I finally feel like our lives are starting to come together again. We deserve it. We deserve to be happy. And I'm so happy right now!*
>
> *Love ya, Cali Cal xoxoxo*
>
> *EEK! I'm so excited.*
>
> *Krissy*

Oh my God. I push myself up from my desk and make it to the bathroom as quickly as I can, hoping no sees me crying this hard. Landon? It couldn't be the same one. What are the odds? Did he go to the University of Texas, too? Everything was supposed to be perfect. She never dated. She didn't give guys a chance. School was too important to her. She was truly happy that day. She was thinking of a future neither of us could comprehend for the longest time. I was always the one trying to make our future plans, trying to pull her out of her depressing funk. Why would she be murdered that night? Why would the world work like that? It's so fucking unfair.

All of my pain is resurfacing, and my hormones are definitely amplifying this. God dammit. How am I going to fucking survive this shit, I can't even make it through a day at work without breaking down. I used to be the strongest woman I knew, and now I'm the weakest. The absolute weakest person I've ever met.

I clean up my face and head back to my desk, immediately starting a new email.

Hey Sash,

What college did Landon go to?

Just wondering.

-Cali

She responds within a few minutes with:

University of Texas. Why?

-Sasha

I have spent the last four hours of my workday staring at a blank screen, contemplating life and the lack of it that remains.

My desk phone rings and pulls me out of my trance, and I debate ignoring it and going home sick, but I answer it anyway.

"Cali speaking?"

"Hey Cali, I have a new laborer starting tomorrow. He'll be meeting with you at nine. Just giving you a heads up."

"Thanks, Jack. I'll be here." I hang up the phone and wonder why my boss is reminding me to be at work on time tomorrow. I've never been late, and I haven't called in sick. Must be a high-level position.

* * *

"Landon, do you remember a girl named Krissy from your business economics class a few years ago?" He thinks for a minute and then his face turns pale.

"Oh yeah, I do. Poor girl," he says, staring through me. "How did you know about her?" His eyes focus on mine, probably puzzled about how I would know of their brief encounter.

"She was my sister. I—ah—I waited two years before opening up her last e-mail to me." I pull out the printed e-mail and hand it to him, then watch as his eyes sadden while he reads each word.

"Oh my—wow. Yeah, that was me. What are the odds?" He nods his head slowly looking at me with sympathy. "I heard she was killed in some alley a few blocks away from where she lived."

I can feel my eyebrows puckering and tears filling my eyes. "You made her really really happy that day. She hadn't been that happy since our mom died. You gave her that." I can't say anything else. I just wrap my arms around his neck and squeeze him. Sasha's on the other side of us, crying too.

We spent the rest of the night sharing stories and Landon telling us about the little hard-to-get game Krissy played with him for two months. He told us how nervous he was to ask her out and couldn't believe when she actually agreed. Landon said she always looked happy and that's what drew him to her. I guess he had no idea how troubled she was. She must have been good at putting on a front when she was in class. She was good at hiding her troubles behind a smile.

Rather than falling asleep with a lump in my throat as I do most nights, I fall asleep knowing that Krissy smiled a real smile the day she died. And it gives me a little closure.

* * *

These mornings are getting harder and harder to pull myself out of bed and drag myself to the office. I'd much rather sleep all day. That's what I should be allowed to do in this bodily state, but instead, I unlock the glass door of the office and step inside. I flip the lights on and turn around to face my desk.

And my heart stops.

And my heart starts racing.

And the tears, they pour down my cheeks.

TAG 247

And the sobs, they gurgle up through my throat.

I walk slowly over to my desk. I walk slowly over to the man sitting in my desk chair. My mouth is hanging open and I've forgotten how to speak.

He stands up and moves toward me.

"I'm here for a job," he says with a jaunty grin.

"I think I might have one for you," I manage to say. I wrap my hands around my swollen belly. "How about being a dad?" I cry again.

His smile grows twice the size and he rushes up to me, quickly closing the space between us. His hands cup around my cheeks and he presses his lips into mine with so much fierce exuberance, I almost forget about the last eight months. "The baby's mine, right?" he asks, sounding worried.

I slap him. "No one else could fill the empty shoes you left behind."

"Wait, weren't you on the—pill?" These don't seem like proper *I haven't seen you in eight months, lets catch up* questions, but I'm sure just as many things are whirling through his head, as are in mine right now.

"Turns out you're not the only one who can be the exception to a rule," I say, biting down on my bottom lip.

"Marry me, Cali. I love you more than I have ever loved anyone in my entire life. I thought of you every single day for the past eight months. I prayed that you hadn't moved on, and that you'd be waiting for me.

"I love you. I've loved you and I will always love you. I would have waited for forever. And yes, I'll marry you." I strangle my arms around him, squeezing so tightly it releases some of the built up pressure in my chest.

"Easy easy. I don't want to hurt—" He places his hands on my stomach. "Do you know if it's a boy or a girl?"

"A girl. I want to name her Tyler Krissy Wright. " For the first time since I met Tango, he's crying. He's crying not because he's dying. Not because he's remembering a horrible memory from combat. Not because he had to say good-bye to me. I think he's crying because he gets to experience a second chance at life—with me, with our daughter.

When the emotions settle down, I can see different thoughts running through his eyes. "I have something for you," he says.

"What else could I possibly need beside you?" I ask, wiping my drippy eyes.

He walks back around my desk and pulls out a large white canvas along with a bundle of cloth-wrapped paintbrushes and paints. "Here," he says. "It's a blank canvas. I want you—I want us to pour a bucket of white paint over this and start over. I want you to fill this canvas with what our lives should look like."

He remembered.

TANGO

I've seen my life flash before me too many times. But for the first time, I see my future flash before me. Beside the thirty-second heart attack I had when I watched Cali waddle through her office door, wondering if she had met someone else and was having his baby, I haven't felt like anything was so right in all my life.

The folks in China weren't so bad. Their only goal was to successfully cure cancer with the new drug they had spent years developing. They treated me well. Treated me more like a friend than a test subject. The only thing they prevented me from doing was making outside contact. But being in the Marines and deployed a number of times, this wasn't a lot to ask. Although, I would have done just about anything to tell Cali I was okay.

I built an unbreakable bond with Alice. She's an amazing woman, mother, and friend. I can see why Cali's heart would never heal from her absence. I can also understand why she remained hidden for so long.

I was notified that Eli turned himself in, and while we all thought he'd be convicted for international theft, he was able to prove to the world that this treatment did work with no side effects. For this he was released and forced to retire, taking up a new residence with Alice in the home she had built for her family all of the years he was busy working.

My lungs are completely healed and I'm cancer free. So is Alice.

The scientists are in the process of getting the drug put through trials. With their eight months of research and testing, they have all the information they need to prove to the world that a cure for one of the most deadly diseases is close to being approved and publicized.

They let me go as they promised they would. They'll come check on me periodically to make sure the cancer doesn't return, but I'm okay with that.

We walk into Sasha's house and Cali leads me down to her bedroom. "So this is where you've been living for the past eight months?" It's small, but I'm glad she was able to stay with Sasha.

"It's been fine. I've saved up enough money to rent my own place, but I haven't found one yet."

I laugh a little knowing that we won't have to worry about money ever. "Not only do I have the money Eli gave me for taking care of Cali, but the company in China gave me a large sum of money to pay for my time spent being their test subject." I think if I help out with a mortgage, we can buy a nice little house near your parents." The smile on her face is so pure and real. I love making this girl smile and I will do whatever it takes to make her smile every day for the rest of my life. "I'm taking you to see your parents tomorrow and to show you the house that I sort of already picked out." I wince, hoping she doesn't mind. It was a long flight home, I had free Internet service, and they gave me a laptop and a phone in addition to the money. I spent the entire trip searching for houses and rings."

"Really? Wait, both of my parents are . . . home?" she asks.

"Yes, your dad is now retired and your parents will finally have their happily ever after."

And more tears commence. "Jeez, Cali. You're like a running hose. Have you been crying like this the whole pregnancy?"

Her tears turn into giggles. "Yes, I can't help it." I wipe her tears away and place a kiss on her nose. She's changed somehow—she's happy and free.

"Wait. What about your parents? Can you tell them you're not really dead?" she asks.

"Not really, but I have an idea . . ."

CALI
SIX MONTHS LATER

My toes crunch into the white sand as I walk toward Tango, deliciously dressed in loose khakis and a white shirt. With baby Tyler in Tango's arms, wearing a tiny little pink dress, they both smile at me as I make my way toward them with a large bouquet of white lilies clenched between my hands.

I glance over at my parents sitting on the left, keeping one chair open for where Krissy would have sat. Mom and Dad are both crying happy tears, which makes me turn my head quickly to avoid my own tears. I look to the right and I see Tango's parents and sister. While Tango couldn't tell them he was still technically alive and that he had set up his own death, I asked them to meet me in Mexico—a place where it was safe for everyone to be together without getting Tango's old Marine officer in a lot of trouble for forging a death. It was tough getting them to Mexico, especially with a plea coming from a complete stranger, but I told them there was something they should know about their son. Chelsea helped.

Tango saw them for the first time in two years today. His mother was angry at first, but she understood what a snap decision after receiving a two-month death sentence could cause a person to do. They made a promise to meet in Mexico twice a year and they would keep in touch through me. Chelsea and I have become very close and we talk daily. Everything is as perfect as it could possibly be.

With Sasha on one side and Landon on the other, one as a maid-of-honor and the other as the best man, I arrive in front of my two loves. Tango hands Tyler to Sasha and fills his empty hands with mine.

"Do you, Carolina, take Tyler Wright to be your lawfully wedded husband? Will you promise to love and trust one another until you both shall part?" the priest asks.

"Yes. I love you. And I *trust* you," I smile, knowing how easy it feels to admit the feeling of trust. "You will always be my exception to *the* rule."

"He *is* the exception to my own rule," my mother shouts to us through tears.

"And do you, Tyler Wright, take Carolina to be your lawfully wedded wife? Will you promise to love and trust one another until you both shall part?"

"I do," he smiles.

"By the power vested in me in the country of Mexico, I now pronounce you husband and wife."

We kissed. We laughed. We kissed again. We took our little girl in our arms and became a family just like that.

EPILOGUE

HE WAS MY WEAKNESS and I was his strength. And we needed each other to survive.

Tango's hand slips inside mine. This type of pain never bothers me. I know it's worth it, so I endure it. We found this little tattoo shop on a side street in Cancun. They're our wedding gifts to each other. Our parents were all busy fawning over baby Tyler, so we took the opportunity to have a little *us* time.

Our chairs sit side by side and he's looking at me with a proud grin. "You are one cool chick, Carolina *Wright*."

"You should have *that* tattooed on your arm instead," I laugh.

"No." He squeezes my hand a little tighter. "The only tattoo I will ever add to my body is this one, the one symbolizing life after death."

I smile at his words, knowing I feel the same way. "Me too."

Doves will now soar out of the old tattooed skulls on his back. And as for me, I won't cover up or touch the tattoo that represents the death of Krissy, but I did promise her I would live for both of us. And that's what I'll do. Instead of a tattoo that represents life, I've chosen to add a man—Tango, to the lonely island on my arm. He is my life after death. He is the exception to the rule. And with my life-long vow: Know everyone. Trust ~~no~~ one.

PREVIEW OF

RED NIGHTS
COMING EARLY 2015

(CONTENT SUBJECT TO CHANGE DURING EDITING)

PROLOGUE

WHEN SOMETHING is your fault, you can do one of two things: deny it or accept it.

I have done both.

Acceptance has never been an issue for me. I accepted the truth from the moment I looked up into my second-floor bedroom window and watched a tidal wave of thrashing flames take away almost everything I had. Even though I was free from the blaze, it was all I could feel inside. I may not have been in the fire, but I was burning from the inside out. I've accepted that I'll never forgive myself, and for that, I've accepted this undying pain—it will never go away. I don't feel like I have the right to be breathing air and feeling life when I took it away from the closest person in my world.

I should have been killed up in that room instead of him. I shouldn't have had to watch the firestorm swallow him whole, leaving nothing but charred skin and burning bones.

I watched as the firemen carried him out on a stretcher. I've never heard him or anyone scream like that before, his voice gurgling from fluid collecting in his lungs—his crying draining every last breath he had. I don't know what happened once they put him in the ambulance. I don't know if he died in pain or if he was unconscious. I only know he survived for two more hours. I remember the paramedics telling me they were sorry. Sorry? For what? For having to live with this blame, or for the loss of my brother? Sorry doesn't fix things. Sorry digs the knife in deeper. And I would have said that to them if they hadn't been rolling me away, too.

After jumping out of my bedroom window and enduring a severely broken leg and a separated shoulder, the sustained agony was nothing compared to hearing the numbing words, "He didn't make it." Those four words made him disappear from my life quicker than I had time to realize it was all my fault. Strapped down to the gurney, staring up into the very same stars I've always looked to for comfort, I knew then it was *all* my fault. All I could do was wonder why those stars stopped providing for me that night.

The social workers tell me this will eventually become easier, but I don't see how. A moment of inattention, just a quick misdirected thought burned my brother to pieces.

The doctors and nurses say I won't feel this type of pain forever, but I can't see that happening. I'm alive, living with my thoughts and memories. My nightmares and flashbacks. There isn't a day that feels better than another. The pain doesn't go away or even subside. Maybe numbness will eventually take its place, but as of now: every day since *that* day, I've woken up feeling worse than the day before.

When I tell those doctors and nurses the pain keeps growing, they tell me I need to heal before the pain will lessen. But I'm smart enough to know that when a piece of your heart has been taken away, it doesn't grow back. It leaves a hole. And the hole has grown. It's taken over, changing who I am and who I've been, ultimately creating a person I might never know again.

CHAPTER ONE

EVERY MORNING is the same: when the red glow fades into daylight, I know I've made it through another starless night. I relish in the minutes before I open my eyes—trying to convince myself I'm waking up from a nightmare rather than real life.

I used to lie in the cool grass, staring up into the darkness above, wondering who was looking back at me. Someone up there had to be granting wishes, and I believed whoever it was could hear me, because my wishes were always answered. The serenity of feeling alone under heaven's vault allowed my mind to wander and think clearly. It's the perfect spot for meditation and contemplation, but I never could wrap my head around the simplicity of the night's sky being able to hold so many answers to life. Maybe it's just the comfort of believing in something larger than anything else in existence. After all, the sky does hold the world together. But as of a couple of weeks ago, I feel like I might have slipped through the cracks.

The sky has all but forgotten me—it's left me without the stars, granted wishes, and answers I so desperately need.

I force my eyes open, confirming everything is real, not a nightmare. I'm still in rehab with no end in sight. The pain never kicks in until my eyes are open, which is when I see the damage left behind. I push myself up on the bed, careful not twist the wrong way. It's been three weeks, and I think my body is developing a tolerance to the pain meds since they don't seem to be working as well as they were in the beginning.

The beginning, meaning, really . . . the end.

It could be the rods holding my left leg together or the plate they had to surgically fix to my ankle bone. It's an all-over type of pain. My leg feels heavy, as if I may never be able to lift it again. And this scares me. Not a day goes by where I don't wonder if I'll be left immobilized forever. But if I am left that way, don't I sort of deserve this type of suffering? If Blake had the option of burning to his death or losing the use of his left leg, I think he'd choose the latter.

I look over the other marks on my body, observing the healing process, determining which scars I'll be left with in the end. Everything is scabbing, except for the contusion on my arm where a rock broke my fall. Because they had to use a skin graft to close it up, it will take the longest to heal. I feel weak and tired, bored and stiff. Every other part of my body beside my left leg wants to get up and run away from this life I'm now confined to.

I reach to the side table and grab my phone and ear buds. I need the music to drown out the silence. Silence creates memories and images in my head, and I have to do what I can to avoid it. With the ear buds in place, I lean my head back against the pillow and lie in a daze, focusing on the darkness behind my eyelids, while imagining the swirls and blurs growing and shrinking along with the beat, like the audio visualizer I used to watch on my laptop. My imagination hypnotizes me until I feel lips on my forehead. I peel open my heavy eyelids and find Mom standing in front of me with two cups of coffee. I remove the buds from my ears and let them fall to my lap.

"What are you doing here?" I ask, keeping my voice soft to avoid scaring her away again. I've only seen her twice in the past three weeks: once the night of the fire and…now. I'm not angry, and I don't blame her, especially seeing the pain behind her eyes, showing the struggle she must have overcome to be here today. Her eyes scan my body, stopping at my left leg. It makes her cringe and clutch her stomach. The look in her eyes turns to guilt. I give her the time she needs to find the right answer. I doubt she'll say it's because she missed me.

"It was wrong of me to say what I said to you that night. I've come to apologize and see how you're doing." She expels a quiet sigh and presses her finger into the center of her forehead. "I've gotten daily updates from your doctor, but I needed to see for myself." Her words come out so cold and very unlike her. Coming from the woman who always acted like nothing bad would ever happen to us, it sounds as if the rug was ripped out from beneath her—which it was. Neither Blake nor I could do anything wrong by her before this.

But that's different now.

"You weren't wrong about anything you said, Mom." I try to push myself up to a better leaning position so I can take the coffee cup she's trying to hand me. It takes a minute to reposition myself, but she's patient and watches me intently. Once upright, I curl my fingers around the hot Styrofoam, feeling the heaviness within my weakened hand. "Thank you."

"I was wrong, Felicity," she says again.

She isn't wrong; I did kill Blake—not intentionally, maybe, but he died because of me anyway. I took away our house, our memories, and a piece of our future. "Mom, it was all my fault. Everything. Honestly, I wouldn't blame you if you never wanted to see me again. Death and destruction change everything. They change love. I know this because *I* don't love me anymore."

She sits down on the guest chair beside my bed and places her purse down on the table. "Sweetheart, let me make one thing very clear: I will always love you, no matter what you do. However, it doesn't diminish my anger or resentment at the moment . . . your dad's, either."

We're both silent while we sip from our cups, using the coffee as an excuse not to speak. "How's Dad?" I ask.

She shifts her weight around in her chair, appearing as uncomfortable and awkward as I feel right now. "Not good. Aunt Laney is driving him nuts and he spends most of the day yelling at the insurance company, trying to get things resolved quickly. He's frustrated. I guess taking his anger out on people makes him feel better, although I'm not sure how." I nod, because I truly understand this. I won't bother asking if he wants to see me. I can assume her response based on his absence.

"How was the funeral?" I ask hesitantly, keeping my eyes locked on the miserable rods puncturing through my skin.

She pulls in a rigid breath. "It was a beautiful ceremony. The church was full with family and friends, and people we didn't even know. Tanner was kind enough to do the eulogy. He did such a wonderful job."

Tanner. I haven't heard his name in years. He was Blake's childhood best friend. They met at the bus stop on their first day of kindergarten and became inseparable. I remember being jealous of their friendship; it was around that time when Blake lost interest in playing with his *stupid* little sister. They did everything together—sports, overnight camp. They even went to the same college. But Blake moved home to save money after graduation, and Tanner moved away for an executive position at a hotel in Vegas. Even though it's only six hours from here, they didn't speak much after that. It happens, I guess. I lost touch with my close high school friends when we all went off to college, and the few friends I made at Northeastern University weren't worthy of keeping in touch with after graduation. I never had a true best friend. Not like Blake had with Tanner.

"It was nice of him to do that," I say, knowing if I weren't immobile in this bed, I would have insisted on giving the eulogy. I assume most people wouldn't have wanted to hear from me, though.

"Tanner is a saint." Mom clutches her hand around the crucifix dangling from her neck. "Would you believe he took a month sabbatical just to help your Dad and me with whatever we need?"

"Wow. That's—that's very sweet of him."

"That boy has always been such a good friend to our family. God bless him." She looks up toward the ceiling as her eyes film over with tears. She grinds her jaw back and forth and looks back at me. "As a matter of fact, he asked if he could come visit you. I told him I needed to speak with you first."

Maybe he'll come in here and tell me how horrible I am, how this is all my fault, and how I should be suffering more for the pain I've inflicted. That might actually make me feel better. I deserve it. "Sure, he can come visit."

"I'll let him know. Visiting hours are eight to four, right?" I want to say, "I don't know," because the truth is: no one has come to visit me in the past three weeks. My sarcasm wouldn't help things.

"I think so."

She looks away from me, finding any other part of the room to look at besides my face. I'm guessing our exchange is over, and I'm assuming I won't see her again for a while. Regardless of the internal struggle between loving her daughter and hating her for what she's done, I can't imagine she'll end up with the desire to be around me much more than she has been. "I want you to take care of yourself, Felicity. I'll come visit again soon." The word *soon* reminds me how long I'm expected to stay here.

"Thanks for visiting…and for the coffee. It was nice to see you." I try to remain strong. I try not to break down in front of her. That would just make this harder for both of us.

She tosses her empty coffee cup into the small trash bin and pulls the thick strap of her purse up and over her shoulder. I notice as she's preparing to leave that her blouse isn't ironed as it would normally be, and her jeans look like she's worn them a few times since washing them last. She's not the woman I once knew. It's evident her grief has taken the place of her usually impeccable appearance.

When she reaches the doorway of my room, she rests her hand on the wall and turns to face me, as if she wants to say something else. She looks at me for a few seconds then forces a tight-lipped smile, turns and leaves. I assume the silence took the place of *I love you*, the words she has always said to me when leaving or hanging up after a phone call.

The pain in my heart is heavy, almost like someone is sitting on my chest, which makes it nearly impossible to breathe. The sensation never eases. Though I can persuade my mind to sometimes think of other things, my body won't seem to allow me to forget, not even for a second. I'm assuming my heart will always know the truth and it remains in a constant state of pain because of it.

I lift my headphones to put them back in place, just as a nurse walks in with a tray of breakfast foods. "Good morning, Sunshine. How are we feeling?" She places the tray down and lifts my chart to review what the last nurse has written. Her auburn curls bounce around over her shoulders as her head bobs from side to side, as if she's read the same thing over and over again. "Okay," she says, her voice full of exuberance. When she places the clipboard back down, her dusky eyes glance up at me with curiosity. "You had company this morning, I saw. Was she an aunt?"

Most moms wouldn't wait three weeks before visiting their critically injured daughter. This is an exception. "It was my mom, actually." The shocked look I was expecting twists along her face. Her gaze speaks of her disappointment. "Better late than never, I always say." It's what people say when they can't think of a proper response. But I know how lame it sounds.

I try to close the conversation on this subject, dreading the *how does this make you feel?* question I keep getting. I wonder if they think I'm suicidal? "So I think the pain meds are wearing off. I'm in a lot more pain today," I say, looking down at the puffy areas of my leg.

"It does look like you have a bit more swelling this morning. I'll see what I can do about the pain. For now, though, eat up. You'll need your energy to begin physical therapy this morning." The thought of moving makes me lose my appetite. Have they not taken a look at my leg? How could they possibly expect me to do physical therapy? Doesn't that involve moving my broken body?

The nurse sees the apprehension in my eyes. She sits in the chair Mom was just sitting in and holds my hand. "It'll be okay. They'll start slow." Slow or fast, the thought still sickens me to the point of wanting to cry. I've never had physical therapy before—never had a need for it. I went twenty-two years without breaking one single bone, not even a toe. I guess everyone's luck runs out at some point. Mine did, in so many ways.

I try to eat the few morsels of food I can stomach, but I'm not one to eat when I'm upset. I'm the opposite. My health is pretty much on a downward spiral, heading nowhere good. I push the tray away as an unfamiliar man in scrubs enters my room. I haven't seen him before. He's either here to take me to physical therapy or he's new.

"Felicity, right?" he asks.

I clear my throat to answer, but my breath has left me. "Yes," I whisper. Until now, the nurses have been female with the exception of a male nurse who was old enough to be my grandfather and looked a little like Dan Aykroyd. But this one looks to be about my age, and the word *hot* doesn't quite do him justice. I've never actually seen a man in real life who could pull off thick black-rimmed glasses, but it's as if the style was created with his face in mind. For a split second, I forget I'm lying in pajamas with rods lining the outside of my leg from my thigh down to my calf. So attractive. I haven't even looked in a mirror in three weeks. I'm sure I'm on the verge of horrifying, if I haven't reached it already.

"That looks pretty painful," he says, placing his clipboard down on the table. He moves around to the left side of my bed to get a closer look. He appears intrigued as he inspects the landscape of damage, then looks right at me. His aqua eyes are piercing; they're like a splatter of colors that blend seamlessly, purposely matched to create the perfect wash of jade, turquoise and hazel. His dark lashes accentuate the whites of his eyes. I have to look away to break our stare. But you know that sensation after you close your eyes after staring at something so bright for too long and your mind creates the identical image within the darkness behind your closed lids? I have that.

His eyes are all I can see now.

"Are you okay?" he asks. His hand gently rests on my wrist and my eyes snap open. I realize I zoned out while he was looking at me. "No. I'm not okay."

Anytime I've been honest with people about my pain over the past few weeks, they've given me their best sympathetic look. Whether it was a detective, a psychiatrist, a doctor or nurse, the looks have been consistent. Everyone feels bad for me, even though they shouldn't. It wouldn't be right for me to take sympathy from anyone right now. Killers don't deserve compassion.

This one doesn't glower or curl his bottom lip into a pout. Instead, he unfurls a pretty perfect smile. "So…you know what's cool about my job?" he asks.

I don't even know what his job is, which makes his question hard to answer. "Not a clue."

"I get to make people like you okay again." I want to tell him that my pain is deeper than what he can see, but if he thinks he can fix me, I'll let him try. "I'm Hayes." He extends his hand. "I'll be your physical therapist."

And I know in this instant, I will never be the same.

MORE GREAT READS FROM BOOKTROPE

Seasons' End by **Will North** (Contemporary Romance) Every summer, three families spend "the season" on an island in Puget Sound. But when local vet Colin Ryan finds Martha "Pete" Petersen's body in the road on the last day of the season, he uncovers a series of betrayals that will alter their histories forever.

Saving Jason by E.J. Hanagan (Contemporary Fiction) Jason Barnes is a walking contradiction, a fun-loving free spirit with a severe case of PTSD. When an accident leaves him in a coma, his pregnant girlfriend must team up with his ex-wife to solve the mystery of Jason's past. What they discover and the friendship they forge will have a profound effect on both of their futures.

Suddenly a Spy by **Heather Huffman** (Romantic Suspense) Thrown into a world of espionage, seduction, and human trafficking, Veronica must fight for the life and husband she thought she had—and she must discover whether they are the life and husband she truly wants.

Pulled Beneath by **Marni Mann** (Contemporary Romance) When Drew unexpectedly loses her parents, she inherits a home in Bar Harbor, Maine along with a family she knew nothing about. Will their secrets destroy her or will she be able to embrace their dark past and accept love?

The Puppeteer by **Tamsen Schultz** (Romantic Suspense) A CIA agent and an ex-SEAL-turned-detective uncover a global web of manipulation that will force them to risk not just their fledgling relationship, but their very lives.

Return to Sender by **Mindy Halleck** (Historical Thriller) A Korean-war-hero turned apathetic Catholic Priest and a religious fanatic serial killer collide with destiny in small town Manzanita Oregon.

Discover more books and learn about our
new approach to publishing at **booktrope.com**.

CPSIA information can be obtained at www.ICGtesting.com
Printed in the USA
LVOW11s1623210115

423771LV00002B/306/P